RICOCHET

~~~~

CATHLEEN COLE

FRANK JENSEN

Copyright © 2023 by Cathleen Cole

All rights reserved.

No part of this book may be reproduced in any form or by any electronic or mechanical means, including information storage and retrieval systems, without written permission from the author, except for the use of brief quotations in a book review.

Any references to historical events, real people, or real places are used fictitiously. Names, characters, and places are products of the author's imagination.

Publisher: C&J Novels LLC

Cover designed by: Kari March Designs

ASIN: B0BS5VBFXH

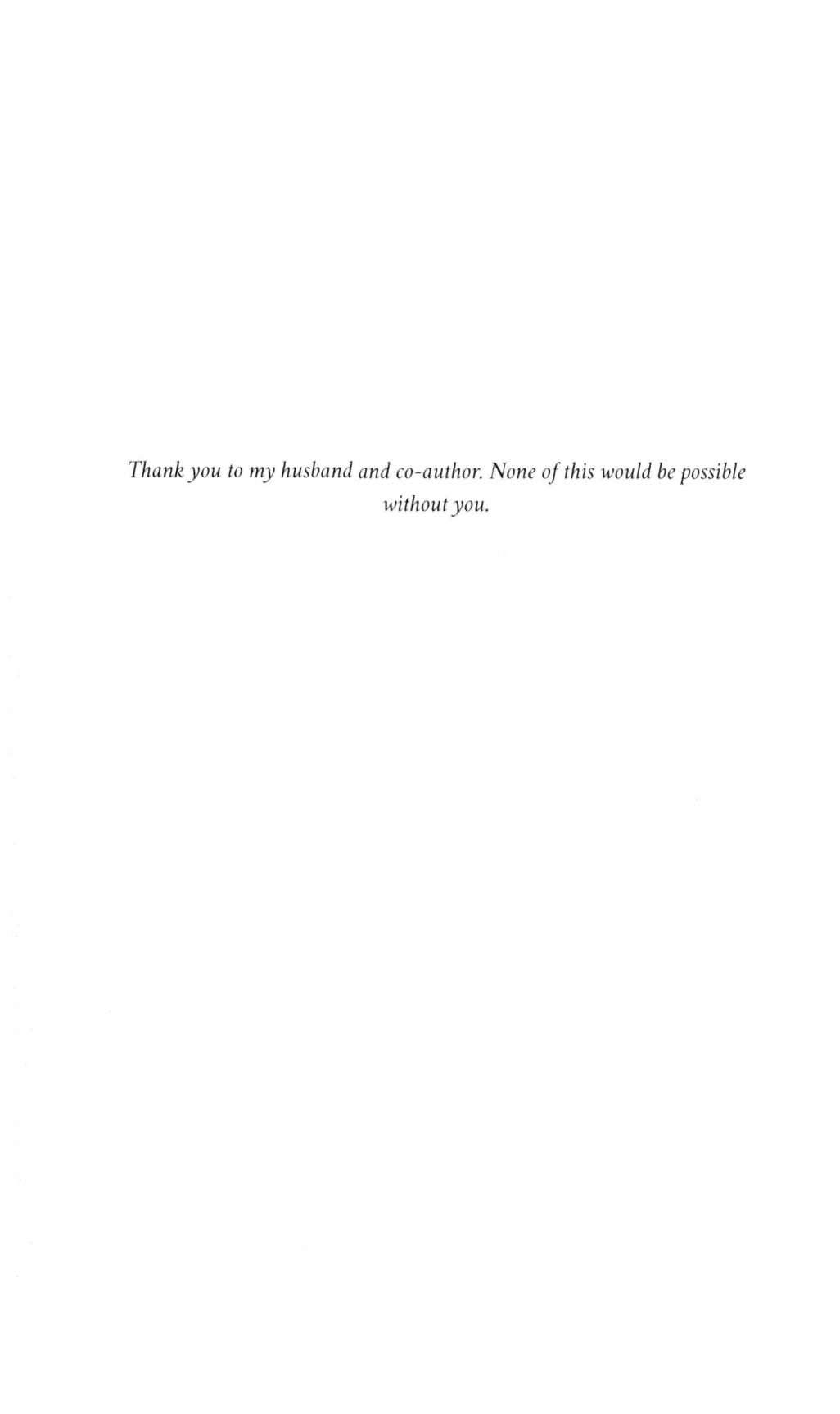

Thank you to my husband and co-author. None of this would be possible without you.

TRIGGER WARNINGS

This book is meant for readers 18+. Some content may be unsuitable for some readers. Due to the nature of the PTSD in this book, there are some heavy topics discussed. Please find the list of trigger warnings below.

Ends in a cliffhanger (Couple gets their HEA)
- Strong language
- Explicit sexual content
- Gun violence
- Knife violence
- Fighting
- Murder
- Death
- Character with PTSD
- Talk of suicide
- Talk of death of a child

CHAPTER 1

Ricochet

My breath hissed out as the cold water sent shivers racing down my back. It created a sharp chill that cascaded throughout my whole body. I reached for the shower knob and rolled it back, wincing as the water got even colder.

I wasn't one of those masochist types or health nuts that took cold showers for the fun of it. I could tell you I did it to cool the rage inside me, to ice down the monster within. That would be bullshit, too. At least it would be *good* bullshit. Almost believable. It made me sound like I was doing humanity a kindness. I wasn't sure I was capable of being gentle or caring any longer.

No, I did it because it was something I could *feel*. Really feel. I didn't enjoy being cold, but I enjoyed numbness even less. And I'd been living without feelings and emotions—besides anger—for too long now.

Letting my skin take the punishment of the cold water, and taking on that pins and needles feeling as the spray hit my body, was far better than the emptiness in my soul. Before all this I wouldn't have subscribed to the theory of souls and shit, but once you fuck up the way I had? You started to believe. The absence of it was driving me insane. I spent my days unable to connect with anything or anyone around me. Not even my MC brothers, and they were some of the most important people in my life. That numb aching feeling was getting worse. I wasn't sure how much more I could take before I did something drastic and stupid.

Standing in the shower, now that I was accustomed to the temperature, I went about the business of scrubbing myself down. Getting worse was an understatement. A black inky weight was slithering over that part of me I once thought was mythical. All I wanted to do was find my enemies and torture them until they writhed in pain. Finish them once they couldn't absorb another moment of torment. Let them bleed out and die. That wasn't normal, right?

My head dropped, heavy with the weight of my urges, and the water pelted the back of my neck. Icy cold fingers spread over my skin, creeping down my body until they disappeared through the drain and it started all over again. I didn't have any enemies at the moment, they were all dead, but the urge was still there. I needed to find new enemies. Someone to expel my rage onto. Needing that couldn't be good either.

Last night we raided the cult. Executed the extremists and freed the women and children. I thought I was ready to get back into the fight. Hell, it sounded easy enough. Crazy cult leader, fanatical men who rape and abuse women. I had no issue with killing those types. That wasn't the problem.

I hadn't been ready for what was actually going to happen. Butcher tried to warn us, warn me, that with these cults it's never that easy. I thought we'd be fighting crazy men. *Adult* men.

I wasn't ready for the kid. Ten, maybe eleven years old. I had a nephew that age. Still playing with Legos but not yet looking at girls. In a different world the kid from last night could have been going to school with my nephew, they could have been friends. In any sane world he should have been in with the group of women and children we were rescuing. The other two—while still young—had been old enough to make their choices. The kid... The kid, though, shouldn't have been there. Shouldn't have shot at Hellfire.

I reached for the knob and rolled it back slightly. A new round of shivers engulfed my body with the colder water. It was the only thing that was helping to chase away the memories.

No. This was the real world. At least the one that boy had lived in. The one I'd helped take down. And he'd been carrying a rifle. He'd gripped that gun, and he'd been ready to use it. He *had* used it. When I saw him I froze. In my life, in all my service with the Navy Seals, my time on the teams, I only ever froze once. When I had, my best friend had been killed. I was the reason his wife was a widow. His children were growing up without their father. My best friend had died because I'd hesitated.

Swallowing hard, I squeezed my eyes shut, as if that could block out Jack's face from my mind. As if that one movement could somehow erase the fact that he was gone. He was buried in fucking Arlington, and I was still here. The cold and memories bled together, making it hard to breathe.

Last night when I saw that kid, I froze again. Hellfire was nearly killed because of it. My limbs had weighed a ton and it was as though I was anchored to the ground, and because of that the kid shot my brother. I honestly wasn't sure for a minute if I was awake, or if I was stuck in the middle of one of my fucked up dreams. Then I'd heard Riptide. I was able to move again. My training kicked in and I killed a kid. Again.

That was when I lost it. I wasn't sure I was ever going to regain my sanity after this. When you're forced to end the life of someone who was so young and should still be innocent of the evil in this world? It did things to you. Things I never wanted to experience again, but they were my constant companions. Voices inside of me, whispering all the fucking evil things I shouldn't think about.

Behind that kid had been a man giving orders. My brain went from sluggish and unable to process to hyper efficient. I saw the man

—Bruce had been his name—and realized he had been the one to arm the kid, to make a child soldier. He had been the one to put me in a position to kill a kid for the second time.

Berserker is what my brothers call it. When I lose my shit the way I did last night. A blind rage overcame me. Some guys called it seeing red. I didn't see much of anything, other than the target of my rage. I'd beaten Bruce to death. With my bare hands. Broke two of my fingers and dislocated two more. This wasn't the first time I'd gone Berserker, but it certainly was the worst. I'd get into bar fights, lose my temper, and take it too far. I'd just lose sight of when to stop. This rage, this fear, always took hold, telling me that if I stop, the person I'm fighting will hurt someone else that I care about. So I didn't stop.

Looking down at my hand, I flexed it. Crash—a special forces medic we'd known from back in the day—had reset the two dislocated fingers and splinted the other two. The pain hadn't registered. Crash was a bit of an oddball. Even Butcher gave him a wide berth, when possible, but the look he'd given me when I'd refused any pain relievers told me he thought *I* was the crazy one. He wasn't wrong.

My knuckles were scabbing over, but a few hours ago you could almost see bone. That was a new one for me. I'd never hurt anyone that badly when I'd gone Berserker in the past. It was building, growing…getting worse. I wasn't sure how deep this rage and numbness could go. Or what would happen when I lost it.

Usually I just beat someone's ass, wounding them, maybe breaking the occasional rib. I'd never beaten someone to death with my fists before. Killed plenty of men, and I wouldn't feel bad for that. Not for killing for my country, or for my club, but men were entirely different than what was haunting me. Or should I say who?

According to Riptide, if anyone deserved what happened to him, it was this Bruce fellow. His death didn't bother me. The blind rage and lack of control was worrying. It was a problem, both for me and for the motorcycle club.

I knew my brothers wouldn't just throw me out. But they couldn't rely on me. Pain stabbed through my heart, making me gasp out loud. It'd been so long since I'd felt a fucking thing besides that rage, the zip of emotion physically hurt me. My brothers couldn't trust me. Why should they? I couldn't even trust myself. Soon we would have to deal with this. And I had no clue how to begin.

Leaning my arm against the wall, I rested my head on it, closing my eyes and trying to block out the images from last night. My ears were filled with the sound of water and static. Nothing penetrated my bubble so long as I was in here. But I couldn't live my life in the fucking shower. At least I wasn't using up all the hot water.

I shut the shower off and stepped out to begin drying myself. Walking past the mirror, I refused to glance over. I was in no condition to look at that guy right now. Instead, I went to my phone. I had a text from my sister. Despite living in the city, I hadn't seen her in some time. She wanted to know if I was free to come visit.

Somehow, she always knew when I needed her. I used to be able to tell the same for her, but that instinct had been silent for a few years now. Ever since I'd gotten home from my last deployment. Since Jack's death. Since the last time a death from my hand had haunted me.

If there was anyone who could calm the raging beast inside, it was my twin sister Gwen. Staying with her and her kids might help me keep myself under control. Fuck knew I couldn't be here right now. All it would take would be one pitying look and I'd lose the tenuous hold I had on my control.

My MC brothers were my world; that didn't mean I didn't need room to clear my head. I always needed space, more and more so over the years as this disease grew inside me. How could I join my brothers and enjoy life when I never knew when the rage would break free?

One thing I knew for sure, I'd kill myself before ever laying a hand on my twin or her kids. They were safe from me. I couldn't say the same for my brothers at this point. It didn't matter how much I loved them, something was broken inside of me. I was afraid, more than ever, that in my spiral I'd take them down with me. They wouldn't abandon me; they would allow themselves to fall before leaving me. I couldn't allow that either. They deserved better.

Decision made, I dressed and packed a duffel bag. I'd stop and talk to Lockout on my way out. He'd understand. He wouldn't stop me from leaving. I knew it would be a short reprieve—because Lockout wasn't going to let me slink off like a dog with its tail between its legs—but I needed it. He'd understand that. My president was far too fucking perceptive for his own damn good. And mine.

CHAPTER 2

Ricochet

I made my way downstairs, moving slowly. Glaring at the lightbulb as it happily shone overhead, I tried to figure out why the room looked draped in shadows. It was noon and I could see the ambient light bleeding through the windows. That one light fixture that needed the bulb replaced was flickering like it always did. So why was it so fucking dark? I rubbed at my eyes, wondering what the hell was wrong.

Lock had forced me to go see Crash last night to get patched up. There was no way I was heading back on my own just to get my damn eyesight checked. I avoided doctors at all costs. Continuing down the stairs, I shoved my hands into the pockets of my jeans. It would have been too easy to say I was creeping around. I just couldn't stand the thought of running into anyone.

As soon as I made it to the main level, I realized there were already people milling around. It was the middle of the day, so it wasn't all that surprising. I'd just been hoping to get the hell out of here without seeing anyone. I knew Riptide and Hush were worried about me. Smokehouse and Kit were still with Hellfire at Crash's as far as I knew, but if they were here my closest friends would be dragging me back up to my room to talk sense into me. That was the last fucking thing I wanted right now.

I moved past the bar, scanning faces as I went, taking stock of who was around today. I didn't see either of my friends. Guilt pinched as the thoughts invaded my mind. I couldn't face them right now. Smoke and Hell knew me better than anyone. When I'd tried to avoid making close friendships, they'd bulldozed right past my defenses. It'd been too fucking hard losing Jack, but those assholes didn't give a shit. They'd forced me to care. As much as I could right now anyway. It wasn't the same way I'd loved Jack. Nothing was the same since I'd lost him.

Still, those two and I had just clicked. All of the MC members were my brothers. I'd give my life for any of them, but the relationship wasn't the same between every man. I saw Lock and Hush as mentors. Men I could go to when I needed something. People I respected more than anyone else. Rip, Priest, Butcher, and Toxic. They were great. I knew they'd go to bat for me. Every member would, but I always held myself back from the rest.

Hell had been the one to approach me on that first day when I'd started prospecting. He'd watched me as I'd completed my first task set by Lockout, guard the gate. No time limit had been given, so I'd sat there for just under twenty-four hours. Hell had come out with a beer. Smoke had later joined us with some sandwiches. Eventually, Riptide had come out, when he realized I'd been forgotten out there, and released me. Ever since that day, Hell, Smoke, and I had been each other's shadows.

I can't handle seeing him.

Bile rose in my throat as the image of him wavered inside my mind. It kept intermingling with the memory of Jack—lying still, eyes open, but empty, staring at nothing—and the idea of losing Hellfire made my stomach roil. The shame was too much. The fear, overwhelming. I'd failed him. Eventually I'd have to face him, just...not right now.

I grunted a hello at the others, but kept my eyes averted and moved forward. My limbs were shaky and wooden, making my gait stiff. I knew any one of my brothers would talk if I asked them to. I could feel Priest's eyes on me, burning into my back as I turned and made my way down the hallway. Some would talk to me even if I *didn't* want to. Which was why I was avoiding eye contact.

In a way, I was fortunate and I knew it. Too many guys in my position had no one. They faced this alone. I had brothers who would support me. Who would talk—or beat—sense into me, depending on what I needed.

Even in Afghanistan, when Jack was killed, there were people there. People from my SEAL team, hell, even some Army pilots became unexpected friends. I'd been surrounded by people who just wanted to help. It'd been a shock, but welcomed.

It wasn't a lack of support. That wasn't my problem. I just couldn't see burdening them. I was a child killer. A lowly piece of shit who didn't deserve help. Damaged goods. These men were heroes. Legit pulled a baby and her puppy from a burning building type of heroes. They were the best men I knew. The last thing they needed was to be babysitting me. I definitely didn't want their pity. Deep down, if I allowed myself the slightest bit of hope, what I really wanted was an end to the numbness. That would only happen through redemption.

Last night was supposed to be that redemption. Instead it was Afghanistan two point zero. I was fairly sure it'd done more harm than good. I didn't know anymore how to fix myself. What could I do? For now, hiding out was my only option. Gwen offered the only safe place for me to go. I could always stay here, but then I'd feel like a burden. It was better that I left.

I got to Lockout's office and knocked on the door. It was open already so I leaned my head in.

"What's up Ricochet?" Lockout asked, motioning for me to come inside.

"I- uh- I just got off the phone with my sister. I haven't seen her or her kids in some time."

"Far too long," Lockout agreed, his sharp eyes watching every move I made.

I swore the asshole could read minds. It made me fucking nervous. I loved the man with every fiber of my being. He'd taken me in, treated me better than I could have ever hoped. He was like an older brother to me, but he still made me nervous. Everyone did. When you had so many secrets you weren't sure you could name them all, you tended not to trust anyone fully. Not with that dark part of you that could snap at any time. No. That got tucked away, pretending like it didn't exist, until it forced its way forward from time to time.

"She wants me to come by, maybe stay with them for a little while. I thought that maybe it would be ok, what with us not being as busy right now."

"I think some time with your sister and family would be good." He gave me an understanding smile, but there was a lot left unspoken. I could see it in his eyes. He didn't need to say more, and I didn't need to ask. We were both hoping that maybe she could help me in ways the club couldn't. If not, we both knew Lockout was going to step in and take over.

I wasn't sure what that meant for me, and I *was* sure I didn't want to find out. Somehow, I needed to figure out how to unfuck myself. That was easier said than done. It was also a problem for another day. I had enough weighing me down right now that I didn't need to contemplate that.

With the small talk over with, I made my way out to my bike. I didn't stop to talk to anyone, I just nodded and grunted as I passed. Stepping outside, I realized how gloomy it was. It was unusual to have cloud coverage this time of year, but today it was thick enough to block out the sun. Fitting. It matched my mood. If those clouds got any darker, they'd match my soul. At least it made me forget about the darkness inside the clubhouse. In a place that should be bright and make me happy, all I knew were shadows and pain. I had to get out of here.

Hopping onto my bike, I made my way across town. The city was quiet, barely anyone was on the road, just the way I liked it. I skipped my way through some red lights. There was no point in stopping. If someone came along and slammed into the side of me, I'd come back long enough to thank them for ending it.

Gwen lived on the west side, near Picture Rocks. It was a beautiful area, and still pretty vacant. Not too many people lived this far outside the city limits, but Gwen preferred to be out here. I'd bought this house as an investment years ago, when I'd still been in the service, and continued to make the payments. She and my nephew and niece deserved the very best. She'd had a rough go of it so far, and I hadn't been about to let my only family struggle. Not when there was something I could do about it. After her divorce, I'd put the house in her name. I didn't need any kind of credit or acknowledgement. It was enough to know they were in a safe neighborhood and happy. I rolled up to her house and shut my bike off.

The thing about a Harley is that you can't make a quiet entrance. I wasn't even off the bike yet before the door burst open and the kids were on their way out.

"Uncle Gage!"

I put on my biggest grin, hoping they wouldn't see through it to the dead man underneath. Despite my mood I had no desire to ruin their happiness. Maybe some of their innocence would rub off on me.

Fake it 'til you make it, right?

I grabbed Sean and swung him up into the air, bringing him full arc and onto my shoulders. The screeching and giggling was a nice change to the silence I normally had.

"Me next, do me!" Grace was screaming from the ground. I picked her up and swung her in the same manner, then held her upside down by an ankle in front of my face. I studied her as she giggled and swatted at me. I tickled her exposed belly. More screeching and laughter filled the air.

"Gage, it's so good to see you! We've missed you." My sister said, walking up with a big smile on her face. She'd known me as Gage her entire life. It was hard for her to remember to use my road name. It didn't bother me. Nothing about my twin ever did. She'd always understood me better than anyone. More than our parents, though they'd done their best while we'd had them.

Her arms wrapped around me, somehow avoiding the kids, and managed to give me a hug. We were a mess of tangled limbs. I gave myself a moment to relax into her embrace. To soak in the love and contentment, so I could almost feel it for myself.

"You look good, Gwenny."

She made a face at my childhood nickname for her. "Thanks." She made no move to release me. It was almost as if she realized I needed this comfort. We'd always had that twin bond. Some didn't think it existed. We knew for a fact it did.

The day after Jack had been killed and I'd been back in my barracks, staring down the barrel of a pistol, she'd called. From halfway around the world, she'd known something was wrong. She'd made me pause long enough to take a walk around the base. Taking that walk had resulted in me sitting down to talk with a man who'd ended up saving my life. So many things had aligned to make sure I was still here when I'd planned to end it all. I hadn't been able to follow through after that.

How could I put my sister through that? We'd lost our parents when we were younger and I wasn't going to be the reason she lost the rest of her family. I made a choice, every-damn-day, to fight and to stay, for her. For my nephew and niece. For my brothers. Maybe one day, I'd want to stay for myself. That was the hope anyway.

Over my sister's shoulder, I spotted a woman walking out the front door of the house next door. Long raven hair and forest green eyes met mine. They reminded me of the trees from back home. The home we'd ended up leaving to come live with our aunt in Tucson. I'd had a treehouse built in my favorite tree on our property. It had been my escape. Her eyes brought me right back to that little wooden shack stuck up in a massive tree.

My heart nearly stopped. The sun had chosen that moment to emerge from the clouds and shine on her hair. It was so dark the highlights almost looked blue. More importantly, the brightness of it made me squint. Whatever was going on with my eyes seemed to have resolved itself. She sauntered down the walkway, smiling at our reunion.

I almost dropped the kids. Grace let out a squawk of indignation, so I set her down, followed by Sean. I nearly walked through Gwen as I moved toward the beautiful woman.

She made her way over to us, ignoring the way I was staring, and waited patiently.

Gwen let go of me and laughed. "Sorry, manners. Ga- I mean, Ricochet, this is Jordan, my neighbor. Sweetie, this is my brother."

"Hey." It was all I could manage to mutter. I reached out and took her offered hand. It was soft and warm. A warmth that spread through my own, up my arm, where it unfurled inside my body. Her cheeks pinkened and she glanced away. It made me wonder if she'd sensed something sparking between us like I had.

I wasn't sure what was happening, but for the first time since Afghanistan it wasn't only numbness, pain, and rage inside of me. Somehow she'd managed to bring out more. Staring into her eyes, holding her hand, I knew this was something I didn't want to let go.

CHAPTER 3

Jordan

He was staring like he wanted to drag me back to his cave and lock me up. Strangely enough, that wasn't a turn off like it would be with most guys. My core clenched and I had to bite the insides of my lips to hold in my gasp.

I've seen men give me this look over the last few years, but I've never been tempted to let one drag me off, until now. Then again, I hadn't ever met such a gorgeous, intense, guy like him. I'd moved in next to Gwen a couple years ago and we'd hit it off right away. She'd talked about her brother many times, but the man standing in front of me—still holding my hand—wasn't what I'd pictured when I thought of him.

Gwen was grinning, her eyes darting between us as she pulled her kids in close and held them against her body. She was caging them in so they couldn't interrupt the moment that seemed to be happening between her brother and me. My cheeks heated and I pulled my hand from his. It wasn't that I wanted to. His grip was strong and for some reason, I felt safe with him. I'd known him for all of a minute, but I knew he was one of those types who were protective over their women.

"Ricochet," I said after a few moments of silence. "That's an interesting name."

"Oh," Gwen said with a laugh. "It's Gage, but-"

"Ricochet is my road name," he said, cutting his sister off with an amused look.

Frowning, I looked at the black leather vest he was wearing. It had patches on it, one of which said his name. My gaze drifted over to the road and I stared at the black and chrome motorcycle sitting there.

"I'm in a motorcycle club." His voice was deep and sexy. Everything about him was intriguing.

"Oh. That's nice." I had no idea what that really meant. I'd never known anyone in a motorcycle club before.

He smiled at me, flashing white, straight teeth. I wanted to throw caution to the wind and take a chance. To cast aside any hesitation. *What is happening right now?* I'd been on a hiatus from men for a couple years, ever since my ex and I had split, and things had been going great. No heartbreak, no fear. Something told me that had come to an end.

"We'd better let you get to work," Gwen said. She gave her brother a quick peek and, since he was still staring at me, wiggled her brows at me.

Narrowing my eyes on her, I fought back a laugh. Gwen and I had become friends almost immediately. She was so warm and open and I adored her kids. "Thanks, Girl. I'll call you later," I told her. My eyes landed back on Ricochet. I had to fight not to squirm as his pale blue eyes roved over me. It should be illegal to look at another person the way he was. "It was nice to meet you…"

"Ricochet," he offered, putting an end to the question of which name he preferred.

"Ricochet," I said with a nod. "Maybe I'll see you around."

"You will."

Swallowing hard at the promise in those two words, I began

backing away. Relief rushed over me as soon as his gaze fixed back on his nephew and niece and released me from his sultry stare.

I hurried over to my own driveway and got into my car. The drive to work was a bit of a blur as I thought over the morning. If I'd known I'd end up meeting such a handsome man, I might have actually done my hair. Instead, I'd thrown the dark tresses back into a high ponytail to keep it out of my way. I might have put on some make-up. Instead, I'd just washed my face, thrown on my jeans and a suitable t-shirt and my comfiest sneakers before bolting out of the house. I was running behind, as usual.

Punctuality wasn't what I was known for. I pulled into the parking lot at The Arizona Wildlife Sanctuary, grabbed my badge and purse, and then hightailed it toward the entrance. I loved working here. It was like an outdoor zoo, except it featured all the wildlife local to Arizona. I'd worked here for years, but used to live further away. One day I'd decided I'd had enough of the commute. Driving over an hour each way was eating into my day. It wasn't that I had much of a social life, not since I'd sworn off men, but I still wanted *some* time to myself.

"You're late," Margie called as I raced past the ticket booth.

I gave her a wave, but kept going. Her laughter followed me as I ran into the park. After a quick stop by my locker to drop my things off, I grabbed my gear and headed out to my area.

As soon as I stepped into the mews, Scuff let out a series of soft chirps. He jumped from his perch and his beautiful wings spread as he soared over to me. He bypassed my gloved fist and landed on my shoulder.

Laughing, I brushed the top of his head. His eyes closed as he enjoyed the contact. "Hi there, Scuff. You're not supposed to land on shoulders. The parents get a little worried when you do that," I admonished him. "You ready for our show?" I glanced at my watch and grimaced. There was only about five minutes before my show started. With him riding around on my shoulder, I hurried and gathered the things I'd need.

Today's presentation was a smaller one. There weren't any other handlers helping me and it was just going to be Scuff and me out there. I didn't mind. I enjoyed the time with my little friend.

I transferred him onto my fist and hurried out to the veranda area where I'd give my presentation. Gasps of pleasure sounded from the awaiting crowds. I smiled as kids tugged on their parents' arms and pointed at Scuff.

"Hi there! Welcome to The Wildlife Sanctuary. We're so glad to have you with us today. Scuff and I are here to teach you a little bit about hawks." I waved at a little girl who squealed and held her hands out toward us. "Does anyone know what kind of hawk Scuff is? Say it nice and loud."

The Sanctuary put a good amount of distance between us and the visitors when we were doing our shows, so I was mic'd up and they were all about ten feet away.

There were a couple half-hearted shouts from the kids, but no one got the right answer. I lifted my fist and sent Scuff soaring off to the perch that was placed high up to our left. The crowd 'oooo'd' and 'ahhh'd' as he flew. He was a gorgeous bird.

"Scuff is a Harris Hawk," I told them. "Harris Hawks are one of the most common hawks here in Arizona. The most interesting thing about them is they are the only hawks that are social. They live in groups and have hierarchies and actively hunt together. This isn't something you typically see with raptors."

I ran through my spiel, letting Scuff soar and dive and entertain the crowd while I gave them facts about his species. At the end there was a segment of time set aside for questions and answers, then it was time for me to wrap it up. The disappointed faces as I said goodbye made me want to stay out there for another hour, or as long as the kids wanted to see us, but it was policy and Scuff needed a break. I waved again to the kids and made my way back to the mews.

"You did so well, Buddy," I told him as I held my gloved fist up to his perch. Raptors could be as different as dogs, personality-wise. You could end up with some like Scuff, who truly seemed to enjoy being around you. Others could be mean and ornery and only want one thing from you—food. I treated all the birds here at The Sanctuary with the respect they deserved. I knew which were looking forward to me coming by and which to avoid. There was one red-tailed hawk who needed to be put in a separate enclosure while her living area was cleaned out. She wouldn't hesitate to attack anyone coming inside, even just to feed her.

Scuff hopped up onto his perch, his dark eyes watching me as he waited for his reward. I gave him a dead quail and watched as he tore into his meal.

The way he'd just been watching me brought blue eyes back to my mind. Maybe that was why I'd felt an instant connection with Ricochet. He watched me the way the birds did, all intensity, interest, and curiosity wrapped into one smoldering stare.

I tried to get him out of my mind as I went around and fed the other birds who called The Wildlife Sanctuary their home. Most of the animals here would stay for life. They were unable to be rehabilitated and released back into the wild, so we kept them here and taught people about them. Sometimes we got lucky with the birds and could release them. It was always a happy day when that was the case.

"Hey, Theo," I called out as I tossed a dead mouse into her habitat. The Great Horned Owl gave a hoot as she watched me deliver her meal, then descended on it, quick as a flash. She stood over the mouse, watching me with slow blinking eyes. "How are you today, Lady?"

"One of these days I swear they're going to answer you."

I jumped at the voice and laughed as I turned. "Hi, Dad."

"Hi, Pumpkin. Didn't see you earlier." He arched a brow at me.

Giving him a guilty grin, I shrugged. "You know me."

"Yes, I do. We have a staff meeting tomorrow. Don't be late," he cautioned. He adjusted the glove he was putting on. He had his own show starting up soon.

The crowds were usually bigger during the summer when the kids were out of school, but the weather was perfect right now. People were happy to walk around outside while the temperatures were cooler, so many were making good use of the gorgeous day. It wouldn't be but another few months and the days would start heating up in preparation for summer.

"I won't miss it," I promised him.

"Wish I could stay and chat, but everyone is eager to see Iggy." He stepped into the red-tailed hawk's enclosure to get her. We currently had three red-tails, one owl, three Harris Hawks, a Cooper's Hawk, and a Rough-Legged Buzzard.

I leaned against the mesh wire separating Iggy's mews from the hallway. "Everything's good?"

"Yup. Your mom is good. Still coming hunting on Sunday?"

"Of course." I smiled at him. Our family took our raptors hunting every Sunday, usually followed by some kind of meal. We rarely missed it. Falconry was a sport we all enjoyed and it kept us close.

"Good." He closed the door to Iggy's area and then leaned over and dropped a kiss on my forehead. "See you later, Pumpkin."

"Have a good show." My dad was the reason I'd become a falconer. He'd started into the sport when I was a senior in high school. As soon as I'd graduated, I'd taken my own test to become an apprentice falconer, and two years later I was hired here, working my dream job with the birds that I loved. I'd been here five years now and I wouldn't want to do anything else.

Dad had helped me secure the job, but I'd worked hard to prove myself so that they'd want to keep me on. I moved around, cleaning out the mews my father hadn't gotten to this morning, making sure everyone who didn't have a show scheduled for the day had their meal and plenty of fresh, cool water.

By the time the clock hit quitting time, I'd completed all my tasks. There was a part of me that wanted to find an excuse to go home and knock on my neighbor's door. Instead, I pulled into my driveway and went inside my house. It wouldn't be fair to take time away from Gwen and the kids, just because I found her brother to be drop dead sexy. That didn't mean I couldn't see if I could bump into him here and there while he was visiting. Shaking my head, I reminded myself sternly that I was on a hiatus. It didn't matter if there'd been enough sparks to start a blaze, I wasn't supposed to be intentionally spending time with men.

Checking my phone, I saw that Gwen had texted me. I'd been so busy at work this was the first chance I'd had to look at it. Her text was filled with heart emojis and she claimed to never have seen an actual flame between two people before.

I rolled my eyes and texted her back before I started making dinner. If I wasn't careful my best friend was going to end up trying to hook me up with her brother. If I was being honest, there were only two reasons I was hesitating. My hiatus from men. And the fact that if something went wrong it could affect my friendship with Gwen. I wasn't willing to lose her. Fine, there was one more since I was being so honest with myself. The intensity he showed frightened me as much as it fascinated me.

The man was gorgeous and any woman would be taking notice, but I wasn't sure if I was ready for the challenge that Ricochet represented. As much as I'd like to get on that ride, it wasn't a good idea. I kept repeating that to myself most of the night. By the time I climbed into bed it'd been a steady mantra in my mind. It didn't stop the heart pounding dreams.

CHAPTER 4

Ricochet

Twin tornadoes landed on my bed and began jumping around. Groaning, I pulled the covers over my face. "Go away," I grumbled.

"Can't!"

"Mama says you gotta get up for breakfast."

I sighed as Sean grabbed my blankets and pulled. Giving him a mock glare, I lunged forward and pulled him down onto the mattress. His laughter spilled out as I tickled him without mercy. His sister jumped on my back and gave an impressive right hook to my ribs for a four-year-old.

"Stop! Please!" Laughter made the words almost unrecognizable as Sean begged for mercy.

"What are you doing?"

All three of us froze and looked up. Gwen stood in the doorway, her hands on her hips, a scowl fixed on her face. I could see the laughter dancing in her eyes, though.

"Nothing," I said, feigning innocence.

Her eyebrows raised. "Nothing?"

"Nope," Grace said.

"Nothin'," Sean continued, finishing her sentence.

We disentangled ourselves while she watched. "It's time for breakfast. Wash your hands," she told me then sailed away.

I waited until she was out of ear shot before muttering, "It's like being in the military all over again."

"Will you tell me about it?" Sean asked, an eager look on his face. At eight years old, he'd been interested in anything military for years, especially since his Uncle Gage had been in.

Fighting against the automatic wince, I ruffled his hair. "Of course I will. But later. Better get downstairs before your mom comes looking for us again."

We trudged downstairs and I sat at the table. The scent of pancakes and bacon hit me like a ton of bricks and I realized I was starving.

Gwen dropped a plate in front of me. "You look like you've lost weight."

She didn't ask the question, but it was there in her words. *Is everything okay?* She knew all about me being discharged from the military and why, and she'd done everything she could to help me with the guilt and sadness of losing Jack. But she didn't know what had just happened.

Years had passed, but nothing really changed for me. I was just existing. The memory of green eyes brought me back to meeting Jordan yesterday. Something had shifted, though I didn't know what or how that might impact me, but for a few minutes there'd been warmth instead of numbing cold.

Shaking my head, indicating I didn't want to talk about it, I looked down at my plate. I poured syrup on my pancakes and ignored the way she stared at me for a few moments before letting it go and turning away.

"Oh. By the way…"

I looked over at her as I shoved a huge bite of food into my mouth.

This was the first time I'd felt hunger since before the attack on the cult's compound the other night. Focusing on Gwen, I realized she looked nervous. Chewing, I watched her struggle to find a way to say whatever she needed to. That's how I knew I wasn't going to like whatever it was.

"I invited Trent over to dinner next Friday night." She gave me a forced bright smile, her eyes flicking over to the kids as though to remind me they were there.

Setting my fork down with exaggerated care, I narrowed my eyes on her. "New boyfriend?" I knew exactly who she was talking about, but a brother could hope she wasn't going back down that road again.

Gwen rolled her eyes and turned back to the stove to flip a pancake. "Ex-husband," she replied, playing the game.

"Why?"

Sean looked up, watching me with a solemn expression. He didn't seem to be thrilled about his dad coming back into their lives either.

"He didn't want anything to do with any of you before," I reminded her.

Her head snapped toward me and she gave me a piercing glare. "He's making an effort. He said he realized he didn't want to go through his life without knowing his children."

I shot another look at Sean. His mouth tightened, then he bent his head and stared at his plate, refusing to look up. The kid took after me in too many ways. Grace was more like Gwen. Sweet, kind, and forgiving.

"What does dinner have to do with that?" I asked her, softening my tone a notch.

She sighed and brought her own plate over to the table. "He's making an effort now. I have to give him a chance to prove himself."

"Bull-"

Her sharp look had me swallowing the rest of the curse.

"Men don't change. *People* don't change."

"Maybe not, but ever since he's gotten this new job, he's really been trying."

"How long has it been?"

"Six months."

I snorted in disbelief and picked my fork back up. "What job?"

"He's working with the District Attorney." Her gaze implored me to be understanding.

Grinding my teeth together, I said nothing about Trent or his new job for the remainder of breakfast. As much as I wanted to give my opinions, she was right. The kids didn't need to hear me bad mouth their father. Even if he was a dick and they knew it. As soon as we changed the subject Sean brightened up, joking and laughing about something funny that had happened in school.

"Speaking of school," Gwen said, cutting off his tirade, "go finish getting dressed so you don't miss the bus."

I watched as they raced up the stairs. "Seems like he's enjoying school more."

"It's so much better out here. This is only his first year at this new school. It's smaller than the one he was going to inside the city and I think that's making a difference for Sean. They're happy here." She smiled and reached over to cover my hand with hers. "Sorry I dropped that on you."

I knew she was talking about Trent. "No problem. I'm the one who decided to come visit with only a few hours' notice. I don't expect you to change your plans for me, Gwenny."

She sighed and her shoulders slumped. "Thanks, Gage. It means a lot to me to have your support."

My jaw flexed as I bit back an angry response. "I don't think you should get involved with him again. He was a complete asshole to you while you were married and through the divorce. He somehow managed to get you and the kids kicked out of the house for fuck's sake." It was the reason I'd bought this house. Gwen hadn't had the money to buy her own place and I didn't want her renting a home in some scummy area of the city, so I'd bought this house out in Picture Rocks. Got them all outside the city limits and further away from Trent.

Working for the DA, is that how he got the upper hand in divorce court? Did he have those connections back then?

"I haven't agreed to anything yet, Gage. We're taking it slow because of all that. But he really seems to have changed." She gave me a hopeful smile.

It took all my self-control to bite back my response to that. It would only cause a fight. "We'll see." It was all I could settle on that was neutral. "I'll make sure to be somewhere else next Friday night."

"Oh. No. I was hoping you'd have dinner with us."

My brows shot up. "Do you think that's a good idea?"

"It is if you behave," she told me.

I stood and began clearing the table. She came to help me and I shook my head. "I've got the dishes. You help the kids."

"Gage." She was standing by the table, looking hesitant. "Are you okay?"

Yesterday I would have told her no. Today? Somehow meeting Jordan yesterday morning had switched on something inside of me. It was as surprising as it was unexpected. Not that all my problems were solved. They still lurked deep down, but at least I was looking forward to something. The thought of seeing her again was weighing on my mind, chasing away some of the guilt that ate away at me.

"I'm working through some shit," I told her. I never lied to my sister. She'd know if I was anyway.

She nodded. She also knew when I was done talking about something, so she left that alone. "Please promise me you'll behave at dinner?"

I appreciated her letting her line of questioning drop enough to agree to her terms. "I'll do my best."

She grinned at me, the same smile Grace usually had on her face, and hurried upstairs.

I wasn't sure how I was going to keep that promise. I despised Gwen's ex. Didn't consider him much of a man. He'd wormed out of taking care of his family and made it that much harder on my sister. All that after he was the one who'd asked for a divorce. They'd met in college and from day one, I hadn't liked him. I'd done my best to keep my opinions to myself while they were married. Once they divorced? It was open season on the man all the time. Not that I saw him much.

One wrong move and he was going to regret coming back into my family's lives. I'd make sure of it. Turning back to the sink, I filled it with hot soapy water. Movement caught my attention and I watched as Jordan rushed out of her house and jumped in her car. The tires squealed as she backed out of the driveway.

My lips twitched in amusement as I watched. Maybe her brand of chaos was what I needed in my life. Someone who was always rushing around, late, and wasn't so rigid with their time.

The military had created that within me. Even if the kids hadn't woken me up earlier, my eyes would have popped open on their own. Sleeping in wasn't a luxury I enjoyed anymore. Just like I'd made my bed before coming downstairs, making sure the corners were tucked just right.

I dipped my hands into the water and began washing the morning dishes. My day needed to be filled. Idle time wasn't something I was used to, though I didn't have to be at work for an indeterminate amount of time. I worked on a construction crew. George, one of our MC brothers, owned the company. Smoke and Hell would often help out if we were short-handed, despite having their own jobs.

I'd already spoken to George about taking some time off and he'd been all too happy to let me do my thing. A few of our other brothers would end up helping him out since he'd lost me for the unforeseeable future. There were quite a few of our brothers who were handy with a hammer.

George wouldn't complain, though. Just like the brothers who took over for me wouldn't say a word. This is what we did for each other. As much as I loved Gwen and her kids, if I didn't have the MC, I wasn't sure where I'd be. My brothers were a big reason I was still here. I knew it without a doubt. Together both sets of my family kept me tethered here, even on the days where it seemed easier to let go.

Looking over my shoulder, I drained the sink and left the dishes in the rack to dry. I grabbed a beer from the fridge and went out onto the front porch. Sitting in the swing, I opened the bottle and stared at the desert surrounding the house. There were only a few houses scattered in this area. Jordan's and one other sandwiched Gwen's home in, but the rest weren't in sight. It made for a nice, scenic place to live.

Gwen and the kids rushed out of the house. She paused, eyed my beer, and gave me a disapproving look as she bundled her kids into the car.

"Have a good day at school," I told them.

The kids waved and Gwen tried to see how long she could keep eye contact as she climbed into her vehicle. I didn't feel any shame, just raised the bottle in a toast to her.

Her laughter was cut off by the closing of the car door. I kicked back and watched them drive down the road.

CHAPTER 5

Ricochet

I was still sitting in the same spot, a few hours later, when a motorcycle pulled up. Shifting on the swing, I watched as Smoke got off his bike.

His brows shot up as he surveyed the ground at my feet. I'd run out of beer and it wasn't even noon. "Have any of those for me?"

"No. Planning on going to the store soon, though."

He shook his head. "Yeah, that's a great idea." He sat on one of the wooden rocking chairs nearby. "I'll get you more before I leave."

Shrugging, I watched as a roadrunner zipped by, chasing some kind of bug. "Guess I need to find something to do besides day drinking. What're you doing here?"

Smoke's gaze bore into the side of my face, but I kept my eyes on the brush. "Came to check on you."

Ignoring the way his words made my gut clench, I changed the subject. Too many people were worried about me. I hated fucking disappointing them. "How's Hell?" Now I met his eyes. The beer swirled in my stomach as it rolled at the reminder of my friend and his condition.

"He's doing well. Crash said he should be up and on his feet again in a day or so. Of course, Hell told him to fuck off and proved he didn't need to be 'coddled', or so he said."

My lips twitched up into a half smile. That sounded exactly like Hellfire. "So is he still in bed?"

"Fuck no. He thanked Crash Cart for patching him up and asked Kit to take him home. He's back at the clubhouse. Lock forced him to go lay down on the couch and all the sweet butts are waiting on him hand and foot."

"Bet he's eating that up."

"Hell yeah, he is," Smoke said with a chuckle. He leaned forward, elbows resting on his knees. "How are you?"

"Fine."

"Uh huh."

I gave him a warning look. "I have no problem kicking your ass out of here if you're going to be a dick."

He grinned at me. "You like me too much to do that."

"The fuck I do." It was true. Smoke and Hell were my best friends. They were older than I was, but emotionally we were all pretty much on the same level. Kit always complained that we had the maturity of eight-year-olds. She wasn't wrong. We got into a lot of shit together.

"How's Gwen and the kids?"

That was one thing about my brothers, they made it a point to know what was going on in my life and my family had become theirs. Any of the men in my MC would protect my sister, niece, and nephew with their lives, even if they hadn't all met them, just like I would for their families. It was what we did for each other.

"They're doing good. Trent's coming back around."

Smoke swore, making me feel justified in my own reaction. "What's that shit stain up to?"

And this was why he and I got along so well. "Claims he's changed and wants to be in his kids' lives." The disgust in my tone was mirrored on Smoke's face.

"Sounds like a bunch of bullshit."

"Agreed."

"Probably just wants some pussy."

Nausea rolled through me at that thought. "Smoke, if you talk about my sister's pussy again, I'll pound you into the fucking ground."

"My bad. I didn't mean *her* pussy exactly."

I gave him a look of disbelief and confusion.

"Well, I guess I did. I just meant-"

"Stop. While you're behind." Shaking my head, I tried to figure out a way to bleach my brain so I'd never have to think of that again.

Smoke cleared his throat. Before he was able to shove his boot any farther into his mouth a car whipped into Jordan's driveway. His eyes narrowed on me as I sat up a bit straighter. "How are the views out here?" he asked, gaze straying over to Jordan's car.

"Fuck off."

Smoke was a player. He'd fuck anything that moved. I'd be damned if I let him near Jordan. Even if I didn't want her, which I did, I wouldn't let him get close.

"Off limits," I said, as he studied her while she got out of her car.

His right brow shot up and interest covered his face. "Really? You haven't called dibs..." he thought back over the years we'd known each other, "since Suzie Hersch."

"I never claimed Suzie Hersch. And I didn't say I was calling dibs," I muttered. He didn't need to know that I couldn't get this woman out of my mind. He'd just give me mass loads of shit, especially after finding out I'd talked to her for a total of two minutes.

"Well if you're not calling dibs, then I can-"

"We're not fucking ten years old," I growled at him.

Jordan pulled a backpack out of the car, spotted us, and waved. Her smile lit up my world. It was like a punch to the gut. The good kind. I didn't know how it was possible to have this kind of reaction to someone I'd just met, but here I was.

Smokehouse gave an aggravating laugh. "Holy shit, Bro. You're into her." Amazement flooded his features. "I was kidding before, but seriously, I haven't seen you chase tail in years."

"I swear to Christ, I'm going to make you eat your words. Shut the hell up." The last came out as a mumble because Jordan was walking over. I kicked the beer bottles under the swing and over toward Smoke.

Her beautiful eyes watched a bottle roll across the porch. "Bit early in the day, isn't it?" she asked with a smile. There was no accusation in her tone. More it was like she didn't know what else to say, even though she'd approached us. It was cute.

"He's an alcoholic," I said, pointing at Smoke.

His jaw dropped and for once he seemed lost on what to say. For a guy that could run his mouth in any situation it was almost refreshing to see him shocked into silence.

"I just got here, you dick," he finally managed to stutter.

Jordan's smile grew at our banter. "Are you brothers? Gwen never mentioned another brother, but…"

"We're MC brothers," I told her. "This is Smokehouse."

She shook her head. "Your names are very unique. It's nice to meet you, Smokehouse."

Smoke stood and leaned over the railing so he could take the hand she offered, holding it close to his chest. I rolled my eyes at his antics. He was just trying to piss me off. He could tell I was into her and even though he fucked anytime he could, even he had a code. He wouldn't put the moves on a woman I wanted. Not seriously, anyway. He'd annoy the shit out of me though by pretending to.

"It's nice to meet you as well, Jordan. Are you new here?" He gave her a look that his sister, Kit, had termed as a smolder. "I could show you around if you wanted."

Uncertainty filled her eyes as she looked over at me. "I-I was born and raised in Tucson."

Standing up, I took Jordan's hand from my friend and knocked his away. I used my free hand to launch myself over the porch railing and landed next to her. "Ignore him," I told her, tugging on her hand.

I walked her over to her door. She hesitated as we approached it. "You have interesting friends."

"Wait until you meet the weird ones."

Her startled green eyes landed on mine. "Am I going to?"

"Yes." I still hadn't dropped her hand, so I used my free one to tuck a piece of her dark hair behind her ear. My fingers trailed lightly down her neck.

Her breathing was choppy and her pulse fluttered against her neck. I wasn't the smooth talker that Smokehouse was, but I could tell when a woman was interested in me. I leaned forward a little and watched as her eyes widened then dropped to my lips.

"Go inside, Jordan."

She looked up at me again and I didn't miss the disappointment on her face. She turned and I let her hand go.

My eyes narrowed as she opened her door. "You don't lock it?"

She looked at me over her shoulder and shrugged. "No one ever comes out here." She walked inside.

"Jordan."

She paused again, turning to face me. I put my hand on either side of the doorframe and leaned in until my face was in hers. Another inch and we'd be touching noses.

"Lock your doors. You don't want strange men coming in here."

I left her blinking after me and hopped back over the railing to take my seat again. What did it say about me that I'd drunk an entire pack of beer and felt nothing? It didn't affect my motor skills in the slightest. We tended to drink a lot when we were bored and today hadn't exactly been full of fun. Sitting out here, away from my brothers, away from the city, with nothing to do while the kids were at school hadn't left me with much else. But like I told Smoke, I needed to find something else to do. I didn't need Jordan thinking I was a lush and Gwen worrying about me.

"Don't," I said as I took my seat.

Smokehouse's grin filled his stupid fucking face. "Don't what?"

"I don't want to talk about it."

"Nothing to talk about," he agreed. "You're already in too deep to talk you out of it."

"I'm not in anything."

"The fuck you aren't," he said, leaning back. "Can't wait to tell Hellfire. He'll enjoy tormenting you."

"As if he can talk. He hasn't shown interest in anyone as long as I've known him." I frowned, thinking about my friend. "I should go see him."

"Nah. He said he'll come visit in a few days. We know you need a bit of a break."

"Not from you guys. Or the others," I said. "It's just…" I swallowed hard. The last thing I wanted was my brothers thinking I didn't want to see them. I could handle them individually. Couldn't be around all of them, though. It was just too much right now.

"We get it, Ricochet. We just want to give you what you need. Sometimes I don't know what that is," he admitted.

Smoke never let his vulnerable side show around anyone other than me and Hellfire. He was loud, cocky, and determined, but I knew that was all a show to protect himself. Not that we talked about this feel good crap. Out of all of us he probably had the kindest heart, he just didn't ever let it show. He always left women before they hurt him. It had become a pattern for him.

I hadn't been around when his fiancée had fucked him over. But ever since, he'd refused to allow any female to get close to him. I did the same thing, but not because I'd been hurt by one. Who needed to deal with the shit I had going on? Why would I put that on another person?

My eyes strayed over to the house next door. It'd always been easy before to stick to myself. I hadn't even fucked one of the sweet butts. Too much damn drama with those girls. That was the last thing I needed. Women always came with a price, theirs was too high. Wasn't worth dealing with just to get my dick wet.

Now that there was someone who piqued my interest I wondered if I was going to find it as easy to keep a part of me separated from her? I didn't want to keep my distance from Jordan. Maybe she was exactly what I needed to take my mind off of things.

CHAPTER 6

Jordan

"I just don't know what the right move is." Gwen dropped her head into her hands. "I thought the kids would be thrilled when their dad finally started coming around again."

"They're not?" I asked. My eyes strayed out the window and I had to fight back a sigh of appreciation for the show of muscles happening outside. Gwen was sitting at my table with a cup of coffee while I watched her brother work on her car through my kitchen window. He had his shirt off, showing off tattoos across his chest, down his side, and all down his arms. It was almost impossible not to drool. Looking wasn't breaking my promise to myself to keep my distance.

"Grace seems okay, but Sean shuts down and is completely sullen whenever he's around. I've tried to talk to him about it, but he just says everything's fine." She let out a sad sigh. "That's all boys ever say, 'I'm fine.'"

Focusing on her, I turned my back to the window and went to sit with her. I picked up her hand and waited until she met my eyes. "He's at that age," I told her. "He's kind of been the man of the house for a few years now and their father hasn't bothered to see them. I can understand his standoffishness."

"Should I tell Trent that this is all too much? That the timing isn't right?" she asked, worry there in her pretty blue eyes. They were a tad darker than her brother's.

"That's up to you, Honey. It's not an easy decision either way. Do you think Trent is doing anything wrong?" I was worried for the kids, too. We'd known each other long enough now that I was completely head over heels for Sean and Grace. At eight years old, Sean took far too much on his shoulders. Something told me he was a lot like the man out in the driveway. We'd only known each other for a few days, but there were mannerisms I'd seen in Ricochet that I'd observed in Sean as well.

"That's why I wanted him to come to dinner tonight. Now I'm kind of regretting it. Gage has never gotten along with Trent. Years of him ignoring us and all the crap he pulled during the divorce hasn't endeared him to my brother." A slow smile spread over Gwen's face. "Will you do me a favor?"

She looked so excited it made me suspicious. "Maybe…"

"Come to dinner tonight."

"What?" I gave a sharp laugh. "If you're not expecting it to go well, why would you want more people there?"

"You can help keep my brother distracted," she told me with a sly smile. "And maybe with a stranger there, Trent will behave, too."

"I-"

"Please, Jordan?" She gave me puppy dog eyes. She knew I couldn't resist when she made that face.

"I've already decided to stay away from your brother, though," I told her.

"Really?" She wasn't offended in the least. In fact, she wore a wide grin. "Why's that?" It was all for show. She and I had talked in length about my decision to quit men, at least for the time being. She was in the same boat. Or had been before Trent had started coming around. Now I wasn't sure what her plan was.

My lips thinned out into a grim line. "He walked me to my door the other day."

Her grin only got bigger as her eyebrows went up.

Giving her a look that told her to behave, I continued, "He got into my face and told me to keep my door locked."

The smile disappeared. "He what?"

"No." I shook my head and took a deep breath. "It wasn't intimidating… It was so hot," I squeaked and dropped my head down into one hand. My elbow rested on the table and I stared down at the wood pattern. I couldn't face her when I admitted this. "I know he's your brother, but I nearly jumped him right there. Wanted to pull him into the house and just…" I swallowed the rest. His sister didn't need to know the depravity that had crossed my mind. Not when it concerned her brother. "Maybe this has all been a mistake and I just need to sleep with someone. Someone other than your brother. Scratch the itch."

That last sentence should have brought a laugh, since jumping into bed with strange men was the furthest thing from something I'd do. Instead, the silence went on for long enough that I peeked up. My heart sank. Gwen wasn't laughing, or smiling. She wasn't saying anything. In fact, she looked a little sad.

"See?" I told her. "That's why I'm going to stay away from him." I lifted my head and motioned at her. "I would never do anything to ruin our friendship."

"I would."

"What?" I asked her, shock making me still.

"Gage has had…some hard times." She seemed to be picking her words carefully. It made me curious to ask more, but I knew better. It wasn't her story to tell. "The other morning when you two met was the first time I'd seen him look so…light. Almost like the ghosts of his past weren't riding him for the few moments he was touching you. Now you're telling me he walked you to your door?" Her blue eyes met mine and there was a sheen of tears there. "Please don't shut him out just because of me. If you're both interested, I think you should go for it."

I shook my head. "It's not only because of you, Gwen. I'm…terrified."

Her brows drew low over her eyes in confusion. "He's in a motorcycle club, but they're good men. They-"

"It's not that," I interrupted. "I actually don't even know what that means."

"There are some people who don't get that lifestyle," she admitted.

"I'd have to have you tell me what it included. I've never met a real biker before. All I know is rumors and gossip." I shook my head again. "No, I mean, I'm scared that he'll break my heart. I don't know if I can take it again."

Her face relaxed and there was sympathy on her features. She reached out and rubbed my upper arm. "Isn't love worth the risk?"

I swallowed hard and looked away from her. "I don't know."

"Gage isn't Dan." She waited for that to sink in before continuing, "How about this? Spend the evening with us. If you decide at the end of dinner that you really do want to keep your distance, I'll help make that happen."

I gave her a warm smile. "Something tells me your brother doesn't exactly do what he's told."

She laughed. "You're right about that. Especially now that he's out of the military. But as his twin, I have the ability to persuade him. Sometimes."

"One dinner?"

"Only the one. Then I can get your thoughts on Trent, too. An unbiased opinion."

"Okay," I agreed. "I'll come to dinner. What can I bring?"

***

My heart jumped into my throat as Ricochet opened the door. I'd barely finished knocking before he yanked it open. He stood there in a t-shirt, cut—that's what Gwen had called his leather vest—jeans, and work boots. His dark blond hair was slightly longer on top and looked like he'd been running his fingers through it so it stuck up in spikes, and his pale blue eyes were fixed on me.

"Hi." Why did I always lose my ability to speak around him? It was like my mind went into hiding. I was an intelligent woman, but you wouldn't know it around him. "Gwen invited me over for dinner."

"Come on in." He stepped aside, only enough that I had to squeeze past him. His grin said, 'Yes, it's on purpose, and I *will* enjoy it.'

The scent of leather and spice hit me and my lower belly tightened. This had never happened to me before, this absolute raw, primal attraction to a man. Usually, I needed to get to know them and understand them before I started desiring them. Not that I had a ton of real experience with guys. But that's what had happened with Dan. Not Ricochet. Lust pounded its way through my system as he gripped my upper arm. His fingers were a brand on my skin, heating me from the inside out.

"Dining room's this way." He used his hold to steer me.

I couldn't even say I minded. He was kind of pushy and gruff, but I really liked it. For some reason, I felt totally safe with him. His grip wasn't hurting me, but the touch of his skin was setting me on fire.

Gwen's eyebrows shot up as she watched her brother lead me to the table. Before I could do anything, he used his other hand to yank a chair backward. He released me and watched as I sank onto the offered seat.

"Thank you."

Another knock came at the door and Gwen started to rise.

"I'll get it," Ricochet all but growled.

Gwen gave me a tense smile, but her eyes followed her brother out of the room. It was clear he wasn't thrilled with the last guest.

"Hey guys," I said to the kids, adding a cheerfulness to my tone.

Sean gave me a small smile, then went back to sulking in his chair. Grace chattered up a storm and Gwen gave her a grateful look that I doubted the four-year-old saw.

The men walked back into the room and the air all but vibrated around them. Tense and awkward didn't begin to explain the atmosphere. It made me wonder if Ricochet had said anything to

Trent. I didn't know him well enough to know for sure, but if I had to guess—based off the angry expression on Trent's face—I'd say he had. And odds were it wasn't flattering.

"Hey," Gwen said, hopping up from her seat. She walked over and gave Trent a hug. She chattered brightly as her brother stalked away from them and took his seat. Next to me.

He was watching them with predatory eyes and I finally understood why Gwen had wanted me to come tonight. He looked like he wanted to strangle his former brother-in-law.

I touched his forearm and had to fight back a gasp when his head snapped to me. My eyes widened and I pulled my hand away. I didn't make it far before his hand was holding mine, pulling it back. My fingers were once again resting on his arm.

"Sorry." His voice was deep, but he kept it soft so only I could hear. "Didn't mean to startle you."

"Jordan."

I jerked my hand away from Ricochet and met Gwen's gaze. She had that crazy smile on her face again. My friend loved love. And she loved her brother. And me. I had a feeling she was already planning our wedding and it was everything I could do not to run away from Ricochet and the emotions he was churning up inside of me.

"This is Trent," Gwen said, continuing on with the introductions.

Rising from my seat, I bent over the table to shake his hand. His palms were soft and smooth, not like Ricochet's had been when he'd grabbed my hands. The man next to me worked with those hands, so they were rough and strong.

"Nice to meet you." Trent gave me a smile that I could only describe as smarmy.

I tried to remember what Gwen had told me he did for a living. When it didn't come to mind, I replied. "It's nice to meet you as well." No brain melting attraction there. Thank God. The last thing I needed was to be attracted to my friend's ex. But that just meant that it really was Ricochet causing all this, not that I needed some male attention. The latter would have been easier to deal with. I could go on a few dates and get it out of my system.

It didn't seem like the guy next to me was going to be easy to ignore or avoid. My gaze dropped to his hand as I sat back down. It was wrapped around his steak knife and his knuckles were white as he clenched it.

My gaze darted over and found Gwen's as I tried to pull enough air into my lungs to force them to work. This was such a bad idea. Every crazy, over the top thing Ricochet did only turned me on more. I should be running and hiding from a guy who acted this way. Instead, my pussy was pulsing with desire and I wanted to invite him over to my place. *Getting it out of my system meant getting him inside of me.* I wasn't sure that was an option. Not with this man. Not if I didn't want to lose myself in him.

I tried to pull myself together. I wasn't about to leave Gwen in her time of need. And I still wasn't sure letting myself go along with my attraction to Ricochet was the best thing for me.

Trent was talking, filling Gwen and the kids in on his day as though he didn't notice the tension in the room. It didn't take long to pick out the kind of man he was. He barely took a breath in between sentences about his accomplishments. He loved being the center of attention.

I frowned and looked over at my friend. She was quietly dishing her children's plates with food and helping her daughter cut her steak while he dished his own plate and just kept spewing words. Why had Gwen been with him in the first place? She was kind and caring and he seemed so... Blah. It was safe to say I didn't like him. It didn't matter that I'd just met him. But I'd try to find his redeeming qualities if I could. There must be *something* Gwen used to like about him.

Something slapped down on my plate, making me jump. I must have taken too long because Ricochet was putting food on my plate for me. My eyes widened at the size of the steak and the amount of potatoes he was spooning onto the platter. "That's too much."

He looked over at me, put the spoon back in the bowl of mashed potatoes, and picked up a huge hunk of asparagus with salad tongs. He plopped them down on my plate as I just goggled at the amount of food.

Once he was done with mine, he quietly began dishing his own plate. He was quick and efficient and ended up with just as much as was on my own dish. No wonder Gwen had made so much food.

"Thank you, Ricochet," I finally managed.

He watched me for a moment before giving me a flash of a grin. It lit up his face and made him that much more handsome, but I noticed it didn't seem to fully reach his eyes. He was an enigma and I was slowly getting sucked in. I wanted to know what made him look so... sad all the time. He put on a mask to cover it, that was for sure. Usually he just looked grim, but I saw beneath it.

I wanted to dig and figure out what made him tick. Sighing, I picked up my fork. I was lying to myself. There was no way I was going to be able to keep my distance from him. I wasn't sure if I should even try, or if I should just give in to my fate, the consequences be damned.

CHAPTER 7

Ricochet

Slowly, I chewed the bite of steak in my mouth and watched as Trent grandstanded in front of the women. He was putting on a show, trying to impress them both. He was also ignoring his kids. Big surprise.

Sean was silently eating, and even Grace was unusually quiet while Trent was here. It didn't take a genius to see that this was a normal occurrence.

"Sweetie, did you get enough asparagus?" Gwen asked Sean. He was notorious for 'forgetting' to add vegetables to his plate. But he hadn't forgotten tonight.

Gwen had interrupted Trent, trying to bring her kids into the conversation. To Trent's attention. It didn't work.

A sullen expression flashed over the man's face, then he turned to Jordan and started back up again. He was talking about his job and how important it was. That they were putting criminals behind bars. His gaze slid over to me and he gave me a combative smile. "We have so many plans for the city and ridding it of crime. I have the DA's ear and soon maybe we'll even outlaw MCs. You know how much trouble they cause."

Jordan's deep green eyes flicked to me, but she gave Trent a polite, if weak, smile. She didn't seem to know what to say. I hadn't had a chance to explain to her what MCs really were and here this dick was, calling us criminals. The muscles in my jaw tightened as I ground my teeth together. I was doing my best to keep it together so I didn't ruin this for my sister, but I couldn't understand why she was thinking about letting this piss stain back into their lives. It wasn't my choice, though.

I was back to strangling my steak knife as he continued on about what a menace motorcycle clubs could be to a community. He was just trying to piss me off. He'd been saying shit like that ever since I'd joined The Vikings. He'd go on rants about how MCs were nothing but filth and should be behind bars. I knew exactly what he was doing. Didn't mean I didn't want to lunge over the table and fuck him up.

Something settled on my thigh. Looking down, I saw Jordan's hand there. Meeting her gaze, I forced myself to relax. She gave me a reassuring smile. Everyone at the table knew what Trent was up to and no one was buying his line of bullshit.

I set the knife down. It was too much of a temptation. Gwen had already lured Trent into another conversation.

"Grace received a reward from her pre-school-" she broke off as Trent slammed his hand down on the table and crowed.

"That's my girl! Good job! You've got your daddy's brains in there don't you?"

Everyone was staring at him in startled silence. He'd gone from taunting me to that outburst. As someone who understood highs and lows extremely well, thanks to all the bullshit PTSD the doctors claimed I had, I began to wonder what Trent's excuse was. I'd known him since he and Gwen had first started dating. I'd never seen him act this way before. The boasting and antagonizing, yes, the self-centered behavior, absolutely. But not the high energy and emotional outbursts.

Gwen seemed a little confused, but didn't mention the switch up he'd just exhibited.

"What about you, Little Man?" Trent asked, looking over at Sean. Like Sean had suddenly appeared at the table and hadn't been here for the last thirty minutes, Trent zeroed in on him. He pointed a fork dripping with mashed potatoes at my nephew.

Red started seeping into the edges of my vision as Sean sank down a little in his seat.

"Nothing," Sean mumbled.

"You're a Baker," Trent stated. He didn't have his pompous nose up in the air, but I could picture it thanks to his tone. "You should be excelling in every area of school and life. You're not going to disappoint the family name now are you?"

"Trent," Gwen said in warning. This wasn't the first time they'd had this argument. That much was clear.

Anger rose up within me until I was almost choking on it. Before I could say anything, Jordan squeezed my thigh again. I hadn't realized she'd left her hand there. That in and of itself told me how much my rage was climbing. A gorgeous woman had her hand mere inches from my dick and all I could think about was killing Trent.

"Kids, you're excused from the table," Gwen said.

Grace stared in shock down at her food. We hadn't gotten very far into dinner. I could see her trying to figure out how she was supposed to get enough to eat if her mom was asking her to leave.

"I'll make it up to you after," Gwen said, catching Grace's expression. Sean had already bolted out of the dining room and up the stairs. Grace followed him more slowly.

As soon as both kids were gone, Gwen glared at Trent. "What's wrong with you?"

"What do you mean?" he asked, wiping his mouth on his napkin. "That boy needs to learn that no one is going to give him anything for free in this life. If he doesn't work hard, he'll get left behind and end up being a loser." Trent's eyes met mine. "I certainly can't afford to have any losers near me."

"You calling me a loser, you fucking prick?" I growled. Fisting my hands, I waited for him to make the worst mistake of his life.

"Stop it," Gwen demanded, then turned on Trent. "You're acting weird tonight. What happened to wanting to be in your children's lives? They aren't going to want to be around you if you treat them this way. Sean is eight years old. Eight!" she came close to shouting as Trent opened his mouth to argue. He closed his pie hole and sat sullen in his chair. "You can't push him like that. He's doing great in school here, making friends, and is very happy."

"Except when you come around," I pointed out.

Trent was trying to swallow back whatever retort had popped up after my dig. It wasn't easy for him. "If you'll excuse me," he muttered, tossing his napkin down and standing. We watched as he walked out of the dining room. Instead of him going upstairs like I thought Gwen was expecting, we heard the front door slam shut.

Gwen lost her rigid posture and she sighed. "Jordan, I'm so sorry-"

"No need to apologize," Jordan insisted, leaning over and giving Gwen's hand a squeeze.

Guilt curled inside my gut. I was supposed to have made this dinner a little easier, but my sister knew I couldn't stand that fucker. Still, now that he was gone I thought maybe I could have tried harder. "I'll walk you home," I told Jordan, rising with her.

She looked startled at my offer, then glanced over at my sister. Gwen gave her a soft smile. "Go ahead. I need a few minutes alone."

I moved behind Jordan toward the door, looking over my shoulder at my sister. I didn't like the sad expression on her face. Didn't like that I'd helped put it there.

The fresh night air surrounded me as I stepped out onto the porch. Trent's car was gone. Typical. Something doesn't go his way and he runs. It was his way of doing things.

"That may be true, but you should give Gwen a break."

I looked down into forest green eyes and frowned. Had I said that out loud? I must have. "I wasn't trying to ruin her dinner."

"She's trying to do what's best for her kids," Jordan said as we made our way over to her house. "She's willing to set aside the old pain that Trent caused if it means her kids would have their father in their lives."

I hadn't thought about it like that. "He's kind of a shitty person."

Her laughter filled the air. "I think you might be right. But isn't it better for the kids to come to their own conclusions about that? Or should she keep them away from him? And risk them resenting her for it?"

"Shit. I don't know."

"Neither does she." She smiled up at me. "She's trying to figure out what's least harmful for the children."

Leaning against the doorframe, I waited as she unlocked the door. I brushed a piece of her dark hair behind her ear, causing her to look over at me. "You're smart." Her laughter filled the evening air and some of the tension inside of me eased. I tried to shove the disaster of an evening to the back of my mind. I pushed my way in after her, looking around her spotless living room.

"What are you doing?" There was wariness in her tone now.

"I should check and make sure no one is inside the house."

She put her hands on her hips and arched a brow at me. "What kind of life do you think I live that people would be skulking around my home late at night?"

"You never know," I told her with a mischievous smile. Stalking toward her, my grin grew as she backed up from me. I made her nervous. I sort of liked it. "You afraid of me?"

"No."

"Then why are you backing up?"

She bumped into the wall next to the door and before she could move, I caged her in, arms on either side of her head. She stared up at me, her pink tongue brushing over her lips in a nervous motion.

Groaning, I lowered my head and took her mouth in a kiss. I didn't ask, didn't have the ability to stop myself. The only time I'd felt any emotions besides anger or pain over the last few days had been because of her. If I wasn't careful, I was going to become addicted to her. Strung out on the way she made me feel.

My tongue followed the path hers had, dipping between her parted lips. Her gasp had me gathering her up in my arms, pressing our bodies together while I deepened the kiss.

How long had it been since I'd kissed a beautiful woman? Too long. Just long enough. I didn't know. Didn't care. She was perfection there in my arms. I didn't want to let her go.

Her tongue brushed mine as she started kissing me back. I listened to the little moans she was making and promised myself I'd stop. Still, I kept going. My hands skated down her back to grab her ass. I squeezed, enjoying the feel of her curves beneath my palms before I released her and cupped her cheeks. I softened the kiss before breaking it entirely.

We stood there, panting, staring at each other in disbelief. I could see the desire and confusion there in her eyes. I wanted her to be confident and sure the first time I took her. I needed her desperate for me.

Stepping back, I let her go, even though it was the last thing I wanted. "Goodnight, Jordan." With that, I walked out her front door.

My dick was hard beneath my jeans and I adjusted it as I walked back toward my sister's house. A smile spread over my face and I paused, staring up at the stars overhead. I hadn't smiled this much in a long time. A long damn time. Usually my grins were forced. Not with her, at least not for the last fifteen minutes or so.

Shaking my head as I realized that Jordan was getting to me, I went inside to apologize to my sister.

CHAPTER 8

Ricochet

Guilt flooded back as soon as I stepped into the dining room and found Gwen sitting at the table with her head in her hands. She wasn't crying, just sitting in the aftermath of the disaster that had just happened.

"Sorry, Gwenny," I told her, as I went to sit next to her. I didn't touch her. She didn't like to be touched when she was upset. Just another thing we had in common.

Her sigh was heavy as she lifted her head, and that's when I saw all the worry Jordan had mentioned etched into her features. "I don't know what to do. He wasn't acting like that before. I thought he'd changed and that he really wanted to have a relationship with them."

I didn't want to be the one to burst her bubble, but she was my sister, my twin, and it was my duty to tell her the truth. "Men will never change. *People* don't change," I reminded her with a humorless laugh. A rueful smile tugged at her lips.

"You thought I wanted to get back together with him." It wasn't a question, but there was no accusation in her tone either.

"If he wasn't such an asshole, I wouldn't blame you if you did," I admitted. "I want the kids to have access to their father, too. But that's the one they have."

This time she did laugh. "He really is a jerk."

"Yeah. He is." We sat in companionable silence for a few minutes. "So, what are you going to do?"

"If that's the way he's going to act around the kids, we'll go back to not having him in our lives. He makes it easy by not bothering to come visit or anything like that most of the time. I'm sure whatever this was will work its way out of his system soon enough. Then we can move on and get back to normal."

I leaned over and gave her a sideways hug. "You're doing a great job with them."

Her head dropped onto my shoulder. "Thanks, Gage. Sometimes I really do wonder."

"You don't need to. They're happy, well-adjusted kids." My phone buzzed in my pocket so I pulled it out. "You okay here? I have somewhere I have to go."

"We're just fine," she said in a firm tone. She straightened up and pulled herself together.

"Leave the dishes," I told her. "I'll do them once I get back." Striding over to the hall closet, I grabbed my leather jacket and shrugged it on. My eyes strayed up the stairs. I wanted to go speak with Sean, but Lock had texted that he needed to see me.

With a plan in my mind to speak with my nephew tomorrow, I left the house. My bike was cold between my thighs as I straddled it. The motor roared to life, and I let it idle for a few minutes, warming up, as I stared at Jordan's house.

There had been a brief blip of a thought inside my head that I shouldn't get involved with her. I was too fucked up. Unfortunately, I didn't have much of a say. The way I was craving her was too deep to deny. The instant attraction didn't bother me. I'd experienced that before. But she brought out something inside of me I'd thought was long gone. I'd been living my life numb for years and somehow she was waking my system back up. How could I walk away from that?

It wasn't exactly fair to her, though I did plan to treat her like the best thing that had ever happened to me, because she was. I didn't have it within myself to be self-sacrificing right now. The last thing I thought when I came out here was to find a woman, and possibly a solution, but I wasn't about to give up either now.

* * *

THE WIND WHIPPED past as I drove out to the spot Lock had asked me to meet with him. It didn't matter that it was nine p.m. by this point. He'd be out here for most of the night. We all knew it was his thinking spot.

The road twisted up the mountain as I started to climb Mt. Lemmon. There were times it'd be helpful if Lock had picked a place that wasn't such a drive to do his thinking, but honestly the ride chilled me out.

The remaining anger faded as I zipped along, leaching out into the cooler night air. That was one nice thing about Tucson, even in the winter, it wasn't impossible to ride. You'd freeze your nuts off on some of the colder nights, but it rarely snowed, or rained. It was the perfect riding weather. Once summer hit, I'd be wishing for these chilly nights to keep my balls from sticking to my damn leg.

I inhaled a huge lungful of cold air and slowed as I saw the turnout where Lock's bike was parked. It didn't take long before I was climbing up over the boulders on the side of the road. The moon was bright overhead, lighting my path. It was a good thing as one wrong step would send me pitching off the side of the mountain. It was a long, long way down. The thought of death didn't bother me. I'd lived with it for too long now to worry much about it. Though right now it was far less inviting than it had been a few weeks ago.

Picking my way out, I dropped down onto my ass next to my president. We were out on the furthest boulder, nothing beneath our feet but air as we sat.

"Prez."

He was studying me, but I just looked out over the city lights shining far below us. He'd speak when he was ready.

"Rip's getting married."

My smile was automatic. "Good." I hadn't gotten a chance to know his bride-to-be yet. Or was it wife? I wasn't even sure if their first marriage was legally binding, but I was glad either way. Smokehouse had caught me up on most of what was going on.

"We'll be going up to Washington for the ceremony." He gave me the rest of the details and my heart tripped in my chest. "We all want you to be there, but you have to do what's best for you at this point," he said, not even giving me a chance to speak.

"I can't miss Rip's wedding." I met his gaze and whatever he saw there had him frowning.

"You can."

Shaking my head, I opened my mouth to tell him again that I couldn't.

"If I have to make it an order, Ricochet, I will."

My shoulders slumped as everything inside me deflated. He was right. The brief emotions Jordan was bringing out in me didn't mean I was fixed. Hell, I might never be. As much as I wanted to be with my brothers and see Rip get hitched, I couldn't go. I'd be an anchor on the entire event, dragging it down. He deserved the day to be happy and carefree.

"They'll understand," he said, turning back to the view.

"I'm sick to fucking death of being a disappointment." Shock held me still. I'd never said anything like that out loud in front of Lock before.

He looked surprised as well. "Who the fuck do you think you're disappointing, Kid? It sure as hell isn't us."

I sighed and scrubbed a hand through my hair. It was a bit longer on top now than I usually kept it, but I just didn't feel like getting it cut. "Hard not to feel like a fuck up."

"What happened out in that desert with Hellfire wasn't your fault. I should have anticipated that they'd recruit women and kids to fight for them. Hell, I'm surprised there wasn't more, now that I think about it. I shouldn't have put you in that position."

Shaking my head, I made a sound of disgust. "You should be able to count on me in any situation."

"I do." He shrugged his shoulders. "All our brothers came out of that mess alive and you did what needed to be done. I just wish it wasn't such a burden to you." He seemed to be picking his next words carefully. "I don't actually know how to help you, Ricochet. PTSD wasn't something I received training on, other than the usual slideshows the military forced on us." He cocked his head. "Would it help if I got someone you could talk to? Someone the club can trust?"

"I have no idea what will help me, Lock," I admitted. It was the first time I'd said the words out loud. "I don't know if anything can. I…I don't know that I deserve it." That might have been the hardest sentence I ever spoke.

"You were put in an impossible situation. Twice. If anything, you didn't deserve to be in that position." He narrowed his eyes on me and nodded, coming to some kind of decision. "We'll try a few things and see what works."

I didn't even want to ask what he meant by that. Didn't want to think about it. The thought of asking for help made bile rise in my throat. It was weak to ask for help. They had their own problems and lives to deal with. It wasn't right to burden them with mine.

Except I knew that was bullshit. They could come to me for anything and I wouldn't hesitate to help. These were my brothers. This was my president. I should be able to go to them with anything. And I hadn't been. I'd been swallowing everything down, doing it all myself. And where had that gotten me? Deeper into the hole than ever before.

"It's time to let us help you, Ricochet."

My eyes closed. He'd just uttered the words that were finally becoming clear to me. I nodded and we fell silent again. Maybe with their help, I could claw my way out of all this. Become the man I should be. That my family deserved. That my brothers thought I was. It was time to take action.

* * *

By the time I got back to the house, it was late and everyone was asleep. The drive home had invigorated me and a part of myself wanted to walk over to Jordan's and wake her up. After that kiss we'd shared I wanted to explore more with her.

Instead, I stripped, dropping my clothes into the hamper in the closet. Walking naked into the ensuite bathroom, I turned on the shower. My hand froze over the cold water knob. Usually dousing myself with freezing water helped, only, I didn't need it tonight. Between my talk with Lockout and thinking about Jordan, I was feeling decent.

Cranking up the heat, I stepped into the spray and groaned as the hot water pelted me. It was fucking nice to take a hot shower. I had almost forgotten what it was like. My eyes were closed and a picture of Jordan just after I'd kissed her came to mind.

My dick swelled to life and I braced one hand on the shower wall in front of me while the other wrapped around it. The little sounds she'd made while I'd kissed her had nearly driven me crazy. I couldn't wait to see what kind of noises I could pull from between her sweet lips when I had the chance to fuck her.

Stroking slowly, I thought about what would have happened if I'd taken her upstairs. Would she have let me lay her back on the bed? Strip her bare?

I hissed out a breath as I thought about all the things I wanted to do to her gorgeous body. It was my intention to lick that sweet pussy of hers until she was a shaking, sobbing mess. I watched as my hand slid over my cock, the head disappearing and reappearing with my movements.

Once I had her quivering with the need to be filled, I'd put her on her knees. My eyes closed as I pictured her staring up at me as she wrapped her lips around my dick. I groaned, tightening my grip to a punishing level as she started to suck on me in my fantasy.

It didn't take more than a few more slick strokes before that familiar tingle in my balls had me growling out in pleasure. I opened my eyes in time to watch my cum hit the side of the shower.

Dropping my head back, I enjoyed the sensations while I massaged my length for a bit. Once my dick became too sensitive, I released it and sighed. The release had been necessary if I ever wanted to get to sleep tonight, but I knew it would be short lived. I used the showerhead to wash all evidence away and then finished up.

Excitement to see her again was already building up inside of me. When had been the last time I'd looked forward to anything this much? A long fucking time. Shaking my head, I climbed into bed, wishing she was waiting for me, and shut off the light.

CHAPTER 9

Jordan

"Why are you so quiet?"

I looked over at my dad and shook my head with a smile. "No reason."

His bushy eyebrows rose and I realized everyone was staring at me. I'd floated through all of yesterday and I still couldn't get that kiss out of my head.

Ricochet had nearly set me ablaze. I'd always heard about that all-consuming lust that people felt. I'd just never experienced it for myself. Not before Friday night.

"What have you been up to?" Mom asked, giving Dad a warning look not to pry. We were spread out as we walked along through the desert.

Dad let out a shrill whistle when the baying from the beagles got too far away. The sound had the dogs circling back to us. My brother encouraged his hawk to take flight so he could squat down as Belle and Ellie ran up. Belle was limping on her front left paw, so he lifted and examined it. He took out a pair of pliers and pulled the cactus spine from her paw. He was barely finished before she was wriggling in his arms, baying loudly, so she could chase back after Ellie and the ever elusive rabbits again.

We laughed as we watched the dogs zig and zag through brush and cactus, noses to the ground as they ran. Bells jingled as my hawk shook out her feathers. She wasn't as impressed with the dog's antics as we were.

"They're restless," Dad said, adjusting his hawk's jesses. The leather strapped to their feet held little bells that helped us locate the raptors when they were down on the ground.

"That's because we missed last week," Jenna replied, giving Noah a dark look.

"Wasn't my fault," my brother replied with a grin. He held up his gloved hand so his hawk could land on it again. It absolutely had been his fault. He'd gotten drunk the night before—not something my parents knew—and overslept. If one of us wasn't able to go out on a hunt, the rest didn't go. We all got up at the crack of dawn, so by the time we got out into the sparsely populated areas we didn't have to worry about the heat. It wasn't getting hot in the mornings yet, but it would soon enough. Noah yanked on Jenna's ponytail, causing her to squeal with laughter. Their hawks danced on their gloves.

Falconry was a family sport for us. It was unusual to have an entire family with their own birds, but once Dad had gotten into it we'd all joined in. We went hunting together each weekend, then had a meal together. It was important to each of us. Gave us the perfect excuse to spend time with one another. With Noah about to turn twenty-nine, me at twenty-five, and Jenna only fourteen, we were all at different stages in our lives. Our parents wanted to keep us close as long as possible.

I was supposed to be going with Noah to pick out a ring for his long-time girlfriend. That was the reason he'd gotten drunk. He and his friends had been celebrating and he'd lost track of time and how much alcohol he'd downed. We all loved Mallory. She was even in the process of being an apprentice falconer. Normally, she was out on these hikes through the desert with us. Her parents were in town this time and she was busy this weekend showing them around.

Mom raised her gloved hand and sent her Harris Hawk flying off into the desert. The rest of us followed suit. Our birds were used to hunting together. It was the reason we'd all gotten this breed of hawk. It was less likely there'd be any territorial disputes amongst our raptors. "Well?" Mom asked me, giving me a knowing look. Somehow she'd already picked up on the fact that something was going on with me.

"I had dinner with Gwen and her family the other night," I said, adjusting the pouch I wore around my waist. It gave me something to focus on so that hopefully my mom wouldn't notice that anything was different with me.

"She's such a nice girl," Mom commented.

"She is," I replied. "I'm lucky to have a friend like her."

"You should invite her and the kids over to dinner at our place one night," Dad suggested. "It's been too long since we've seen them."

"Oh, well, she's been busy. Her brother is staying with her right now." If it was just Gwen and the kids, I would have jumped on the invitation. The kids loved coming over and my parents were obsessed with them.

My sister raised her head and gave me a lascivious smile. "Is he hot?"

"Jenna!" Mom snapped, then gave her a look of disbelief.

Jenna may be the youngest, but she was by far the most outgoing. Not that Noah and I were wilting wallflowers. Noah and I gave each other an amused look. My mother continued to scowl at Jenna, then asked me, "Well, is he handsome?"

"Yes," I answered, as innocently as I could. "He's hot."

"Jordan," Mom sighed, realizing her control over this situation was slipping away faster than she could reel it in.

Dad wiggled his eyebrows at me. "Ah, got your eye on him, huh?"

I laughed and shrugged. "I don't know, yet." Honesty was always the best policy with my family. It was like my mother had a divining rod for lies. She always knew when her kids weren't telling her the truth.

"Yet," Noah echoed with a laugh, elbowing my dad in the ribs. "Looks like we're going to have to set up more space in the mews before long."

I laughed along with my family. Only we would see one of us getting a new girlfriend or boyfriend as a chance to get a new hawk to add to our brood.

A sharp cry rang out and I shaded my eyes against the early morning sun. One of the hawks split off from the group and flew back toward us. We all raised our gloves, but Haze landed on mine. She eyeballed me, tilting her head this way and that before launching back into the air. It wasn't an unusual behavior for her. She liked to check in on me while we hunted.

Our birds all had different personalities, as all animals do. True to the breed we went with, our raptors all seemed to love and care for us, but Haze was as devoted to me as I was to her. Dad had once had a hawk that didn't care about him at all. Dad had only been a food delivery method to it. He'd found a better suited home for that bird. With so many of us hunting together, we needed birds who were friendlier.

They weren't dogs, though. Most raptors would never give the loyalty a hound would. I bent and scrubbed my hand over Ellie's back as we walked past the dogs. They'd momentarily lost the trail and were resting, waiting for us to catch up.

Between us and the dogs walking through the brush, we soon scared out a jack rabbit. The hawks dipped and soared as they worked together to direct the terrified rabbit into a position where one of the birds could swoop down on it.

We all broke into a jog to keep up as they hunted. As soon as one of the birds went to ground, the others began landing in nearby mesquite trees and on saguaros, focused eyes watching as their family member killed breakfast.

It was Delilah, Mom's hawk. She approached slowly and tossed a skinned piece of rabbit she'd pulled from her own pouch off to the side. Delilah immediately hopped over to the new meat and swallowed it down. Mom used the moment of distraction to stuff the dead rabbit into her pouch, out of the birds' view. If we allowed the birds to gorge themselves on the first kill of the morning, they wouldn't want to hunt anymore. They always happily took the already skinned meat we kept on hand, over having to do the work on the fresh kill.

Putting a piece of meat between my thumb and finger on my gloved hand, I whistled for Haze. She landed and set into her treat immediately. I watched as she tore into the strip, shaking her head when blood and a fleck of sinew got stuck on her beak. Laughing, I ducked as the gore went flying. Watching these birds eat wasn't for the faint of heart. I loved this. Loved the sport. Loved the birds. Adored my family and our time out here together.

Taking a deep breath of cool air, I wondered if this was something Ricochet could eventually enjoy? Shaking my head at myself for even thinking that far into the future, and for the fact that he was in it, I released my hawk once again. It'd only been one kiss.

Not quite. It was far more than that. It had been an invasion of my senses and a deposit, a promise of what was to come. One soul twisting, pulse pounding, delicious kiss. A part of me couldn't wait to see him again.

It didn't matter that I was on a sabbatical after the last boyfriend had broken my heart. I couldn't seem to convince myself that thinking about Ricochet in any way was a bad idea. He was just there, in my head.

"Hurry up, Slow Poke!" Jenna called out.

I pushed all thoughts of the sexy biker from my mind. There'd be time enough later to figure out what I was going to do about him. For now, I was going to enjoy the rest of the time with my family.

CHAPTER 10

Ricochet

"You look like shit," I called out as Hellfire made his way up the driveway.

Kit was walking beside him and she shook her head and gave me a sharp look. I gave her a wide smile as Hellfire flipped me off.

"Fuck off, I could say the same to you," he muttered as he flopped into one of the deck chairs. "I got shot. What's your fucking excuse, Princess?"

"I can feel the love around this place," Kit said with a snort. "No wonder he's been hounding me about coming to see you."

Hellfire shot her a quick look and Kit zipped her lips. They tried never to talk about being worried about me in front of me. I knew they always were.

"I'll leave you two to it," she told us, starting to turn.

"Hi."

She looked over her shoulder at my sister, who had appeared and was now standing in the doorway to her house. "Hey."

"Gwen, this is my friend Kit. She's Smokehouse's sister. Kit, this is *my* sister, Gwen."

"Heard a lot about you," Kit told Gwen with a smile. She spun around and shook the hand my sister was holding out.

"It's nice to meet you," Gwen replied. "Hi, Hell."

"Hey, Gorgeous," Hellfire told her. "I'd get up but…"

"Gage told me you'd been shot," Gwen said with a frown. She went over and fussed over Hell for a minute before pressing a kiss to his forehead. "You need to be more careful."

Gwen knew most of what we got up to as a crew. I didn't hide much from my twin, but I also knew she'd take the information I told her to the grave. I never gave specifics, just honestly told her when there was a shoot-out, and when we helped people. When I'd first told her I was joining a motorcycle club, she'd tried to talk me out of it. It took a few tries before I was able to explain to her that I needed to be a part of something more. The military had instilled that into me. I had to be a part of a group. These men were more than just club members to me. They were my brothers. Sometimes I got the feeling she still didn't totally get it, but she'd worked past the worry and understood. At least enough to leave me be about the dangerous situations we found ourselves in.

"I will," he promised in a solemn tone.

Gwen looked back over at Kit. "If you wanted to stick around, I was about to go hang out with my friend." She pointed over to Jordan's house.

I sat up a bit straighter, glancing over, trying to catch a glimpse of the elusive beauty. I hadn't seen Jordan in a few weeks, not since I'd kissed her and later jerked off to the thought of her in my shower. It wasn't hard to see that she was avoiding me. I was going to have to do something to fix that. Couldn't have my sunshine slipping away, leaving me to my cold, dreary existence.

"I'd love that," Kit told her. "You girls would be way more fun than these two." She stuck her tongue out at me, but she squeezed my forearm as she walked by.

Kit was Smokehouse's sister, and they came together as a set. The MC knew that. They were a lot like Gwen and me, only not twins. Kit was twenty-eight, and drop-dead beautiful. He may only have two years on her, but he was the typical older brother. Smokehouse had pounded more than one face in when too many bikers had paid attention to his sister. Any man that wanted to date her would likely have to fight Smokehouse, repeatedly, for the honor.

Stretching my legs out, I watched as the girls walked over to Jordan's place. My eyes narrowed as the door opened and the object of my every fucking fantasy stepped out onto her porch to meet Kit. Everything brightened for a brief moment.

"Smoke wasn't kidding," Hell commented. There was amusement etched on his face. "You seriously found yourself a girl way out here."

It was true enough, though I wasn't sure Jordan understood where my head was at yet. How could she when I barely understood it myself? I grunted in response to Hellfire's observation.

"Shit." There was disbelief in the word. "Never thought you were going to find anyone you were interested in. You stick to yourself too much."

"You're one to talk," I shot back. I wasn't watching the girls anymore. Instead, I was focused on my friend. His dark brown eyes were latched onto the women. One side of my lips quirked up. I knew his secret. One that no one else did.

"You really do look like shit," he said, changing the subject. He turned away from the three women and focused on me.

I chuckled. "You're the one who was shot," I reminded him, giving him back the excuse he'd thrown at me only a few minutes ago. The fact that there wasn't any judgment coming from him had guilt pinging through me. "How are you?"

"I'm fine, Ricochet."

Looking down at the decking, I frowned. "I'm so damn sorry I didn't…take those shooters out before you were hit."

"It wasn't your fault."

Glaring up at him, I sat up, leaning forward. "The fuck it wasn't."

"It was a battle, Brother," he said, shaking his head. "We all knew what we were getting into when we went. Knew the potential risks."

"But I hesitated. I froze." It didn't matter that I'd had a good fucking reason. If anyone knew that a kid was just as able and willing to kill in a war like that, it was me. Still, I'd seen that ten-year-old boy and I'd frozen up as everything from before, with Jack, had come rushing back. In the end, I'd done what I needed to, but not before Hell had been injured. The guilt from knowing that I was the reason he'd been shot was eating me alive.

The man was built like a fucking bull. He was massive. Seeing him lying on a cot at Crash Cart's place had nearly made my knees buckle. Seeing Crash cut into him to get the lead out had one dire consequence after another flooding my mind. I could have lost one of my best friends. One of my brothers. In order to save him, I'd killed another kid and it'd shoved what was left of the tattered remains of my soul even deeper into the abyss.

A loud boom sounded nearby and suddenly I was caught in the grips of my memories. Gunfire rang out. My hands started to shake as my mouth went dry. I closed my eyes, lights flashing behind my lids as shouting filled my mind.

"Hey."

The vision of two young kids, lying side by side in the dirt, vanished. I blinked, trying to figure out where they'd gone. Where I was. It took me a minute to realize that Hell was crouched down next to me, his hand on my shoulder, his injured shoulder in a sling.

"It's fine. Ricochet. It was just a car backfiring," he growled, trying to get my attention. To pull me out of the flashback.

"You're not supposed to be moving around that much," I gritted out through clenched teeth as the fear and doubt slashed at me. This was why I didn't like talking about what happened. It had the potential to bring me right back to either of the events where I'd been the one to end two young lives. Of the fact that I'd lost one best friend years ago, and had nearly lost another. It was bad enough I relived both fights each night in my dreams. I didn't need this shit while I was awake, too.

"It'll give Kit something to yell at me about on the drive home," he said, shrugging his behemoth shoulders. A wince pulled at his mouth after he made the move. He'd forgotten for a moment about his injury. Blowing out a breath to ease the pain, he turned his attention back onto me. "You with me?" His eyes searched mine.

"Give me a minute." I looked over to Jordan's house, I could see her laughing, through the window, with Kit and Gwen. I locked onto her smile and slowly all the anxiety started to drain out. It felt like water rolling off my body, a tidal wave emptying out. I wasn't sure why she affected me this way, but I wasn't complaining. My heart was slowing in my chest, my palms had stopped sweating. I knew I had to be careful. Once I had a flashback the threat of another was much more likely.

Hellfire nodded and backed off. He went back to his chair, but he was watching me like a hawk. Out of everyone, he was always the one who knew when a fucking attack was looming down on me. I wasn't sure how he always knew, but he always spotted it first. He always seemed to know what I needed.

Most people thought he was this quiet, brooding guy. He was if he didn't know you. What you'd find out if you took the time to get to know him is he was funny as fuck. He was always joking around, playing pranks, and he was the first to laugh in any situation where he was comfortable. You'd also come to realize how fucking dangerous he was, but that was usually if you and he weren't friendly. I was lucky enough to call him a friend and brother.

I kept my focus on Jordan. Shaking my head to clear what was left, I was able to escape the grip of the memories. I unclenched my fingers one by one. My muscles began to relax. The shaking was what always pissed me off to no end. Such a weak fucking response, yet every time I wound up trembling like a fucking newborn baby lamb.

"This shit doesn't get fixed overnight."

I glared at Hellfire, trying to swallow back my anger. It was mostly directed at myself, but if he was going to insert himself into my issues he could bear the brunt a bit as well. "The fuck you know about it?"

"Nothing," he admitted. "But I've watched you struggle with this for years. You know what else I've learned?"

Rolling my eyes, I muttered, "Like I can stop you from telling me?"

"Ignoring it doesn't make it go away. How long you going to keep trying the same thing over and over again? Didn't someone say that was the definition of insanity?" He tilted his head as he thought about it. "Einstein or some other egghead."

I frowned at him, surprise prompting the reaction. "I would've never pegged you for a guy who knew something Einstein said."

"I know shit." He chuckled and leaned back in the chair once again. He was relaxing because I was. There'd been more than once I'd come out of an attack with his bulk crushing me into the ground. Somewhere along the line he'd appointed himself as my guardian, protecting me from myself. Didn't matter how much I'd told him to fuck off, he'd stuck around. Him and Smoke. Someday I would make it up to them. Thank them properly.

"So what's up with your girl?"

Sighing, I didn't bother to deny it. There wasn't much I kept from Hellfire and Smokehouse. Plus, it kept my mind off what had happened to him and what I'd done. "She doesn't know it yet, but she's going to be my old lady."

He barked out a laugh. "You fucking move fast."

Shrugging, I smirked over at him. "Just know what I want when I see it."

"What's the plan?"

"Haven't figured it out yet," I admitted. "She's avoiding me."

"Probably waiting for you to make a move," he suggested.

"How do I make a move if she holes up inside her home?" My brows drew together as he grinned at me.

"Gotta go where she is. Kick the door down, chicks dig that."

My brows shot up. "You telling me to break into her home? Pretty sure that's not going to make her want to trust me."

He chuckled. "You're probably right. But what the fuck? If she's going to be your old lady she's going to have to get used to the way we do things."

I shook my head, but couldn't help the laugh that rumbled out of my chest. The look on his face made me pause. "What?"

"Just haven't seen you smile or laugh this much in… Ever."

"Used to all the time," I told him with a sigh. The year after I joined the military my sister begged me to end my contract. She had no idea what she was asking or that it wasn't possible, just that I was changing.

The military had made me into a man. It'd taken a young, arrogant kid and spit out a dangerous, arrogant man. I'd be forever grateful for the time I spent serving our country. But all Gwen had been able to see at the time—and for a long while afterward—was the way I'd changed. It hadn't really been a problem until that one mission.

The sound of engines revving caught our attention and I was grateful to see a few more of my brothers rolling up on motorcycles. We watched as Smokehouse, Butcher, and Toxic parked and walked up the drive.

"Figured you hadn't found anything to do yet and were still bored out of your mind!" Smoke called out as they approached.

I stood and exchanged a back slapping hug with the other two. "Not a lot to do," I admitted. "You all want a beer?"

"Absolutely," Butcher said.

"Dragged us out to the middle of the damn desert," Toxic replied, "least we could do is drink your fridge dry."

I should have been happy to see them, excited to have them around. But something was off. It was getting darker, not from cloud cover or sunset. The tunnel vision was coming in. I'd thought I'd shaken off the flashback, but these things had a way of invading my mind when I least expected it.

My footsteps faltered as his words hit me. Middle of the desert. Grabbing onto the door jamb, I took a deep breath as my vision wavered. *Fuck. Not again.* Everything was too fresh. I'd had vicious flashbacks for over a year the last time, and it'd only been a few weeks this go around. I knew this was going to happen, it was why I'd come out to stay with my sister. I'd been hoping to avoid some of these reminders. I didn't expect them to come on randomly like this.

"Ricochet."

Clearing my throat, I forced my heavy limbs to move and walked inside, ignoring whoever was behind me.

CHAPTER 11

Ricochet

My eyes should have adjusted to the darker lighting in the house, but I was getting sucked back into the memories. It'd been dark as hell out in that desert, at least until some of the buildings had caught fire. Passing by the window on my way to the fridge had sunlight flashing into my eyes. I hissed out a breath as they registered to my mind as truck headlights. They'd blinded us as the group of insurgents had surrounded us.

Shaking my head, I tried to get a handle on my breathing. No. Not insurgents. Cultists. Wait. Who had it been? My chest was heaving, heart racing as I grabbed the kitchen counter to keep from going to my knees.

"Don't," someone snapped from nearby. "Don't touch him."

Looking over, I saw three pairs of boots. They blurred, merging together, then disappeared. Sand. Everywhere. Gunfire. Blood. Fuck. I had to help Jack. Hellfire. Someone needed me. I squeezed my eyes shut, trying to will my mind to let go of the past. It was fucking impossible. My brain kept leaping between events and then back here to the present.

"You're safe here, don't try to fight it." That was Toxic.

My eyes opened and landed on his face. He was squatting down in front of me. When had I ended up on my ass?

"Just let it play out," Toxic suggested.

What did he know about it?

"The more you fight, the harder it's going to hang on. We won't let you do anything stupid," Toxic promised.

Sighing, I stopped fighting. My head slammed back into the cabinets as I watched Jack's body jerk with each round that pierced through him. He fell in a pool of his own blood, lying too still on the sand. The sound I made was more of a roar than a wail, but it was agonizing. In the moment, I didn't know if it had only echoed inside my own mind or if it was bouncing off the walls of my sister's kitchen.

Time was all distorted and I didn't know how long I sat there, lost in the grip of the nightmare my life had become. But eventually, it began to fade.

"Get out of my face," I huffed out as I realized all four of my brothers were hovering around me. Embarrassment sent heat sliding over my skin. I hated losing fucking control like that. It was bad enough when it happened in the privacy of my room at the clubhouse, but each time it happened in front of others the shame built. This wasn't the first time I'd lost my shit in front of them. It didn't matter that they were family, I didn't want anyone seeing me like that.

Butcher held out a hand and with a sigh, I took it. He hauled me to my feet.

"Let's get those beers," Smoke suggested, already raiding my sister's fridge.

That was one good thing about my brothers, they knew when I didn't want to talk about it and they were good at not prodding me. We each took our beer and walked back outside. The remnants of the memories were still there, but the guys kept up a constant stream of shit talking that prevented me from dwelling too much on the past.

I caught Toxic giving me considering looks every once in a while, but he didn't say anything. Something I was grateful for. I wasn't even sure where to begin with asking for help. It wasn't something I did often. I knew Lockout was planning something, but I hadn't asked for specifics. Until I figured out a next step, my plan was just to stay out here and as far away from the memories as I could.

My nerves were frayed thanks to having two attacks in one day. I listened as the guys laughed and talked, only joining in once they realized how quiet I'd gotten.

"We leave tomorrow for Rip's wedding," Smokehouse told me. He and Hellfire were watching me closely now.

I couldn't believe over a month had passed so quickly. Forcing a smile, I told them, "That's going to be a damn good time." I swallowed down my disappointment at not being able to go. Just seeing a couple of my brothers had set these attacks off. I could only imagine what would happen if I went and was surrounded by them all, plus their families. As much as I loved them, Lock had been right. I couldn't go. "Tell him sorry I can't be there," I muttered. The beer washed down the emotions that were rising from within my chest.

"He knows," Butcher replied.

"He wanted to come out here today, but they had to get on the road this morning," Toxic added. "He hasn't had a lot of time since bringing everyone back from the compound."

"I bet." I understood. The people we'd brought with us out of the desert needed him. They'd been thrust into an entirely new world and Riptide and Sloane were the only rocks they had to cling to. It was all new to Sloane, too, so that left Rip.

Feminine laughter floated in the air and we all glanced over. Butcher let out a whistle from between his teeth, it was low so only we heard it. "Who're the babes?"

Smokehouse shot him a dark look, but Butcher just shook his head. "Kit may as well be my sister, too," he said with a shudder. "Don't think of her that way."

"The blonde is *my* sister," I told him with my own narrow eyed look.

"Well shit," Toxic muttered. "Everyone's just related to everyone. How about the gorgeous-"

"Taken," I snarled.

They all froze, eyebrows up, identical shocked looks on their faces. My anger wasn't unusual. They saw it often, but the jealousy that was searing my gut was new. And they could easily see it.

A smile formed on Butcher's face. It was devilish and I knew it meant trouble. "Well... Maybe we should go introduce ourselves, Toxic." His eyes were glued on me as he spoke to his friend.

"You deaf, Old Man?" I asked. "She's spoken for."

"I heard you," he replied, his tone upbeat and bright. He was doing this just to piss me the fuck off. "Doesn't mean we shouldn't meet your old lady."

"Old lady?" Smoke asked, looking over at me. "Did you end up-"

"No," I answered, cutting him off again.

"But he's going to," Hellfire added, in what he clearly thought was a helpful tone.

Butcher and Toxic were already hopping over the porch railing. One minute they'd been sitting there, the next they were gone. "Those fuckers," I hissed and went after them.

The women stopped as the five of us approached. Jordan's eyes widened as they bounced between us.

"Hey there," Butcher called out. His voice was pitched lower and he had his eyes on Jordan.

"Um..." She looked over at me, unsure of what was happening.

"I'm Butcher," he continued on, not at all fazed by her uncertainty. "This is my manservant, Toxic."

Toxic flipped him off and moved in close and grabbed her hand. His thumb rubbed over the top of the hand he held as he shook it. "Hi, Sweetheart."

"Hi, I'm...Jordan," she answered, glancing down at where he was brushing his thumb over her skin.

Butcher gave my sister a bright smile. "And what's your name, Beautiful?"

"Gwen," she replied with a smile. She knew what they were up to.

Gwen hadn't met anyone but Hell, Smoke, Lock, and Rip, but she was already picking up on the game Butcher and Toxic were playing.

"Knock it off," I growled at them.

Their grins only got bigger. Toxic stepped up next to Jordan, facing me, and wrapped his arm around her shoulders. "Knock what off?" He asked. His tone was going for innocent, but came off as instigating. "We're just introducing ourselves to your friend."

Jordan frowned, looking between me and Gwen, searching for an explanation.

Seeing Toxic tugging Jordan's body into his side had red seeping into the edges of my vision. I loved these men, but right now I wanted to rip their fucking balls off. All my emotions were jumbled up and too close to the surface to be fucking around like this.

Honestly, the bullshit pranks and jokes these two liked to play helped keep me in check. It was hard to take everything so damn serious when Butcher and Toxic were around. If they weren't fucking with us—their brothers—they were usually starting fights with other people. Either way, I ended up being able to crack heads and take out some of my frustrations.

This time was different. I glared at Toxic and reached over, grabbing Jordan's arm. It didn't take much to pull her toward me and angle her until she was wrapped under my own arm. "No need to touch."

Jordan looked up at me, confusion sparking in her gaze. "What's going on?"

"Ignore them," Kit said, rolling her eyes. "They're giving Ricochet a hard time." There was laughter, but also annoyance in Kit's tone. "That's what Butcher and Toxic do, give everyone a hard time."

"Ouch," Toxic replied, putting a hand over her heart as if she'd damaged the organ.

"Oh please," Kit said with another eye roll. "I'm pretty sure you don't have a heart." When Toxic gave her a pouty look, she laughed. "Fine." She walked over, rose onto her toes and went to give him a kiss on the cheek.

Toxic being who he was, shifted just in time so her lips landed on his. His hand went to the back of Kit's head, holding her there, though he didn't do anything but keep their lips pressed together.

Kit gasped as Smokehouse grabbed her by the waist, yanking her away from Toxic.

"Hands off my sister, Asshole," Smoke snapped. Hellfire looked like he wanted to break Toxic in half.

Toxic and Butcher hooted with laughter. They'd managed to piss off all three of us and confuse the girls completely. Kit played peacekeeper and stepped between her brother and the man she'd just kissed. Her eyes darted over to Hellfire, then quickly away. "Enough. I swear if you two were left alone and bored the world would end," she scolded Butcher and Toxic.

"Just having a little fun," Toxic said, tossing me another grin.

It took all my self-control not to introduce my fist to his face. Since they were so keen on meeting new things. Not that this would be the first time we'd fought. We all took turns sparring with each other with enough regularity that it wasn't a new concept.

"We'd better go," Kit said. She waved at the women. "It was nice chatting. You'll have to come by the bar sometime."

Kit worked at The Bunker, our club's bar. The thought of Jordan going there and mingling with all the bikers and patrons who came out regularly, put me right back on edge. My arm tightened on her shoulders, pulling her more firmly against my side.

She wasn't struggling in my grasp. She just put her arms around my waist, and laid her head on my shoulder. I looked down at her in surprise and she gave me a soft smile.

Fuck. A man could get used to having her in his arms.

Kit herded my brothers out toward their bikes and her car. I could hear Butcher complaining about her ruining their fun. My lips twitched into a smile. Despite the attacks—and their poor excuse for joking—I was glad they'd come out.

"I'd better get going or I'll be late to pick up the kids," Gwen said, hurrying away from us.

We watched as she bolted toward her own house, leaving Jordan and I wrapped up in each other.

"That was subtle," I said with a laugh.

Jordan tugged against my hold, trying to pull away. Though I didn't want to, I let her go. She smoothed down her shirt and gave me a shy smile. "Your friends are...interesting."

Barking out a laugh, I nodded. "That's one way of putting it. Calling them assholes is a better way."

Her mouth opened, then she closed it again as she hesitated with whatever she'd been about to say. I waited for her to work up the courage to voice her concerns.

"Listen, Ricochet..." she started. "I don't know what your intentions are-"

"I want you."

Her eyes widened. "What?"

A smirk settled on my face. "I want you," I repeated.

Her eyes narrowed. "I'm not in the habit of sleeping with men I don't know."

"That just makes me want you more," I replied. "But I didn't mean I want to fuck you. Well," I amended, "I do, but I meant I want you to be mine. To be my old lady."

"Old lady?" she huffed. "I'm not old."

I chuckled at that, noting the way she'd started blushing when I'd mentioned fucking her. Her cheeks were pink and she kept flicking her tongue out to wet her lips. It was easy to see it was a nervous habit, but it had my cock straining against my jeans as I thought about what else she could do with that tongue.

"It's what we bikers call our girlfriends and wives," I explained. I made a mental note to ask Kit to have a talk with Jordan about all this. She and the other women would be able to explain a lot of it to her. I had no problem doing it, but until I convinced her to be mine she wasn't going to be as open to hearing it from me.

"I- You're great," she said. "I mean, you seem like a really...good guy-"

"I'm not," I told her, cutting her off. Stepping forward, I eliminated the space between us. Despite her height she had to tilt her head back to keep eye contact as I stared down at her. "I'm not a good guy. I'm...

complicated. If I was being fair, I would stay far away from you, Sunshine. But I've always been a selfish son of a bitch and I don't see that changing anytime soon." It was amazing. Being around her, my flashback may as well have been a lifetime ago. Now all I had was a possessive desire to take her. To keep her. To wrap myself up in her until I wasn't sure where she started and I ended.

She shook her head, her breath coming out in shuddering pants as she tried to make sense of what I was telling her. It was a stroke to my ego that she was clearly as attracted to me as I was her. My eyes dipped down to where her nipples were hard and straining against her shirt. It was my turn to lick my lips as I thought about sucking those rosy tips into my mouth.

Her eyes followed mine and she gasped, crossing her arms over her chest. She glared at me. "I don't know what you're talking about. This is a bad idea."

"It is," I agreed, "but I don't give a fuck." I dipped my head, watching her eyes widen as my nose brushed hers. "You're mine. Soon enough you're going to realize that."

Moving back, I gave her space. She blinked at me, shocked into silence. Giving her a nod, I turned and walked away. My dick was hard in my pants and all I wanted to do was scoop her up into my arms, bring her back into her house, and fuck her until she was screaming. Instead, I forced myself to leave.

She wasn't a one-night stand. I needed to figure her out because by the time we had sex, I needed her to be falling in love with me. Otherwise, she'd bolt and I'd never convince her to be mine.

I was going to have to wear her down. A smile settled on my face. She didn't realize it yet, but I was very single minded when presented with a challenge. She'd been about to tell me that she didn't want anything to do with me. I just hadn't let her. Just like I wouldn't let her walk away. I didn't need to look to know she was still standing there confused, watching me go. This was going to be fun. It was exactly what I needed.

CHAPTER 12

Jordan

My life used to be so simple and easy. I went to work, hung out with my family, and hung out with my best friend and her kids. That was it. Now my insides were all twisted around like a pretzel.

Three days had passed since Ricochet had claimed that he wanted me. I'd been busy with work and hadn't seen much of Gwen, let alone her brother. We'd gotten a call from a concerned citizen about a hawk out near Three Points. Dad and I had gone out—we were rehabilitators on top of being falconers—and we'd found an injured Red-Tailed Hawk, caught up in some netting.

I'd offered to take the night watch since we weren't sure if she was going to succumb to her injuries or not. This morning she had started taking food and acting normal, it showed she was finally out of the woods.

Yawning, I hit my blinker, waiting for traffic to pass as I pulled into the parking lot for the local school. It was only an elementary school. Once the kids got old enough Gwen would have to find them a high school inside the city.

I got out of my car and stretched. Gwen had texted me that morning that Sean had a city league soccer game and wanted to see if I could make it. The school season wouldn't start until late spring, but the parents liked to get the kids together before that to keep them busy. The city league teams allowed kids to show up as they had time and was almost like a large pick up game each time. It worked out really well, especially for overworked parents who had energetic kids at home.

We'd been friends for long enough that I was basically her kids' honorary aunt. That's why it'd surprised me that I hadn't met her brother before now. She'd only ever mentioned that he'd been busy and hadn't been able to visit much in the last few years.

Now that I'd met him and he'd said those things to me—my core tightened as I remembered him talking about fucking me—I wanted to know everything about him. To know everything, but also to run away. My emotions were all balled up and hard to untangle when it came to him.

"Jordan!" Gwen waved at me from her seat in the stands.

I made my way up and plopped down next to her. "Hey."

"Hey." She studied me for a moment. "You look exhausted."

"I've been pulling night shifts, but I did a double and worked my day shift today as usual so that I can get back into the normal swing of things."

"That sounds awful," she said.

I told her about the injured bird and smiled when she gave me a worried look. My friend had the softest heart. It was why she'd become a vet tech herself. She loved helping animals. She gave friendship and love to any in need. "She's going to be just fine," I reassured her before she could ask.

"You didn't have to come," Gwen said, eyes still worried. "You should be home resting."

"This is going to be so much better," I told her. The kids ran out onto the field and I let out a giant whoop.

Sean's strides stuttered and he looked up into the stands. His grin was easy to see even from up here. He waved at me and then continued on, getting in line to warm up.

"He seems better," I commented.

Gwen sighed. "I told Trent if he couldn't treat his children with respect he could just fuck right off."

My eyes widened and I turned to her, mouth hanging open. She laughed at the look on my face, but I couldn't help it. "You actually said that?"

"Damn right I did."

"Go mama bear," I told her with a wicked smile. "He was totally out of line with the way he was treating Sean."

"And Gage," she added. "He isn't welcome in my home if that's how he's going to treat family."

"How did he take it?"

"About as well as you'd expect." She gave me a sour look. "First he screamed, then he whined. I really don't know what I ever saw in him."

"It's never easy trying to see into the heart of a person," I replied, watching as the kids ran around on the field. "Some people are really good at hiding who they are. They isolate you, without you even realizing it, and then one day… Bam. They reveal the dickhead they've been hiding."

Gwen's brows rose. "Is this about Trent or Dan?"

My lip curled in disgust as she mentioned my ex's name. "Either. Both. Just people in general. Girls can be dickheads, too," I defended when she gave me a bemused look.

"That's true enough." Gwen gave a thumbs up when Sean looked up to see if we'd seen him kick the ball.

He grinned, then looked around the stands. His face fell, but one of his teammates called out his name, distracting him. The game was about to start.

"Gage is late," Gwen said with a sigh.

"Was that what the long face was about?" I asked. Inwardly, I scolded my heart which was bouncing around inside my chest at the mere mention that Ricochet was going to be here.

"Yeah. Trent was always promising to come to one thing or another and never made it. Sean can be a bit sensitive to being lied to now."

"Can't blame him."

"I didn't want to miss the kick off, so I asked Gage to pick up Grace from pre-school. Hopefully everything is okay." Gwen frowned down at her cellphone, as if giving it a probing look would force it to reveal a text from her brother that it had been hiding.

The game had only been going for a few minutes when the rumbling sound of a motorcycle echoed through the air. Everyone in the stands turned to look as Ricochet parked his bike in a spot up front. He reached behind him and held Grace's hand as she scrambled off the huge Harley.

"Oh my-" a woman sitting in front of us said. She and her friend looked at each other with wide eyed looks.

A quick glance around the bleachers showed all the soccer moms gaping in his direction. I bit the insides of my lips to keep from laughing at their reactions. It was warranted. Ricochet grabbed Grace's pink My Little Pony backpack and held it as they walked over toward the bleachers.

He was in his usual jeans, t-shirt, leather cut, and boots, but he wore it so damn well. My mouth dried out just watching him protectively eye his niece while she maneuvered the stands. His hand was out in case he needed to catch her should she fall. My heart melted in my chest. I was positive every other woman's was doing the same.

"Ladies," he rumbled out as he climbed up behind Grace. He was oblivious to the hungry eyes following his every move. No, those pale blue eyes were too busy latching onto me. My heart sighed, my libido rejoiced. The tiny part of me that was conflicted only grew more worried.

Quickly looking away from him, I caught a dirty look from one of the mothers sitting nearby. I would be lying if I said I wasn't thrilled when he chose to sit next to me, his shoulder brushing mine. Grace took a seat on his other side.

Gwen leaned around me and glared at her family. "What? No one wants to sit next to me?"

They just gave her matching smiles and it hit me how much Grace and Sean looked like Ricochet. Which made sense, since he was Gwen's twin, but that devilish look the kids got all the time? That was one hundred percent gifted to them by the tattoo-covered hunk sitting next to me.

I stared down at the field, trying to ignore him. The scent of leather and some kind of spice I couldn't identify hit me and I had to fight back the urge to rub against him like a cat.

"Where have you been?"

Looking over, I met his gaze. "Huh?"

"You haven't been home the last few nights." There was something dark and dangerous there in the blue depths that had me swallowing hard.

"That's none of your business." I didn't know why I wasn't telling him about the bird. The way he had asked just rubbed me the wrong way.

Let him rub you the right way then.

I had to mentally slap my inner hussy down. The way he was watching me right now, like a hawk eyeing a rabbit, made me squirm on the hard metal bench.

"Not sure you quite understood what I was telling you the other day," he replied, keeping his voice low so Grace didn't overhear.

"What? You mean about you wanting me to be your old lady?" I shrugged. "Nowhere in there did I hear you *ask* me to go out with you," I reminded him. "And I didn't agree to anything."

"I don't need you to agree, I've already claimed you." His eyes narrowed. "Where have you been the last two nights, Jordan?"

His words came out as a growl and loud enough that everyone sitting around us was now watching us. Gwen's eyes were wide as she looked between her brother and me. There was a half-smile on her face, like she couldn't believe he was acting like this, but it obviously delighted her that he was.

"I already told you, it's none of your-" I swallowed the rest of the words and let out a little squeal as he stood, jerked me out of my seat, and then my world tilted on its axis.

I twisted so that I was staring at Gwen and Grace's shocked faces—not to mention everyone else's—as this barbarian carried me down the bleachers over his shoulder. My embarrassment didn't allow me to pound my fists against his back, though I very much wanted to. Self-preservation also kicked in and had me holding still so he didn't drop me. I wasn't a tiny woman. It took effort to carry me like a sack of potatoes, though he didn't seem to be struggling.

"What is *wrong* with you?" I hissed at him as he cleared the stands and walked away toward a few trees back behind the field.

"I asked you a question. You didn't seem to want to talk about it in front of others, so I took care of that." There was amusement in his tone.

"You think this is funny? Those women are going to be gossiping about this for weeks." I wasn't sure if it was self-consciousness or hanging upside down that was causing my cheeks to heat.

"Let 'em." He gently bent forward and placed me on my feet near one of the large mesquite trees.

I slapped at his hand when he reached out to steady me. "Don't touch me. You're an asshole."

His grin was fast and sharp. "Tell me something I don't know." He cocked his head. "Like where you were the last few nights."

"Oh my God!" I glared at him as I swiped at my hair, running my fingers through it to comb the tangles out of it. "You're relentless."

"I know."

Placing my hands on my hips, I scowled at him. "I had to work."

He glowered right back at me. "Where do you work that you have to be out all night?"

I sighed and shook my head. This hadn't needed to go this far, but I never would have imagined that he'd do something crazy like cart me off in front of a whole group of people. "I work at The Arizona Wildlife Sanctuary."

"Last time I checked, visiting hours ended at ten p.m."

Giving him a look of bewilderment, I tried to sort through my emotions. I'd never had a man act so…jealous over me before. A tiny buzz raced over my skin at knowing he was being this way because he thought I'd been shacking up with some other guy. Another part of me was angry that he thought he could behave this way toward me. He didn't have the right to question me. It didn't matter that he was claiming me. I'd never agreed to anything. "I told you. I don't do one night stands."

"Who said anything about one night? I'm just making sure you know who you belong to now."

Pure shock held me still. "Do you even hear yourself when you speak?" I asked.

He chuckled. "You'll get used to it." He purred the words out, a promise more than anything. He stepped closer to me, forcing me to back away.

"Go away. I'm mad at you, Ricochet."

"Never going to happen."

My back hit the trunk of the mesquite tree and I looked up into his triumphant eyes. I was in so far over my head with this man. And I couldn't get enough.

CHAPTER 13

Ricochet

Moving forward, I pinned her against the tree. She stared up at me with a mix of emotions flashing over her face. She wasn't sure what to do about me. I liked that. My fingers slid over her soft skin until I was gripping the back of her neck.

Neither of us had been looking for the other, but here we were and I wasn't about to let her run off just because what was between us was so heavy. Especially not since she seemed to chase away the shadows that were my constant companions these days. Being around her I was my normal self. I loved this feeling. I'd almost forgotten who this man was, buried beneath the memories and shadows.

Before she could think to shove me away, I dipped my head down, taking her mouth with mine. Her soft curves pressed against my body and I knew I wanted to spend the rest of the day showing her exactly how much I wanted her.

Her lips moved beneath mine, but she hadn't opened her mouth to me fully. I bit her full lower lip, causing her to gasp. Groaning, I slid my tongue into her mouth. My dick swelled beneath my jeans, aching to press into her sweet body. Her thigh was in my hand and I pulled her leg up over my hip so I could grind between her legs.

She moaned at the action, then mumbled something. She broke the kiss, panting with desire. Unable to stop, I trailed kisses over her cheek and down her neck.

"Ricochet." My name came out breathy and soft. I wanted to hear her say it while I filled her for the first time. Wanted her to scream it as she came.

"Mmmm?"

"We can't…"

My hand moved around to the front of her throat, my thumb stroking her jaw as I licked and sucked at the pulse there. She laid her head back against the tree, eyes closed. She was rocking against me, completely overtaken by her body's desire.

"Why not?" I growled, irritated at the idea of stopping.

"There's people… Kids around."

Shit. Reality check.

I'd forgotten where we were. Why we were here. She had that effect on me. Pulling back, I stared down into her dazed eyes. "Do you get it now?"

She shook her head, as though she was about to deny what she felt. Her lips were swollen from my kisses, she had a small dark bruise starting on her neck from my attention. There was no dismissing this.

"Be mine, Jordan," I urged.

"It's not that simple."

My eyes narrowed and I cupped her cheeks in my hands. "I don't know what the hell that means, but yeah, it is. I want you to be my girlfriend. My old lady. Mine."

She licked her lips, a nervous energy returning as the fog of passion left her mind. "I'm not dating anyone right now, Ricochet."

"Good, then I don't need to track down any men and kill them."

Her jaw dropped. It was clear by my tone that I wasn't kidding.

"But what do they have to do with me?"

Her laughter broke free and she shook her head again, forcing me to drop my hands. They landed on her hips. I wasn't ready to let her go fully yet.

"You're impossible." She sighed. "I haven't had very good luck with men. Call me gun shy if you want, but I don't jump into relationships blindly. Not anymore."

It wasn't easy to bite my tongue. I wanted to ask her to explain. To find out who had hurt her and put this wariness in her beautiful eyes. Instead, I listened.

"I- I feel it, too," she finally admitted.

I didn't need to ask what she meant. The connection between us had nearly knocked me on my ass that first day. Only a few weeks had passed, but it was a race to see who would fall first. I knew it. She knew it. The question was, why was she trying to avoid it? What was the point?

"What do you want to do about it, Jordan?" Normally, I would just take control. I'd already tried that by claiming her. My sunshine wasn't having any of it, so I knew I needed to change my tactics with her. She was nervous. Probably thought I was going to break her heart. Little did she know I'd break every bone in my body before I hurt her.

Surprise filtered over her expression, then appreciation. "Maybe we…could get to know each other. Without any pressure," she added, giving me a pointed look.

"Sounds good." That suited me fine. I planned on getting to know every single thing about her anyway. I didn't care for the no pressure bullshit, but it didn't matter. She was mine. I wasn't going to let any other man near her and I planned to have her fall in love with me. At least she was agreeing to spend time with me. The rest would happen in due time.

"We need some ground rules." She managed to slip from between me and the tree, putting space between us.

I scowled at her, unhappy with not being able to touch her. "Like what?"

"We'll agree to a trial period. We won't see other people during that time-" She broke off as I growled in anger at the thought of her dating another man. "I don't know if that was a sound of agreement, or…"

"It was." I motioned for her to go on.

"No trying to have sex with me."

I gave her an incredulous look. "What?"

Humor danced in her eyes as she smiled at me. "I can't think when you're kissing me. Touching me. Hands off during the trial period."

"That's fucking stupid." I crossed my arms over my chest and pinned her with a dark look.

"Take it or leave it."

"Fine," I muttered. "What else?"

She scrunched up her face as she thought about her list of demands. "No lying." She said the words so softly, I wasn't sure I'd heard her at first.

"I don't lie, Sunshine."

Her eyes were fixed on the ground at my feet. "I've heard that before."

It was starting to make sense now. Her not wanting to jump into a relationship, not wanting sex to cloud things. Someone had lied to get what they wanted and then hurt her.

"You have my word. I won't lie." I hesitated as I thought about the shit show that was my life. "There are a few things I won't be able to tell you in regards to my club."

"I have so many questions about that," she remarked, "but I'll accept it if you can't tell me some things."

Closing the distance between us again, I put a finger under her jaw, tilting her face to mine. "A kiss to seal the deal?"

"That goes against rule number two," she replied.

"Well, we can't shake hands. Not for an agreement like this."

"Fine. One kiss."

She made a startled noise when I grabbed her and yanked her against my body. Crushing my lips to hers, I gripped her tight.

Her hands were on my biceps, steadying herself, while I took the last kiss I knew I'd get for a while. When I let her go, her pupils were blown, and she was looking at me in a way that made my ego swell.

"We should get back to the game. I promised Sean I'd be there cheering him on." My voice sounded huskier than normal, even to myself.

She nodded, remaining mute, but let me take her hand. Our fingers linked together, we walked back to the bleachers. Gwen raised her eyebrows at me as we climbed up toward where they were sitting. I just winked at her. She'd end up grilling me later on at home. It was a time honored tradition between us.

The whole time we watched the game—and cheered Sean on—I watched Jordan out of the corner of my eye. She was so bright and open the majority of the time. It made me want to murder someone knowing she'd been hurt so badly she'd pulled away from relationships. Though, I guess I benefited in the end. It would be a whole lot harder to get her to be mine if I had to take her from some other schmuck first.

Sitting here with her almost eased the guilt of missing Riptide's wedding. Today was the day for my brother. I'd call him in a day or two to tell him congratulations. I knew he wouldn't hold it against me that I wasn't there, but fuck it wasn't easy being on the outside like this. It made me wonder if that was how he'd been feeling while undercover. He'd been secluded out there in the desert, cut off from us all.

We cheered as the game ended. Sean's team won by a couple of points. He came running up to us—a victorious smile on his face—as we climbed down from the bleachers.

"Great game," I told him, giving him a high five. The women from the bleachers were crowding around and I had to side step a few who tried to brush up against me. Jordan was the only one I wanted to be touching.

"Did you see my goal?" he asked, excitement making his voice pitch upward.

"I did. You killed it." I tousled his hair as we all started walking back toward the parking lot.

"Can I ride home with Uncle Gage? Please, Mom?" Grace begged. She gave her mom what I liked to call the angel eyes. I wasn't sure how she managed to look so sweet and innocent, but it almost always worked. At least on me.

Gwen laughed. "Sure, as long as he doesn't mind."

"I never mind having a gorgeous lady on the back of my bike." My eyes met Jordan's. From now on she'd be the only one behind me besides family.

Her cheeks pinkened and I knew she'd caught the message in my look. She studied my bike. "Is it safe for such a young kid to ride a motorcycle?"

I chuckled. "Grace has been riding with me since she was old enough to walk. I'd never do anything to put her in danger."

"Oh, I didn't mean it like that." Jordan looked genuinely upset.

"Don't worry, Sunshine. I know you didn't. Come on, Gorgeous," I called out to Grace. She was busy waving to her friends.

I pulled the kids' helmet out of my saddlebags and fitted it on her head, adjusting the straps. The rest of the kids on the soccer teams were almost to the parking lot. It was amusing, watching the boys' mouths fall open as they saw Grace scramble up onto the bike behind me.

Mothers were shaking their heads in disapproval. It was damn near impossible to keep from flipping off the busybodies. I didn't want to cause any trouble for Gwen, though, so instead I blew them a kiss. Worth it to see the scowls. Starting up the bike, I revved the engine a few times. The kids standing around were wide eyed and looked jealous.

Grace ate it up. She waved at them like a princess as I backed the bike out and then sped off down the road. My laughter was drowned out by the engine, but I knew in that moment, I'd needed to come here. I'd made the right call. I was hopeful it would be the first of many.

CHAPTER 14

Jordan

My shoulders drooped as I cleaned up in the kitchen. I'd eaten an early dinner and was planning on being in bed in the next half hour. I was completely wiped from a week of taking care of the sick hawk. I'd ended up working a few more night shifts as she'd relapsed. She was finally on the mend, but it had been an exhausting rehab. Staying by the new hawk's side had been worth it, but I was paying for the lack of sleep. As long as she kept improving we'd be able to release her in another few weeks. It made me so happy knowing she'd be able to go back to living a wild, free life.

I paused in the act of wiping the counter as I thought about the soccer game and, more importantly, the man who'd lingered in my thoughts since. If I was being honest with myself, he'd been on my mind since I'd met him. I couldn't seem to shake this attraction I had for him. That's why I'd given in and proposed this plan to get to know each other.

It was still risky and I should be running in the opposite direction every time I saw him, but I couldn't bring myself to do it. If anything, he drew me in closer. He was like my own personal black hole, sucking me into his vortex. It was dangerous.

Correction, he was sucking me in because he *was dangerous.*

I should have learned from Dan that handsome, charming men weren't to be trusted. But then again, I wasn't sure Ricochet was all that charming. At least not in a conventional sense. He didn't have pretty words that eased all my worries. He was blunt. Told me exactly like it was, or how he perceived it to be. He came off as very…honest. Something I hadn't experienced much with men of my age.

Thanks to my dad and brother, I knew exactly the kind of relationship I wanted with my future husband. Men who were like them. Kind, caring, protective, and loved their women more than anything. I'd just started to give up on finding it. It didn't help that I'd locked myself away like a princess in a tower.

Was Ricochet my prince? I frowned at that. He was no prince charming, but somehow it just seemed right. Maybe he was a fierce beast. One who'd rip past every barrier I erected around my heart. Time would tell whether I could truly trust him.

A sound caught my attention right before my front door was yanked open. A gasp tumbled from my lips as I reached over and grabbed the largest knife out of the wooden block on my counter. I was too far away to get to my shotgun.

"I thought I told you to lock this door." Ricochet stepped into my home, shutting the door behind him.

The breath wheezed out of me, my heart thrumming inside my chest at a rhythm that was double its normal tempo. "Ricochet!" I was still holding the knife out in front of me, but I slapped my empty hand to my chest as if that would force my heart back into a normal pace. "You scared the shit out of me."

He was still scowling at me, his eyes surveying the room, when the sound of jingling echoed in the space. "You were supposed-" He froze, staring down at the floor in the living room. "What the fuck is *that*?"

I hurried around the low wall that divided my kitchen and dining room from the living room. That was the only aspect of this home that I disliked. I loved the open floor plan that was common here in Tucson, where one room bled into another with nothing in the way. It hadn't been an option and I'd loved this place too much to pass it up for one wall.

Hurrying over to Haze, I crouched down. "You're okay, Lady," I murmured to her. Using a finger, I stroked her head. It was more for myself than her. She merely tolerated the handling, but I loved that she let me pet and soothe her. She fluffed out her feathers, eyeing the large man standing there gaping at us, before starting in on preening herself.

"That's a fucking hawk."

I couldn't help but laugh at the disbelief in his tone. Standing, I faced him. "She is. She's a Harris Hawk." I cocked my head at him. "I told you I worked at The Sanctuary. What I didn't mention was that I'm a falconer."

"You treat sick birds?" A look of fascination passed over his face as he moved closer to Haze.

"No, the veterinarians do that. Though we do go out and pick up injured raptors when people find them. Mostly, I fly them. Use them to hunt rabbits for sport. At The Sanctuary I take care of them, feed, water, clean their mews, and I teach the public about different types of raptors."

"That's pretty cool," he said, crouching down near Haze. "Can I touch her?"

"Sure, but go slow. She's friendly, but these birds aren't pets. They-" I broke off in shock as I watched Ricochet reach forward and press his finger onto the tip of Haze's beak.

She arched her head back, then sent me a bewildered look. I was as surprised as her. "Did you just…" I trailed off, trying to hold in my laughter.

"Booped the snoot. I do it to all animals." He told me, as though it was completely normal for him to touch the nose of a predator. He was now stroking his fingers down Haze's chest.

She was being patient and letting him. That or she was still in shock over what had just happened.

"Her feathers are a lot softer than I figured they'd be." He brushed her chest again, then stood and gave her some space. She settled back down on her perch. "Do you always have her in the house?"

"No. Her mews are out in the backyard, but since I haven't been home much in the last few days I wanted to bring her in for a bit. She's a really social bird and gets depressed if I don't visit enough."

"This is seriously interesting," he told me, a glint in his eyes making me a little nervous, "but I'll have to ask you about it later. For now, I want you to explain why you haven't been locking your door?"

"I…forgot. It's a habit to just leave it unlocked once I get home. I'm still trying to change that," I admitted to him.

"It's not safe to leave it like that, Sunshine."

Shaking my head in exasperation, I explained, "I've never had any issues. We're far enough out here that no one usually messes with us.

"Until the day someone decides to," he countered. He sighed, visibly trying to rein in his patience. "Do me a favor and please keep it locked." He raised a questioning brow when I grinned at him.

"Something tells me you don't typically ask so nicely for something."

"Rarely," he admitted.

I moved back into the kitchen, with him close on my heels. "Would you like something to drink? …Eat?"

"Naw, I'm good." He leaned back against the counter. Somehow the open space of my kitchen seemed so much smaller with his broad shoulders filling it.

"What brought you over to break into my house?"

"Can't break in somewhere where the door isn't locked. That's just called coming inside. Open invitation."

Rolling my eyes, I conceded, "I get it. I'll keep it locked."

"Good."

He shifted to move out of my way as I reached past him to put my now dry dishes away. His hand ran down my back as I moved past. Shooting him a mock glare, I scolded him. "Remember our deal?"

"Yeah, yeah," he muttered. "Wanted to see when your next day off was."

"Day after tomorrow," I replied, bending down to put the pot I held away. It didn't require me looking to know he was staring at my ass. My smile was sly as I pushed the pot all the way to the back of the lower cabinet.

"Wanted to see if you'd come with me."

His voice was thick and deep. My lower belly clenched at the huskiness of his words. "Where to?"

"To meet my family."

Straightening up, I frowned. My hands found their way to my hips. "Your-"

"My *other* family," he elaborated. "They got back from a wedding a few days ago. Almost all of them anyway. I want to introduce you."

"I don't know, Ricochet," I said. My nerves were already jangling.

"You already met, Kit," he pointed out. "And Butcher and Toxic. It's just a few more people."

"It just seems to be moving fast..."

He didn't try to force the issue. There wasn't any whining or manipulation, a tactic that was Dan's go to move. It was just another way he was proving he was nothing like my ex.

At some point you're going to have to learn to trust again. Men and yourself.

My mother's words of wisdom echoed through my head. Because of all that, I relented. "Okay. I'll go." It didn't matter that my hands were suddenly sweaty and it felt like I was diving into the deep end. What better way to get to know a man than to meet his family? Speaking of, I needed to clear all this with Gwen.

My stomach began tangling itself into knots at the thought of us discussing me possibly having a relationship with her brother. She'd heard all of my woes over the years, just like I'd heard hers. She might not approve of me for her brother even though she seemed open to it the other day. Maybe she'd changed her mind after the dinner. Just the thought made an acrid taste pop up inside my mouth.

If nothing else, maybe meeting more people that knew Ricochet would help settle this internal debate that was warring inside me. It was incredibly difficult to be at odds with myself like this. Nothing before had ever prepared me to be so torn.

"I'll let you get some sleep." He'd moved closer while I was lost in thought.

I hadn't even noticed. His palm covered one half of my face as he cupped my cheek. His thumb brushed lightly underneath my eye. I had bags big enough to hold all my trauma and those of half the people living in Tucson. If I wasn't so exhausted, I'd be embarrassed that he was seeing me this way. Though, it was only now occurring to me the state I was in.

My old sweat pants hung low on my hips and the shirt I wore stopped just beneath my breasts, leaving my stomach bare. I hadn't bothered with a bra since this was what I'd wear to bed. My hair was tossed up in a messy bun and I'd long since wiped off the light coating of make-up I'd applied that morning.

"You look so damn good."

My eyes widened at his compliment. How had he known what I was thinking?

"You have a really expressive face," he told me, answering my silent question. "Bet you're a shit liar."

"I am," I confirmed. "But I'm not a fan of lying or liars."

"Good to know. I don't ever plan on lying to you. For instance, if you hadn't made me agree to that stupid deal I'd be carrying you upstairs right now, Sunshine. The things I want to do to your body have me hard as a rock." He leaned in closer, letting the proof of his words brush against my lower belly.

Danger!

I was milliseconds away from letting him do whatever he wanted. He was waking my body up from a dormant state. I hadn't been this horny in a long time. I knew hopping into bed with this man would be the end of life as I knew it. Only, I wasn't ready for that. So I did what came naturally, I deflected. "Why do you keep calling me that?"

He blinked at me, caught off guard. "Sunshine?" I nodded, hoping to keep him talking in order to give my raging libido a chance to ease.

I eyed my freezer, thinking about dumping ice down my pants to cool off. "Because you chase the clouds away."

My brows drew low as I mulled that over. "I'm not sure what that means."

"Ask me again the day after tomorrow. If you're still interested, I'll tell you then."

"What-" I stopped talking when his hands skated down my sides. When he reached my ribs and coarse fingers ran over my naked flesh, I shivered. Oh God. It had been so long since I'd been touched by a man. Since strong hands had wandered over my body. Every cell of my being was rejoicing in the feel of those calloused hands on me. "Ask you later," I managed to squeak out. "Got it."

His fingers squeezed my waist in agreement, or appreciation. It didn't matter. All that mattered was that this didn't stop. I longed to feel him touch me. My nipples were hard little points, straining against cloth. My panties were quickly dampening beneath my sweats and all he had done was touch my sides. I needed to get a grip. I just didn't know how to while he was touching me.

"I'd better go." He sounded as tortured as I was. At least I wasn't in this alone.

As much as my body was screaming at me to make him stay, I nodded. There was a reason I was doing this and it wasn't just to put us through hell and back. I couldn't trust myself to be impartial. Not when I was this insanely aroused by him. I needed to make sure that he wasn't like my ex. Only then could I allow myself to imagine the things he said he wanted. To be his old lady. To belong to him.

I walked him to the door and the look he gave me as he stepped out into the night air nearly scorched the fuzzy socks I had on. As much as I wanted him, I was afraid. Scared to let myself get involved and to allow feelings to grow. That was a surefire way to get hurt. Dan breaking my heart had been bad enough. Ricochet, given the opportunity, would shatter it. He had the potential to destroy me on a level that there would be no returning from.

And how damn scary was that? I'd just met the freaking man and already I knew the consequences of loving and losing him would be catastrophic. Leaning against the door frame, I watched as he bounded up over the railing in a single leap. It didn't matter that there were stairs nearby. He seemed to take the jump as a challenge. There was probably a metaphor somewhere in there that I could take some lesson from, but I was too damn tired and wrung out to analyze it. Shutting the door, I locked it before I returned Haze to her mews and made my way up to bed.

CHAPTER 15

Jordan

Grabbing my purse, I stepped outside my door and turned to lock it. A smile made my lips twitch as I remember Ricochet barging in the other night. I'd waffled back and forth about walking over to Gwen's house and telling him I'd changed my mind. In the end, I didn't bother.

I seemed to have no willpower when it came to that man, and seeing him face to face I knew he'd convince me to still go with him today. We were supposed to be leaving in an hour. There was something else I needed to do first.

It was Gwen's day off as well, so I walked next door and knocked. When she pulled open the door and frowned at me, I smiled. "Hey."

"Hey. Come on in." She patted her pockets, looking for her cell. "Did we have something scheduled for today? I thought you were going with Gage to his party?"

"Party?" I asked, eyes widening. "He said I was just meeting some of his family."

She laughed as I followed her back to the kitchen. "You will be." The way she said it held some mystery and my nerves were back full force.

"Um… I just- Hi, Sweetie," I said to Grace when I saw her at the counter. They were baking cookies. The house smelled divine and my mouth watered. I had a soft spot for chocolate chip cookies.

"Hi, Jordan. We were going to give you cookies later," Grace chirped, giving me a wave. There was more flour down the front of her shirt than in the bowl sitting on the counter.

Gwen and I grinned at each other. "Thanks, Sweetie. I love your cookies."

"Uncle Gage does, too," she said with a giggle.

"What brought you by?" Gwen said as her daughter turned back to the bowl of flour.

My eyes strayed back to her, unsure if I should say anything.

"Don't worry about her. She's mashing the flour." Gwen gave me a mischievous smile.

"Mashing the flour?"

"It's the secret of the cookies," she informed me with a serious look on her face. Her eyes danced with laughter. "Gives me a few minutes to get the mess cleaned up before we start baking," she muttered under her breath.

"Ah." Laughing, I sat down at the table. "I…wanted to talk to you about Ricochet."

She sat down next to me and put a hand over mine. "I think it's wonderful."

"Really?" I asked, relief making the word nearly catch in my throat. "I wouldn't want to do anything that would strain our friendship."

"You're going to be in my life even if things were to go sideways with my brother," she promised. "You're stuck with me." She squeezed my hand. "But Jord, he's not going to let this go sideways. I haven't seen him look this… light… in years."

Frowning, I tilted my head. "What do you mean?"

"That's his story to tell you. Just know that you're good for him and I'm completely on board. He'll give you everything you've been searching for. That relationship you said you've always wanted? The one your parents have? You'll have that with him. He'd put you first before almost everything in his life. He'd die to make you happy. Kill to protect you. No one would ever hurt you again." She gave me a rueful smile. "He's still a man, so I'm sure he'll make some mistakes along the way, but he'd never do what Dan did."

The sigh shuddered out of me as I admitted the dark secret I'd been holding onto for a long time. "I'm terrified of finding that kind of love."

Concern filled her eyes. "Why?"

"Because if a man loves me that way and leaves…"

"I understand."

"You would. I guess I can take hope from you that I'd be able to move on and make it work," I told her with a smile.

Her laughter made me blink in surprise. "I wish I could tell you that's what happened. I never felt that way about Trent. And he never loved me like that. I was just deluding myself all those years. And I was more miserable than I could admit. Even to myself." She shrugged. "I'm still looking for that kind of love, Jord. Don't deprive yourself of something that's so hard to find just because you're afraid."

I nodded. "That's why I'm doing this. Despite my fears, I have this feeling that he and I can be so good together."

"I think so, too. Plus, then I get to officially have you as my sister." She grinned. "There's still a lot you need to know about him. About his…lifestyle, but that will come in time."

"Or you could tell me."

"Oh boy. I don't even know the half of it, but if I told you what I knew it'd send you running."

"That doesn't ease my mind…"

"Just remember what I told you. He'd die for you. More importantly, he'd kill for you."

"Metaphorically… Right?"

Her smile was alarming as she stood to go help Grace mix the final mashed flour into the rest of the ingredients.

* * *

"I don't think this is a good idea," I said, eyeing the motorcycle like it was a coiled snake ready to strike. "We could take my car."

"Why would we want to do that?" Ricochet asked. "There's nothing like being on a motorcycle." He looked over at me, arching a brow. "You can't tell me you're scared of something you saw my four-year-old niece doing just last week?"

I grumbled under my breath about that four-year-old being fearless, but moved closer to his bike. "What if we fall?"

He chuckled. "Trust me. We're not going to fall. Just hang onto me. Lean into the turns with me. Other than that, just enjoy yourself."

I watched the powerful muscles of his thigh flex beneath his jeans as he straddled the bike.

"I won't let anything happen to you."

The engine rumbled as he started it up. Knowing he wanted to have me ride with him I'd opted for a pair of jeans and a cute flowy top. I'd stuffed my phone, ID, some money, and my lipstick into the pockets of my jeans so I wouldn't have to hang onto my purse. I'd backtracked to my house and tossed it through the door before locking up.

He was watching me with an amused look on his face while he waited for me to make up my mind. That was something I appreciated about him. I knew he was a take charge kind of man. He'd proven that. Yet, time and again he'd given me the opportunity to make up my own mind. I always decided to go along with him. How did he know it was what I needed? So many men were afraid to let a woman decide for herself, he just knew I would choose him. I nodded in agreement to riding the bike.

He reached out and took my hand, tugging me closer so he could put a spare helmet on my head. His fingers brushed over my jaw and throat as he adjusted the strap, making me shiver. I wanted to feel them there again as he kissed me.

I swung my leg over his bike as he put his own helmet on. My hands went to his hips, tentatively hanging on. My gasp was loud inside the helmet as he grasped my wrists, pulling me forward until I was clutching him around the waist. It caused my breasts to flatten against his back, so I jerked backward, going back to my previous position.

His head turned and though I couldn't see his eyes behind the shaded visor of his helmet, I could tell he was scowling at me. He didn't say anything, just pulled out onto the street. Without any warning he hit the brakes.

Squealing as I slid forward on the seat toward him, I wrapped my arms around him like he'd shown me. It was that or fall off. My breaths were loud in my ears as I tried to process what had just happened. It was his way of showing me why hanging on tight to him was safer.

He reached back and patted the outside of my leg. "Good girl!" He shouted so I could hear him through our helmets and the engine.

Jerk.

Still, I bit back a smile. He got the bike moving again and soon we were zipping along the roads, heading toward the freeway. After the first few minutes, I relaxed the stranglehold I had on his waist and started to look around. Everything was flying past and it was so strange to see it without the windows and steel of a car between me and the landscape.

My heart soared along, leaping when he'd lean into a turn. I'd glued myself to his back, so whatever he did, naturally I was forced to do the same. No wonder these guys liked these machines. It was exciting and fun riding through the desert on the back of one.

I didn't know much about motorcycles and hadn't ever thought I'd ride one, but being with Ricochet somehow made me feel safe. It was like nothing could touch us while I was hanging onto him. We darted in and out of traffic and once we made it onto I-10 he poured on the speed. My laughter and wonder was whipped away by the wind. I could stay on here all day.

The ride ended too soon as he pulled into a parking lot. The property was surrounded by a chain link fence. On one side there was a huge brick building sitting there. The name on the side read The

Bunker. The other building was three times the size and didn't have any distinguishing marks. Beyond that was a field of grass, brown and dormant for the winter months. When spring gave way to summer, if they maintained it, I knew it would be lush and green.

People were everywhere. My heart leapt into my throat as I saw them. There were families with kids spread out on the grass. Two huge dogs romped around with the children. The doors of the bigger building were open and music blasted out through the air.

Men wearing leather jackets like Ricochet walked around with beers or cups of alcohol. There weren't as many women, but there seemed to be two kinds. There were those dressed like me. In jeans, or even cute sundresses, despite the fact that it wasn't summer yet. And women dressed in… My eyes widened as a girl sauntered past in heels so high I worried she'd break her neck in the gravel parking lot. Her skirt was as short as her heels were tall.

I climbed off the bike and handed my helmet back to Ricochet. Trying to smooth out my hair, I watched as he put them away in the bags attached to the side of his bike.

"You said there would only be a few people," I told him, eyes wide, surveying everything.

"Looks like they invited a few more friends," Ricochet replied with a shrug. There were at least fifty people here. He put an arm around my shoulder. "No need for you to be nervous, Sunshine. They're going to love you."

Normally, I wasn't a shy person, but that was when I was in my element. I had no control over this situation. This was his world and I was about to find out whether I really belonged, or not.

CHAPTER 16

Ricochet

We watched as Lockout walked across the parking lot toward us. "That's my president."

She frowned first at Lockout, then looked up at me. "President?"

Damn. I had a lot I needed to explain to her. I probably should have done it before we came out here.

"Do I call him Sir, or something?" she asked.

Barking out a laugh, I shook my head. "He's the president of our motorcycle club. You're not in the club, so you can just call him Lockout. As an old lady there are certain rules you follow, but it's not the same as being a member."

She opened her mouth to say something, but Lock reached us by that point, so she snapped her mouth shut. I was pretty sure she was going to say something about not being an old lady. I knew she thought that, but in my mind, she already was. I was only going along with this plan of hers so that she'd feel comfortable.

"Damn, Brother. I haven't heard you laugh like that in a while."

Lockout grinned at me. "We must have you to thank" he said, shooting Jordan a softer smile.

One side of my mouth tipped up into an answering grin. Very slowly small pieces of myself were returning. That didn't mean that everything was fixed. I was still beyond fucked up, but it felt damn good to be myself again, even if it was only for minutes at a time.

"Lock, this is my…" Jordan shot me a narrow eyed look, "Jordan," I amended.

Lock's grin only got bigger. "Nice to meet you, Jordan." He reached out and shook her hand.

"It's nice to meet you, too, Lockout." She licked her lips, her tell that she was nervous, and gave him a questioning look. "What does that mean? Lockout?"

He chuckled. "It's a flight term. In a helicopter you can override the engine power controls, making them go uncontrollably to full power. It's called putting the engine into 'lockout'."

She blinked at him, trying to figure out why that would be his road name. She didn't know him well enough to know this man lived his life in that red zone. He was always pushing himself, striving to be the best, to provide those he loved with everything they needed. He pushed himself to the limits in every aspect of his life. His road name fit him perfectly.

Someone called out to him and he glanced over his shoulder. "Hey, I have to go deal with something," he told me. "I'll find you later. Catch up."

"Sounds good."

We watched as he walked away, heading over toward a group standing near the bar. He was strolling like he had all the time in the world, but I could see the rigidness in his back. Whatever he was about to handle had him on edge. Priest met him halfway and together they walked over to rest of the men.

"Welcome back, Kid."

I glanced over and grinned as Hush walked up. The older man reached out and as soon as his hand was on my shoulder he yanked me in for a hug. His hand pounded on my back, making me wince, but I returned the favor. "Glad to be back, Hush."

"See you have a friend." He let me go and held out a meaty paw for Jordan to shake.

"Jordan, this is Hush. Another one of my MC brothers."

"Isn't everyone here one of your brothers?" she asked.

We both laughed at that. "Not this time," I told her. "Looks like Lockout invited a few of the weekender clubs out to celebrate."

"Weekender?"

"They're a formed club, but they don't really live the lifestyle. They ride on the weekends and have their own type of brotherhood," Hush explained.

"How does your lifestyle differ?" she asked, looking between us.

Hush gave me a curious look and I shook my head. I hadn't explained it all to her yet. I planned to. It just wasn't something we did until we were sure the woman was going to stick around. We didn't need a bunch of people knowing our business. I knew Jordan was the one, but wasn't positive she wasn't going to run in the opposite direction yet. "We're more dedicated," is all I said by way of explanation.

"Why don't you come meet the other old ladies?" I asked, putting an arm around her and using pressure on the small of her back to steer her.

Hush fell into step beside me. He arched his brow. "*Other* old ladies, huh?"

"Not now, Hush," I muttered.

He shut his trap, something Hush excelled at, and I was grateful for it. Jordan and I were in this weird limbo for the moment, and I didn't want to freak her out. It was hard enough getting past her defenses as it was. I didn't need to make it more difficult on myself.

"Ricochet!" Seek struggled to shove to her feet from where she'd been sitting in the grass. At almost five months pregnant her belly was gently rounded now and seemed to be getting in the way just enough that it was hard for her to get off the ground. Hush stepped over and helped haul her to her feet. She popped a kiss on his lips, then hurried over to me. Well, not so much of a hurry as waddling enthusiastically. Though I'd never utter those words to her.

I caught her in a hug, careful not to bump her stomach. Looking over her shoulder, I saw Jenny jumping to her feet as well and waiting for her turn at a hug. These women were simply amazing. My brothers were lucky to have them and I had to admit that, prior to Jordan, they were the only blips of light in my otherwise darkened world.

"Quit hogging him, Seek," Jenny said with a laugh.

She didn't get a chance at her hug. "Uncle Ricochet!" Four little tornados blasted through the crowd of people and latched onto my legs.

Laughing, I lifted Caitlyn and Cassie up, one in each arm. They wrapped their own arms around my neck while Taylor and Gabby kept hugging my waist. "I missed you four. How was Washington?" A quick glance over showed Jordan standing there with an incredulous look on her face. So far she'd only seen me with my sister and her kids. Little did she know I fucking loved kids. I was damn good with them, too.

"It was good. The wedding was so beautiful," Gabby replied. As the oldest—she'd just turned ten—she was starting to get to the age where she was noticing boys. It was all of our biggest nightmares, but none so much as Priest, I was sure. I shared a grin with her step-mom, Jenny.

"Uncle Butcher fell into the ocean," Cassie said, covering her mouth as she giggled.

"That doesn't surprise me in the least."

"Hey now, tell the truth," Butcher grumped as he walked up. He gave Cassie a mock glare. "I didn't *fall* into the ocean. You and these three other hellions pushed me. Thanks a lot," he muttered at Toxic.

"It wasn't my idea," his friend said with a wry grin. "They came up with that all on their own."

"And you helped them execute," Butcher told him.

"Well, yeah. We have to do our part to make sure they're equipped to handle whatever comes their way in the future."

"Uncle Ricochet," Caitlyn said, tugging on my cut to get my attention. Her voice was soft, and a little hesitant. She was still getting used to being here with all of us and the chaos that came with living with a bunch of outlaws.

"Yeah, Sweetie?"

"Can I see your necklace?"

The shadows crowded in as her sweet voice asked about the only reminder I had of Jack. The adults crowded near went quiet at her request. Jordan's brows drew together and the smile she'd been wearing slipped off her face as she tried to understand the sudden shift in energy.

"I'm so sorry," Jenny said, coming over, arms out to take Caitlyn from me.

I handed Cassie to her instead, and used my free hand to dig the dog tags out from underneath my shirt. I dropped the chain over Caitlyn's head. "It's fine," I told Jenny with a quick twitch of my lips. It was the only comfort I could offer. "She's fine."

Caitlyn played with the double set of dog tags and smiled up at me, unaware of the unease she'd caused. Everyone around me was watching to see how I'd handle things. My own fault because in the past this was when I'd distance myself from the group. I had to quit doing that. This was my family. I wasn't about to let her innocent question backfire on her, or ruin anyone's day. Glancing at Jordan, I knew I could handle it.

"Do you want to wear them for a while?" I asked, eyeing the chain that held both my and Jack's tags.

Her smile was bright. I set her down and watched as Seek's dogs came over to investigate. Jecht did a flyby, licking Caitlyn's face as he ran through, making everyone laugh. Kids and dogs were great for breaking the ice. Auron, the older dog, leaned against my thigh, instinctively offering comfort. Scratching his head, I listened as the others all started relaying how the wedding went.

People came and went as we talked and I introduced Jordan to most of them. I knew her head had to be spinning by now with all the names and faces, but she took it all in stride. She greeted everyone with a warm smile, and she was already getting along great with Seek and Jenny.

"Where are the other girls?" I asked.

"On their way. Daisha and Tori had to work today and Kit was still sleeping since she worked the late shift at the bar last night. Susie had to run home to change Dex's clothes."

Which explained where Smoke was. He and Kit both worked at The Bunker, for the club. Kit loved being a bartender, so her brother insisted she work where he could keep an eye on her. At some point she'd given up arguing with him about being over protective. You'd think he'd realize a woman raised in this life could easily take care of herself. She knew exactly how to handle bikers with bad attitudes.

My name drifted over the din of the music. Lockout motioned for me. "You good here for a few minutes?" I asked Jordan.

"She'll be fine here with us," Seek insisted, rubbing a hand over her belly.

"Yeah, go away so we can get to know your girl," Jenny told me with a smile.

Jordan just laughed and nodded in response to my question. She looked relaxed and happy, falling into conversation with the other two women. The kids had abandoned the adults and were running around with some of the other children who'd been brought to the barbecue.

Butcher and Toxic fell into step with me. I saw my brothers all start gathering around our president. My instincts went on full alert even though I wasn't sure what was going on. Maybe *because* I didn't know what was going on.

We passed the other women as they finally got to the barbecue. Susie, Tori, Daisha, and Kit all met and gave each other hugs in the parking lot, then bee-lined for their friends. This was what every biker hoped for, that their old ladies would become the best of friends, and so far all my brothers who had women had gotten their wish.

"You two know what's going on?" I asked, turning my attention back to the meeting that seemed to be happening next to the bar.

"Nope," Toxic said, shoving his hands in his jeans pockets. Butcher just shook his head.

Priest handed me a beer as I walked up, then reached down into a cooler that was next to his feet and did the same for Toxic and Butcher. I opened the bottle and took a swig to wet my suddenly dry throat. Everyone was staring at me.

CHAPTER 17

Ricochet

"What's up?" I asked, looking over at Lockout.

"Wanted to run something past you." He tossed his phone over to me.

Catching it, I grinned when I saw Rip on the screen. "Hey, Rip."

"You look good." He was studying me over the app that allowed us to see each other.

"This is so sweet," Butcher attempted a sugary tone. Coming from him, it was more a high pitched raspy tone, making him sound more insane than usual.

Glaring at him, I shook my head. "Thanks. Congrats on the wedding, Brother."

"Appreciate it, Ricochet. We have a proposition for you."

"Oh yeah?"

"My angel asked if we could possibly make a school for the kids." He didn't need to explain that he meant the kids that we'd pulled out of the desert cult. "I spoke to Lock about it immediately and he and

Static have been looking into what that might entail," Riptide explained.

I frowned, wondering what that had to do with me. School had been something I'd endured until I was finally out. I certainly hadn't enjoyed it.

"Static jumped on it right away and has been helping us by talking with the Arizona State Board for Charter Schools. Seeing what they require," Lockout explained.

Holding the phone up so Rip could still see, I waited. They'd eventually tell me how this was going to connect to me. "Sounds like a good idea," I told them. "A way for these kids to get educated and a taste of life here in the city, without exposing them to a regular school. They essentially need to be deprogrammed from the cult and educated in normal life."

"Unfortunately, it can take a few years to get everything done, but Static thinks he has a buddy who can help with that," Lockout continued. For whatever reason, Lockout sounded disgruntled at that, though I couldn't figure out why. He was usually on board with getting help wherever we could. "We'll worry about the accreditations, permits, and timelines. We wanted to know if you'd build it for us?"

My arms dropped as though they each weighed a hundred pounds. The phone dangled in my right hand and Rip was getting a great view of the ground. I glanced over at George, who was grinning from ear to ear. "Why wouldn't you ask him? He has the construction company." I'd gotten my own contracting license years ago, but I'd always just worked for George rather than striking out on my own.

"They did ask me," George replied, "but I'm booked up on jobs for the next six months. You'd still be working under my company, I'd just be promoting you to foreman and you'd be taking the lead on this job. You'd have your own crew."

This time it was my jaw that dropped. That was a lot of fucking responsibility. It wasn't that I couldn't handle it, more the fact that they were willing to trust in me to get the job done. These men never once let my age or my PTSD dissuade them from including me. I swallowed down the love and affection I had for each of them before I blurted out something stupid. "Fuck yeah, I'll do it."

Smoke slung his arm over my shoulders. "This is going to be fun."

Lock narrowed his eyes on us. "We're going to have Smokehouse join you, and Hell when he has the time."

"What about your job?" I asked Hellfire.

"I have some time off coming up this summer. I'll be pitching in then."

"Doing construction in the middle of summer on your time off," Butcher said with a lift to his lip. "That sounds like fucking torture."

It wasn't fun. It was hot, sweaty, miserable work, but we wouldn't complain because we were doing it to help our family. Sloane's family now belonged to us.

"Thanks, Kid," Rip said, pulling my attention back to the screen as I lifted the phone once more. "We want to get it going as soon as the permits get approved. We appreciate you taking it over."

"Shit. I appreciate the opportunity. How long until we start?" I asked both Lock and George.

"Static and his friend are like wizards," George said with a shake of his head. "They're slicing through the bureaucratic bullshit with impressive speed. I hit a couple of walls myself when I went down to permitting and thought it was going to end up taking months, or longer."

"That's why we pulled Static in," Lock remarked. "Having him on board is helpful in and of itself, but the list of people he knows is fucking priceless."

"Who's his friend?" Toxic asked.

Lockout tensed up. "A friend he knows who lives in Idaho. The guy's an investment guru. He's good at what he does. Static trusts him to get this done. He's gotten the paperwork finished and in place in a few days' time, that's all I really care about."

Frowning, I studied Lock's face. There was something he wasn't telling us. Something about this new guy was riling him up. His tone said the matter was closed, though, so I didn't push. I wasn't sure whether the others had really noticed.

"Can we really trust Static?" Hell asked. He winced when Lockout focused on him. "Sorry...but how well do we know him?"

"You don't know him at all," Lock conceded. "But I do. So does Riptide."

"Good enough for me," Hush said before our president could even utter another word.

"Same," Priest said, leaning back against one of the cage rides that was parked in front of The Bunker.

The others all nodded. We knew that Lockout and Riptide both had some connection with Static, but the rest of us didn't know him well yet. He'd been included in the last mission and it didn't seem like he was going anywhere for the foreseeable future. Hush had mentioned at one point that Lock had tried to convince Static to join the club. I wondered if that was what was happening now.

I hadn't spoken to Static much yet. I'd been mostly keeping to myself, but he seemed like a decent guy. He certainly had skills that the MC could utilize. Being helpful to our club was important to us all. It was why Hellfire was willing to use up his yearly vacation just to come work for us.

"We'll go over the plans, and who your crew will be over the next week," George told me. "That way you'll be ready to jump in once those permits are approved." He hesitated, clearly not wanting to ask the next question. He didn't need to; I knew what it was.

"I'll be ready," I said, before he had the chance to voice it. It'd actually help to have something to focus on. Something that was important to the club. Not just to the club, but to the victims of the cult. This might be the most significant and impactful thing I'd ever been tasked with. It could be a way of atoning for what I'd done. I wasn't going to let anyone down.

"Too bad you can't get time off sooner," Butcher told Hell with a wicked grin. "Better to be up on a roof than shoveling shit."

Hellfire chuckled as he rolled his eyes. "I don't shovel shit, Dumbass."

"He pumps it," Toxic said helpfully.

"Yeah, that's better," Butcher muttered.

Hellfire's family owned a local septic company. He ran a pump truck, and as the oldest son would eventually take over once his father retired. He didn't mind the work and it helped his family out. It was hard finding good workers, so the company was mostly family owned and run. Hell's three brothers, two sisters, and four cousins all worked for his dad. They were a pretty tight knit family so they all enjoyed it, even though, as Butcher pointed out, they worked with shit.

I'd rather stick with construction, but would do whatever it took to make it. After being medically discharged from the military, I'd needed something to keep my mind busy and off my troubles. George had taken me under his wing and taught me everything I knew. I liked working with my hands, creating something new from disassembled pieces.

"Thanks, Ricochet," Lockout said, drawing me back into the conversation. "This is going to be a big project, but we knew if anyone other than George was going to oversee it, it had to be you."

I wasn't tooting my own horn or anything, but I was damn good. This job wasn't being given to me because they felt sorry for me, it was because I was the next best. George was planning on retiring in the next few years and he'd already started grooming me to take over. It's why I'd gotten my license already. It just made sense that they were asking me. That didn't mean that it didn't make a warm sensation take up residence in my chest. And the timing really was perfect. With Jordan here, and now this project, life was more than just bearable, I was looking forward to tomorrow. I hadn't had that sensation in years.

"Just wanted to make sure you were on board," Rip said from the phone, "before we got too far into making plans."

"Like I'd say no," I told him with a chuckle.

He grinned at me and we said goodbye as I passed Lock's phone back to him. This was turning out to be a good fucking day. My thoughts turned to the woman I'd get to enjoy the rest of the day with.

"That's it," Lock said, dismissing everyone. "Go enjoy the barbecue." He watched as everyone started to walk away. "Ricochet. Give me a minute."

I waited, and we watched as Priest's girls charged Butcher and Toxic. Lockout laughed and shook his head. "How long before you think they've got those girls trained up on everything from self-defense to lobbing grenades?"

Snorting, I shook my head. "You think they haven't started already? The second one of them has a crush on a boy you'll find them shaking down a twelve-year-old. They have those two wrapped around their fingers."

"Not just them," Lock murmured.

He was right. We would all give up our lives to protect them if need be. "Something tells me they'll have the girls target shooting long before Priest is ready for it."

Lockout laughed. "Damn straight they will. Priest will eventually give in and teach them his deadly accuracy."

"I almost feel sorry for whoever they end up marrying."

"I don't," he said. "They'll have to get through all of us before they have a chance. It's just the way it goes. Those girls will be worth it. Any man worth his salt will know that."

Nodding in agreement, I shoved my hands inside my jean pockets. "Thanks for the chance to do this."

His hazel eyes met mine. "You know we wouldn't be asking if you weren't the best man for the job."

"I know."

"I see the change in you since Jordan came into the picture. I can tell you're ready for something more."

"I am. I still plan on staying out at my sister's place for a while, but I'll be here every day, ready to work."

One corner of his lips kicked up into a smirk. "Something tells me that it's not about needing space anymore. You're staying out there to be closer to your old lady."

He wasn't wrong. That was the thing about Lockout, he didn't miss a damn thing. "She wants to take things slow."

His chuckle was low. "Then you take it at her pace. You've got the rest of your lives together."

"That's what I'm doing. Doesn't make it any easier. I just want to-" I shook my head.

"We're used to getting what we want. Makes it hard as hell to adjust to someone else's timeline." He gave me a piercing look. "She worth it?"

"Fuck yeah."

"Then you'll do whatever you have to in order to get her on board." He slapped me on the shoulder as he started to walk away. He paused, looking over his shoulder. "Don't wait too long. There's a difference between giving her time to adjust and giving her time to talk herself out of things. Sometimes you just have to take what you want."

"How the hell do I know when to do one or the other?"

His teeth flashed through his grin. "That's on you to figure out."

I watched him join the others down in the grass. We always kept a few acres green, so the kids had a place to run around and play without worrying about cactus. "That was real helpful, Lock," I muttered. He hadn't told me anything I didn't already know. He just hadn't helped with the one part I could have used advice on. The timing of it all.

Wanting to give Jordan a chance to get to know the women, I headed over toward the others. I grabbed the beer Butcher handed me and we caught up on everything I'd missed out on. Eventually my mind wandered back to what Lockout had told me.

Like he said, I'd have to figure it out. Enough time had passed, so I went over to the bar. I opened the door and leaned against the doorframe, watching as the women laughed and talked. It only took a few minutes before I knew that the women were already connecting. That made me relax a bit. The family aspect of our lifestyle was one of the things a lot of the women craved. They loved the friendships they made almost as much as they loved their bikers. It was going to make it easier for me to convince Jordan she couldn't live without me.

CHAPTER 18

Jordan

"Jordan! Hey. Fancy seeing you here." Kit gave me a mischievous smile.

That look told me she wasn't at all surprised to see me here. I blushed at the implications of that. Knowing that Ricochet was talking to his friends and family about me caused equal parts delight and worry to work their way through my mind.

Kit quickly introduced the other women she was with, then motioned for us to follow her. "I'm making mojitos," she announced as we headed toward the bar.

Seek groaned. "I love mojitos. That's not fair."

"Sorry, Girlie, you'll just have to wait until after you pop that baby out."

We all laughed at Kit's wording. We were closing in on the bar, and the group of bikers having their meeting, when one of the women, I think her name was Susie, called out to one of two men walking our way.

"Done with your meeting?" she asked as he approached.

"Our part of it."

"Good. You have kid patrol."

His jaw dropped and horror washed over his face. "All of them?"

"Don't worry, Dash, Bear will help you," Daisha—I remembered her name because it was so unique—said, offering up Tori's old man as a helpmate. She gave the man a huge, innocent smile

The men just shrugged and Bear took Tori's baby from her before they walked back toward where the kids were playing. Seeing these huge burly guys with kids surrounding them made me smile. It was actually really sweet. And it was just as clear they were over the moon for the kids.

I looked around as we walked into the bar. It looked exactly like I'd expect a biker bar to look. Kit flicked on the lights and got busy behind the bar. Sitting on one of the stools, I smiled at the others, feeling a bit awkward as all attention turned to me.

"Tell us everything about yourself," Jenny requested.

My eyes widened. "Um. There's really not a lot to tell…"

"Oh please," Tori said, waving a hand at me, "you managed to catch Ricochet's eye."

The tone in which she said it made me curious. "That doesn't happen much?"

"Girl. I've known Ricochet since he prospected into this club and I've never seen him bring a woman to one of our barbecues," Kit told me with a significant look.

"Bringing you to the barbecue is his way of claiming you," Seek told me with an air of confidence.

I watched in shock and a bit of disgust as she lifted up a bottle of lime juice and poured some of it into her mouth. We were all watching her in utter bewilderment.

"Sorry," she said, a sheepish look on her face. "I've been craving really sour things lately."

"I don't know how you just downed that." Susie shook her head.

"What do you mean, claiming?" I asked, getting back to the matter at hand. "He's mentioned stuff like that before. That I belonged to him-"

The others started laughing and giving each other knowing looks. "When did he tell you that?" Kit asked.

"The day you were at the house…"

I watched as five of the six women groaned and Kit whooped with delight.

"I win!" she declared.

"Win what?" I asked in confusion.

They all gave me looks of shame, though their eyes were sparkling, so whatever it was they didn't feel that badly about it. "We bet on how long it would take for him to claim you," Daisha told me.

My mouth dropped open. "How did you even know about me?"

"Kit told us everything," Jenny replied.

"I knew from the minute I met you that Ricochet was interested," Kit stated. "Partly because my brother let it slip, but I also caught him staring at you. It was more than just checking you out, he was hooked."

My cheeks heated with embarrassment. "We're not dating or anything."

"That's what you think," Tori said with a snicker of laughter.

"We're just getting to know one another."

They all just blinked slowly at me, like owls.

"He agreed to that?" Seek asked, looking dumbfounded. "The boy *must* be in love."

"I- Look," I said with a sigh when the silence stretched on, begging for an explanation, "I'm not ready for whatever…this…is."

"It's a lot," Jenny admitted. She frowned at me. "Do you know what you've gotten yourself into here?"

"What do you mean?"

Seek and Jenny gave each other pointed looks. Then Seek sighed. "Will Ricochet mind if we fill her in?" she asked Kit.

The woman behind the bar shook her head. "He's hoping we will, guaranteed. There are some things that are just easier to hear coming from old ladies."

"Who's old lady are you?" I asked her.

Kit shook her head. "My dad was a part of this club way back when. Since Smoke is a member now, Lockout lets me hang around, but I don't belong to anyone."

There was a glimmer of sadness in her eyes. I wondered if she had her eye on someone? Was that why she seemed disappointed that she wasn't an old lady? I didn't say anything. She didn't seem to want anyone to know about it, because she quickly turned away to hide her expression.

"This is going to take some time," Jenny said.

"Good thing we have all night," Susie chirped.

"And plenty of drinks," Kit said, setting a pitcher of mojitos in front of us.

Looking around, I gave them an uncertain smile. For some reason I knew I was going to come to love these women. That didn't mean I was completely on board with what all that entailed.

* * *

My eyelids were heavy as we polished off another pitcher of mojitos. The last time I drank was with Gwen on her birthday last year. We'd both sworn off alcohol for a while after that night. I smiled as I remembered the way we'd stumbled into her home shushing each other and giggling, so we didn't wake the kids. The babysitter had put us to bed and I'd been passed out in the guest bedroom before she'd made it out the front door.

Even with the amount of alcohol we'd consumed, I had a decent buzz going. Just enough to be relaxed and no longer self-conscious, but I was heading toward drunk and somehow the cup in front of me kept refilling itself. These women had been telling me some of what I needed to know about the club life. There were so many rules. Thankfully, most of them applied to the men, but the old ladies had a few as well. Something I would need to know if I decided to take Ricochet up on his claim. Though the girls didn't seem to think I had much choice in the matter.

I'd found out that meant he was telling his brothers that I was off limits and belonged to him. Really that should disgust me, I wasn't property after all, but according to these women, I was. Ricochet's property. Why did that make my heart jump for joy? And my core clench in anticipation? It was ridiculous to be happy that someone wanted to claim me, but he was so damn handsome, and sweet, and demanding, and…and…sexy. I sighed, resting my chin on my hand.

The women surrounding me gave each other knowing looks. "So why are you making him wait, Honey?" Susie asked.

I straightened up, looking around at their curious faces. Deep down, I knew I could tell them anything. They'd already explained the girl-code between old ladies—and that it didn't apply to the sweet butts. The woman I'd seen earlier had been one. They hung around, hoping to get a biker to make them an old lady. I couldn't blame them. These men had a huge appeal. All decked out in leather and tattoos, looking as good as…

Someone cleared their throat and I laughed. "Sorry. Uh…" I couldn't tell them my hang ups before I told Ricochet. That just didn't seem right. "I had an asshole ex," I settled on telling them the partial truth. What Dan had done to me was so much worse, but that was a story for another day.

All their eyes softened. It drove away the unease. "It's made me a little hesitant to trust men again."

"How old are you?" Seek asked. "You look too young to have been through heartbreak."

I laughed. "I'm twenty-five. Plenty old enough."

They nodded. "Pretty sure we all have dickhead exes in our pasts somewhere," Kit said. She gave me a pointed look. "No reason to resist a man who'd hang the moon for you."

"No. I guess not. The problem is, how do you know that's the kind of man he is? How can I trust that?"

"That's fair enough," Jenny retorted. "You don't know Ricochet very well yet. I was hesitant at first too, when I met Priest. Ran out of the Austin Chapter clubhouse the next morning 'cause I couldn't believe I'd stayed the night. I hadn't meant to." She laughed at all the whistles and catcalls. "I didn't sleep with him. Well, have sex with him," she replied in a prim tone.

"I have a question."

The women settled down and focused on me, though Jenny's cheeks were still pink from all the teasing.

"Gwen told me that Ricochet would…kill…for me." I tucked my hair behind my ears and leaned forward on my elbows on the bar top. "She wouldn't really elaborate. But she was very specific with her words."

It was like all the humor had been sucked out of the room. No one was really looking at me. Tori, Susie, and Daisha were studying the bar top, while the other three seemed to be having a silent conversation with each other.

"That's hard to explain," Kit hedged.

"It's sort of best to let Ricochet tell you about that himself," Jenny agreed.

"There are certain things that only old ladies are allowed to know," Seek said, expanding on what they were saying. "And there are things even *we* aren't allowed to know."

"Something you have to understand about these men is they are fiercely loyal, to their family, to their community, but especially to each other. You guys may be their wives and girlfriends, but you're not members," Kit told me. There wasn't anything mean in her tone, just honesty. And a seriousness that was not meant to be questioned.

I understood what they meant. Gwen had mentioned that Ricochet and all his MC brothers had been in the military. It seemed to reason that they would look for another brotherhood like that one. "Are women allowed to join?" I asked.

"Not this club. There are some all-female MCs out there, though," Tori replied.

Not that I wanted to join an MC or anything. Mostly I just wanted to learn everything I could about the man who'd caught my unwilling attention. His life was fascinating. I hadn't known anything like it.

"Us old ladies—and honorary sisters—" Seek said, giving Kit a soft smile "sort of have a club of our own, though. We'll be there for you through thick and thin."

My heart softened even more. I loved the idea of that. I had my family, and Gwen and her kids, but I didn't have a close knit group of friends anymore, not since we'd all graduated high school and sort of went our separate ways. It was hard to make friends as an adult. The idea that I'd have a built in circle of friends was a huge check in the plus column. It wasn't enough to completely change my mind, but it was a nice bonus.

"I get that there will be things that he can't tell me," I said. "He already explained that. But part of the problem I had with the ex was the lying and manipulating." And that was only scratching the surface.

"Ricochet won't do that," Seek promised. "None of them do. Secrets, yes, by necessity. But never any lies. Whenever there's something Hush can't tell me, he just says so in no uncertain terms." She cleared her throat and deepened her voice. "Woman. You know I can't tell you what that meetin' was about."

Having met Hush earlier, I laughed at her impression. She'd done a pretty good job.

"Talk with him about it," Jenny suggested. "Explain to him you'd rather he tells you that it's not allowed, than to lie."

"A lot of the time they don't tell us things that would implicate us if the cops came sniffing around," Daisha said. Her eyes widened as the realization of what she said sank in.

"Cops?" I asked, looking around at them. "Why would the cops be…" Understanding dawned. "Wait." The conversation at Gwen's dinner party echoed through my mind. Specifically, what Trent had been saying. "Are these guys criminals?" When Gwen's ex had thrown that out there I'd just thought he was trying to rile up Ricochet. Was it true?

"I think that's my cue to have a talk with my date."

Cringing as the deep voice interrupted our little bubble of solitude, I glanced over my shoulder and met Ricochet's gaze. Uh oh. He looked upset.

"Don't worry," Kit told me as she came around the bar and hugged me. "His bark is worse than his bite."

"At least where you're concerned," Seek agreed and she wrapped me in a hug. Her belly bumped mine.

They passed me around, one by one, giving me hugs. It was meant to be supportive, but really it was just coming off like I was headed to the gallows.

I walked over to Ricochet, looking down at his strong, calloused hand as he held it out to me. Wrapping my fingers in his, I glanced over my shoulder and gave my new friends a weak smile. They waved at me as he pulled me out of the bar.

CHAPTER 19

Ricochet

The families were clearing out because a whole different kind of party was starting up. The sweet butts who worked for us had stuck mostly to the clubhouse while the barbecue was happening. They knew to keep out of the way while we had everyone's families here.

Sylvia was the one exception. She was out on the grass, playing with the kids, and speaking with the old ladies. No one had ever treated her like a sweet butt. We all knew it was only a matter of time before some guy came to one of our parties—maybe a weekender—saw her and fell head over heels for the older woman. Anytime we went on a run to help out our brothers or friends, we kept an eye out for a man worthy of Syl. She was incredibly kind and deserved a man who would take care of her. We wouldn't let her go to just anyone.

There'd been more than once where Syl had sat with me after the nightmares had woken me and sleep was a far distant memory. I usually headed downstairs to drink my troubles away. It was as though she had a sixth sense about when one of us needed something. Us younger guys considered her an honorary mother, while the older men thought of her as a beloved sister. Either way, she was as much a part of our club as Kit was. Both women had a place here for as long as they wanted one.

I detoured over to her, because she was holding a sleepy Caitlyn. Jordan came along with me, though I could tell she was a little tipsy, so I slowed my pace. A grin tugged at my mouth. I was glad Jordan had enjoyed her time with the others. It hadn't even bothered me when I heard what they were talking about, though I'd put a glower on my face. I had a lot of explaining I needed to do for my old lady.

As soon as I approached, Caitlyn smiled. She lifted my dog tags over her head and handed them over.

"Thanks, Kid," I said, ruffling her hair.

Her eyes were heavy, and she was resting her head on Syl's shoulder.

"Jordan, this is Sylvia. Syl, this is Jordan."

"Hi," Sylvia said, giving Jordan a warm smile and juggling Caitlyn's limp body so she could shake my girl's hand. "It's so nice to meet you."

"It's nice to meet you as well," Jordan replied. "I wish we had a bit more time to talk." She motioned to the little girl, who was now fast asleep in Syl's embrace.

If only I could fucking sleep like that.

Out loud, I said, "Next time." I nodded a goodnight to Sylvia and Jordan gave her a little wave.

"You're so good with kids," Jordan murmured as we walked away, toward the clubhouse.

I wasn't dragging her along anymore, not now that I'd noticed her unsteady gait. She was happy and relaxed though, so I owed the girls for that. Her fingers were wrapped up in mine and she was strolling next to me. My mind settled, letting go of the ever vigilant state it was usually in. All it took was the touch of her hand.

Jordan leaned into my side and I caught the scent of citrus. She was like a warm sunny day. Fresh and unburdened by the horrors I'd seen in my life. Again the thought that it was selfish of me to drag her

RICOCHET

into my world crossed my mind. Part of me thought, hoped, that it would be the opposite. The more time I spent with her, the more she was pulling me into her world. I might escape my darkness after all, and she would be my motivation to do so.

She was the only thing that was keeping the encroaching darkness at bay and while I didn't want to let her go, I knew for a fact that even if I tried, I wouldn't be able to. Wrapping my arm around her shoulders, I tucked her up against my body.

We walked into the clubhouse right as Butcher switched the music over to something less suited to the family atmosphere. He gave us a nod and a grin as a pair of young women walked through the door.

Shaking my head as he went over to 'show them around', I reached over the bar and grabbed a bottle of vodka.

Scarlett laughed as she handed over two shot glasses. "Looks like you two are going to have your own party." She winked at Jordan. It was a friendly gesture, unlike Pixie who was huddled up in the corner, staring down at her phone. Ever since Pixie had picked a fight with Seek, and Hellfire had been forced to put her in her place, she'd been sullen and quiet. It was better than her being sullen and loud about it. Hell had put the fear of God into her that day, though, so she was behaving. All it had taken was pointing out the fact that she was going to lose the one thing she wanted, being connected to this club, and the shot of losing out on finding a biker of her own.

"Thanks, Scarlett," I called over my shoulder as I led Jordan upstairs.

"We're not staying down here?" she asked, looking up at me.

"Fuck no. This party isn't for old ladies." The single guys liked to let loose at these things and a lot of the bikers from other clubs were going to be here tonight. I didn't want to spend the night hovering over my woman to make sure no one tried shit when I could be with her upstairs.

She narrowed her eyes at me as I waited at the top of the stairs for her to pass me, but she didn't say anything about me calling her my old lady.

"Fourth door on the left."

She led the way and opened the door to my room before stepping in. "This is nice," she said, going over and sitting on my bed.

"It's fine for now." It was a dorm style room that was big enough to fit my king size bed, dresser, and the rest of the meager belongings I kept. I didn't need a lot of space, or a fancy place to live. That would change once I had a wife and kids—one day—but for now, I was just grateful that it had an ensuite bathroom.

Setting the glasses on the dresser, I poured a shot. My eyebrow arched up as she stood and sashayed over to me. The flirtatious look in her eyes amused me.

"Is that for me?"

"I think you've had enough," I countered.

Her full lower lip poked out in a pout so adorable I couldn't resist. I handed the shot over. Pouring myself one, I kept my eyes on her. She was waiting for me to finish.

"Do you know how long it's been since I cut loose and got drunk?" she asked.

"How long?"

A frown marred her pretty face. "Too long," she responded as though she was just doing the math now. "Four years."

"You haven't partied since you turned twenty-one?"

We both tossed back our shots and a predatory feeling crept over me as I watched her lick the alcohol from her lips. Jesus she was going to kill me. I was willing to bet she had no clue how she was affecting me.

"Oh! No, a year. Last year with Gwen. But before that was another year." She gave me a satisfied smile. She was proud even though her math wasn't adding up. I didn't mention anything as she handed the glass back to me. "Another, please."

My eyes were glued to the little strip of flesh that her flowy top exposed as she reached her arm out. Who knew an inch wide swath of skin on a woman's stomach would have my cock aching in a matter of seconds. It was because it was *this* woman. *My* woman. It was going to be damn near impossible to play her little game. She didn't think it was a game, but that's what it was. She was testing me to make sure I wasn't going to get what I wanted and bail. If only there was a way to convince her that *she* was truly what I wanted. Time. That was the only way of winning this wary creature over.

Not so wary now.

I planned to take advantage of that so I could get to know her more. I handed back the shot glass and chuckled when she immediately tossed it back. "Better catch up."

"You'd better slow down."

"Nope." Her smile was dazzling, and I knew she was close to her limit.

"How about we play a game?"

Interest sparked in her eyes. "I'm good at games."

"And not competitive at all," I told her with a grin.

"Oh, no. I am," she said, going back to sit on my bed again. "My brother says I'm..." She paused and I watched her for signs that she might throw up. But she just leaned back on her hands and continued, "He says I'm no fun."

"Something tells me he's wrong."

She let out a heavy sigh. "No. Noah's right. I'm a stick in the mud. I have been ever since-" She bit her lower lip and I had to hold back a groan.

I wanted to be the one biting and licking at those lips. Not to mention the things I wanted to do with the rest of her. "Ever since what?"

She shook her head. "Not drunk enough to talk about that."

"About what?"

"Dan the Douche."

My eyebrows shot up even as anger boiled in my gut. I didn't like another man's name passing her lips. The last thing I wanted to know about was some guy she was with, but I had a deep-seated need to know everything about her. I had to know so I was aware of any threats in her life. So far, I knew she was a falconer, worked at The Wildlife Sanctuary, and had a brother named Noah. If she didn't start opening up to me, I'd have to learn about her another way. I'd rather *she* told me everything.

Before I could say anything, she started talking. She'd already forgotten that she wasn't drunk enough, according to her, for this story.

"I used to be a lot of fun." Her tone was defensive. "We dated for two years. *He* used to be a lot of fun."

I folded my arms over my chest to keep her from seeing the way my hands were bunching into fists. I wanted to use them on her ex. There was hurt there, buried in her eyes. Her tone was tight as she spoke. She didn't like reliving this.

"Then we turned twenty-one and all he ever wanted to do was drink. He'd be out at bars and clubs until all hours of the night. The cops brought him home more than once. He'd convinced me to move in with him, then he started spending all his time and money on booze. I was struggling to keep everything going," she admitted, her voice soft and filled with shame.

As if any of that was her fault. Sounded like she'd hooked up with a guy who decided it was more fun to sow his wild oats than maintain the commitment he'd made to his girlfriend. I wouldn't know shit about that. I'd been in the military so young, there hadn't been sowing of much of anything until I joined the MC. I had a feeling I knew at least a portion of what was coming next in her story.

"He started getting into fights. He wasn't paying his portion of the bills. I kept having to go pick him up from either the police station or bars in the middle of the night. Then he started borrowing money from friends and family to fund his drinking. They'd call me, trying to get back some of the money he'd blown."

"Fucking idiot."

"That and more."

"Him, not you."

"Oh, I know." Her gaze turned fierce. "He was the one who fucked up. I don't blame myself. I know I didn't do anything wrong, other than staying with him for too long." She sighed again. "Can I have another?"

"Last one." I shouldn't even give her that. She was already drunk, but I wasn't planning on taking her anywhere else tonight. She was safe up here in my room with me. Not that my brothers would ever act inappropriately toward her if she did happen to wander downstairs, and they wouldn't allow the friends Lock had invited to this party to do shit either. They already knew she was off limits. I handed her the shot and took another for myself. I wasn't even feeling the buzz yet, but I wasn't planning on getting wasted tonight. A few shots before bed just helped me sleep better.

"I did do one thing wrong," she admitted. The sad expression on her face was nearly unbearable.

I wanted to fix all her problems, erase all her worries. Walking over to the bed, I got on it with my back resting against the wall, then dragged her onto my lap. Arranging her so that her back was against my chest. My cock was digging into her ass, but there wasn't much I could do about that. "Tell me."

Her cheeks were pink from the realization that I was hard, but she settled back into my arms. "Dan called me one night to pick him up from the bar. It was still relatively early for him. I was having dinner with my family. Dad insisted on coming with me." Her body shuddered against mine. "When we walked in it was utter chaos. People were hitting each other. Some lady broke a bottle over a guy's head." She looked over her shoulder at me. "I've never seen anything like it." Her lips twisted ruefully. "Granted I've never even been in a fight before. Seeing an entire roomful of people going at it was crazy."

She turned back around, arching into my touch as I ran my hand up and down her thigh. It was meant to be a soothing gesture, but it did nothing to diminish my lust. If her breathing was any indication, it was having an effect on her, too.

"We made our way through the crowd, trying to find Dan. Dad wanted me to go back out to the car to wait, but I didn't want to leave him in that place. Thankfully, I didn't listen because Dan came stumbling out from the area that had the pool tables. Three men were chasing after him. Dad tried to reason with them, but they were drunk and said that Dan had ripped them off. Dad even offered to pay them, just to smooth over the situation."

Anger was rolling off her in waves as she recounted the next part of the story. "Dad had managed to calm everything down. The guys were going to take some money and leave the situation alone."

My eyes closed and I silently called Dan every name in the book. I knew where this was headed. I'd gotten into far too many of my own fights not to know. The difference was, I always won. Sounded like Dan picked fights he couldn't finish, then expected his girlfriend and her father to de-escalate the situation. *Fucking loser.*

"He started smarting off to the guys. I tried to get him to stop, but the damage was done." Her body shook as she recounted the next part, her voice thick with unshed tears. "One of the men hit Dad with the pool cue he was holding. Broke it over his chest." She reached down and grabbed my hand. "I thought he was having a heart attack. That he was going to die in this shitty little bar on the outskirts of South Tucson. That I'd have to live with the fact that my piece of shit boyfriend had gotten my father killed."

Wrapping my arms around her, I pulled her back tight into my embrace. I kissed the side of her face. "Then what?" She needed to get the rest of it out as much as I had to hear it. The need to comfort her while she did was too strong to resist.

"Thankfully, the force of the blow just knocked the wind out of him. Once he was able to breathe, I helped him up and drove him straight to the hospital. I spent the next six months apologizing every day." I could see the smile on her profile as I looked over at her. "My dad, being who he is, never accepted the apology because he said it wasn't mine to make. It was Dan's. Not that I'd let him anywhere near my family after that. After I dropped Dad at home, I went back to our apartment and packed up everything I could fit into my car. I've never been back."

"What happened to Dan?"

"Last thing I saw, he was getting the crap beat out of him by those three." She nibbled on her lip. "Sometimes I feel guilty for leaving him there-"

"Don't. He deserves exactly what he got."

"I know he lived because he tried calling. For months he left voicemails explaining his side of things. I never took his call. Eventually he gave up." She heaved a breath, as though talking that out had released a heavy burden.

I hoped it did. She didn't need to be carrying that around with her. "You did the right thing," I reassured her. I didn't go into my thoughts on starting shit you couldn't finish; she didn't need to hear that.

She turned in my arms, her knees on either side of my legs. My breath caught in my chest as she kissed me. Without even giving them the order, my hands were in her hair, positioning her head so I could take the kiss deeper.

I let the sensations roll over me as I enjoyed her taste. Her body crowded closer and I allowed one hand to free itself from her silky soft tresses to cup her ass and grind her against my dick. Fuck, I was so damn horny.

Her hands slid down over my chest, but it wasn't until she was undoing my belt that reality returned like an ice cold bucket of water hitting me. I caught her wrist and stared into her deep green eyes. "What're you doing, Sunshine?"

Her smile was hesitant. "Proving I still know how to have fun."

My eyes narrowed on her face. God damn it, I wanted to let her prove that, all night long if she wanted. But sober Jordan had wanted to take this slowly. To have time to get to know me before she jumped into a relationship. It made sense now. A kid she thought she knew, who she'd dated for years, had made a drastic change overnight. And one of the people she loved most in this world had been injured because of it. She didn't need to verbalize the way she felt about her family. It was there in her words for anyone to hear. She loved them more than anything else.

As much as I wanted to fuck her. To put my mark on her and prove to her that she belonged to me, I couldn't. Not like this. Not while she was drunk. And not before I told her who I really was and all the fucked up baggage that came along with me. I wasn't going to let her run from me, once I told her, but she deserved to know all the same.

CHAPTER 20

Jordan

Oh God. He's going to reject me.

I could see it there in his eyes. In the rigidness of his body as he held me. He still had my wrist in a tight hold.

Embarrassment stole over me, heating my cheeks and making me want to cry. Maybe he'd changed his mind and he didn't really want me after all. Maybe I'd been way off base. My reasoning skills certainly weren't up to par right now, but I could tell he was putting the brakes on.

I didn't really understand it. Even now his dick was hard where it was rubbing against my thigh. He'd kissed me like he wanted to devour me whole.

"Listen. This isn't easy for me to say," he admitted, voice a harsh guttural sound. It was deep and husky, another sign of how turned on he was.

He wasn't the only one. My pussy was wet and throbbing and I sort of wished he'd stop talking and just push me back against the bed.

That he'd take this choice out of my hands and allow me to lose myself in the response he managed to drag from my body.

"You don't want me," I said, voice barely above a whisper. Humiliation had me forcing the words out, as though they were stuck in my throat.

"What? Fuck no." He finally gave me what I wanted. Well…part of it. He pushed me back, towering above me as his hands pinned my wrists to the mattress. "I mean, yeah, I want you."

He was nestled between my thighs and I could only gasp as he rolled his hips against mine. The proof of his words was grinding against my pussy through our clothes. I couldn't hold back the moan that bubbled up from within my chest.

Ricochet dropped his head down and buried his face in the spot where my neck and shoulder met. "You're fucking killing me, Jordan."

I liked the way he said my name. The growled confession made a shiver of desire skate over my skin. "Then why did you stop me?"

"I don't want you regretting this in the morning."

Somewhere deep in the recesses of my alcohol soaked mind I knew he was right. It wasn't fair to ask him to give me time and then try to jump him the first time I got drunk. That didn't seem to matter to my inner wild child, who was currently controlling things. "But I'm so wet," I told him, turning my head so I could see him, so I could look him directly in the eyes.

His pretty pale blue eyes closed and a tortured look crossed his handsome face. "Fuck me."

"That was my plan," I teased, even though I knew he hadn't meant the words that way. Seeing him with his family had cracked some of the defenses I'd kept around my heart. It reminded me of how my family was together. His were a bit more boisterous and chaotic, but that just made them seem that much more fun. Seeing him with his nephew and niece, and with his MC brothers' kids… Something had begun to bloom inside me. Hope. If he truly wanted me, maybe this was my chance to be happy.

A muscle in his jaw ticked and I wanted to scrape my teeth over it. The alcohol was making me bold, but he had a tight grip on me, and I wasn't going anywhere while a portion of his weight was pinning me down. His arms flexed as he held the majority of his weight on his forearms so he didn't crush me. He was a big man, not that I was complaining.

I tilted my head up as he started shifting my arms until he was able to capture both my wrists, over top of my head, in one hand. My breathing sped up as his free hand cupped my breast over my shirt.

He squeezed, staring down at me. "How wet are you, dirty girl?"

His words made my eyes widen, but he just gave me a wicked smile. I'd been so young when Dan and I had gotten together, and then after him I'd sworn off men, so he'd been the only man I'd ever slept with. Wild sex to Dan had been missionary position with the lights on. I'd listened to all my friends giggle about the things their boyfriends did to them in bed, but I'd never experienced it for myself. Something told me a man like Ricochet was leaps and bounds ahead of me in that department. I licked my lips, unsure how to answer his question.

"That fucking destroys me every time you do it."

I blinked in confusion before I realized he meant me licking my lips. His confession left me breathless. Had I ever affected guys like this before? If I had, they'd never told me. The fact that Ricochet was currently growling everything he wanted to do to me into my ear, in between kisses and bites to the lobe, had a blush rising up on my skin.

"I'm going to release your wrists. You're going to leave them exactly where they are."

"O-okay." He'd paused as though waiting for something. That was all my over-sensitized system had allowed me to stutter out.

"You asked me to give you time," the stubble on his face scraped over my skin, making me shudder, "but I'll be damned if I'm letting my girl go to bed wet and aching. I'm not going to fuck you. Not until you're sober and begging me to. But I'll happily eat out that tight little cunt until you come all over my mouth."

I gasped as his words caused a firestorm of sensation to rocket through my body. My pussy clenched, as though it was tired of being empty and needed to be filled. I tried to rub my thighs together, to get the pressure I so badly desired, but his body was in the way. My movement had me brushing up against his cock. Moaning, I flexed my hips, forcing them up so that we rubbed together again. It was so good I knew if I kept going I could come just like this.

Ricochet's groan was long and deep. His lips were still near my ear. "I can't wait until I can push my way deep into your body. Until you realize that you belong to me, Sunshine. I'm going to fuck you so good when the time comes, you won't ever want it to stop."

His words were building a frenzy inside of me. "Please," I murmured, tossing my head on the mattress.

"Anything my old lady wants."

I could hear the smile in his voice. The satisfaction. But I could only stare at the ceiling and gulp in breaths as he slid down my body. Hands and lips and teeth marked his path, but I was glad he didn't linger long. It was all too much. I just needed to have him between my thighs. To ease the aching throb that had taken up residence there.

He flicked the button on my jeans, and the sound of my zipper dropping echoed in my mind. *Yes, please.* I honestly didn't know if I said those words out loud or in my head, but it didn't seem as though I needed to urge Ricochet along anymore.

His hands gripped the waistband of my pants and he pulled downward. He took my panties with the jeans, baring me from the waist down.

Any other time I might have been shy and embarrassed, letting him see me for the first time, but the lust for him that had been simmering inside of me since I'd first met him didn't allow for it. I wanted him too badly.

He shoved my shirt upward and yanked my bra down, my breasts spilling out from the fabric. His eyes darkened in pleasure as he stared down at my body. He didn't even need to say anything and he had me feeling like some gorgeous sex goddess.

"Fuck, Jordan. You're so damn sexy." His mouth covered my nipple, forcing anything I might have said to come out in a low cry of pleasure.

His teeth scraped over the tender tip, making my back arch up into him. I wanted more. Needed so much more. My cry was louder this time as his fingers found my pussy and stroked. I slapped a hand over my mouth, not wanting anyone to hear me.

Everything stopped. My eyes widened as he lifted his head. My hips strained, trying to get his fingers to move again. Why was he stopping?

"Hands over your head, Gorgeous." He must have seen the worry in my eyes. "No one in the surrounding rooms is up here. This part of the clubhouse is for the single guys. They're all down at the party. You can make all the noise you want." He leaned in until his nose almost bumped my own. "You *will* make all the noise *I* want. I'm going to make you scream my name before I'm finished. If you don't the first time, then you'd better when you think you've had enough. I'm going to eat this pussy until it's dripping for me and you're a puddle on my bed."

The squeak that passed my lips wasn't exactly sexy, but he just had this way of completely disarming me. I wasn't used to any of this. To a man who was so aroused by me that he wanted to do…*that*…for as long as Ricochet was speaking about. Dan had treated it like a chore. In fact, I wasn't even sure I liked it. I never had before.

Ricochet seemed to understand that I couldn't articulate anything right now. Whether it was the alcohol or the desire, I didn't know, but I put my hand back up over my head, holding my own wrist in order to remind myself to keep them both up there.

As soon as I obeyed, he gave a grunt and positioned himself between my thighs. The sight of his huge shoulders wedging between my legs had my mouth drying out. He was still fully dressed.

Why hadn't I gotten some of his clothes off? I knew there were muscles, I'd had the pleasure of feeling them on more than one occasion and had seen him working with his shirt off. And the tattoos. God were those sexy. I wanted to trace all his tattoos with my tongue. I studied his face as he stared down at my pussy. All embarrassment was gone. His strong jaw was tight, as though clenching it was the only way to keep control of himself. The light shone off his dark blond hair.

I didn't get the chance to admire him more than that because he buried that handsome face between my legs. My head fell back onto the bed as I let out a long moan.

His fingers spread my pussy apart and that strong tongue lapped from my opening all the way up to my clit. He gave the bundle of nerves at the top of my pussy a flick before he closed his mouth over it and sucked.

Stars. I'd never really understood the expression of seeing stars, but here they were. Little fire bursts of light behind my darkened lids were lighting up my world.

My toes curled into the bed as my orgasm barrelled toward me. I'd been so worked up prior to this, all it took was a few draws from his mouth and my body imploded. I was shaking and crying out as the most incredible feeling overtook me.

When I floated back into my body, I looked down and found him watching me as he lapped lazily at my pussy. He licked his lips, they were wet and shiny with my release.

"You taste so damn good."

Who knew that was a thing?

"I could eat this, and only this, every day for the rest of my life." His tongue probed lightly inside of me, filling my pussy for a brief moment before he retreated.

The sensation made me gasp and lift my hips, offering for him to do that again. This was nothing like what I thought it would be. Like what it'd been before. I was pretty sure that Ricochet had just ruined me for any other man. I wasn't upset about it, not when his lips and tongue were still playing with my sensitive clit.

"Who does this pussy belong to, Jordan?"

I blinked down at him, not knowing whether I could answer him.

"Sunshine." The nickname was growled out in warning.

Biting my lower lip, I shook my head. Maybe the orgasm had knocked some sense back into my head, or maybe I just wanted to see what consequences he'd dole out.

He dipped his head and started flicking his tongue over my clit as though he was on a mission. He licked and sucked in a way that made me wonder how he knew my body so well.

I knew a part of it was him listening to my gasps and sighs of pleasure, but he was tearing me apart, thread by thread. He'd put me back together again, eventually, I knew it. So I let go and enjoyed it. When his finger filled me, I groaned and arched my hips into his tongue. Now his fingers and mouth were working together. But it seemed like every time I was about to reach the top of my climb, he'd pull back or slow down.

After the third time of not being allowed to orgasm, I raised my head and glared down at him.

He was watching me with an evil grin. "Answer my question, naughty girl."

What had his question been? My mind was running slow and thick.

"Who does this pussy belong to?" He cupped it and squeezed to accent his words.

"You," I whispered, desperate to come. It was the truth. I knew it. I was just scared to admit that this thing between us was real. It'd happened so fast and was so strong I was afraid it would consume me.

"Say it."

"My…pussy belongs to you, Ricochet."

"All of you belongs to me, Sunshine," he corrected. "You're mine."

Before I could argue, he lowered his head again. His finger began moving inside of my body. He made a movement that scraped it against the front wall of my pussy as he flicked his tongue in circles over my clit. It was like he was reaching inside of me and telling my orgasm to 'come here'. He didn't stop.

My body coiled tight and worry crept into my mind. This orgasm was going to be too much. "Wait. Ricochet," I moaned.

He didn't listen. His free arm pinned my hips down, spanning them like a thick band. He held me still as I thrashed below him. It was too much.

The pleasure was white hot. He was right. This time I ended up screaming his name as that wave of bliss crashed over me. The throbbing waves of pleasure dragged me down and all I could do was feel. I didn't know how long it lasted, but by the time I surfaced he had crawled up my body and pulled me into his arms. My nose was smashed into his chest. He still had his t-shirt and cut on, the smell of leather was nice.

My eyes grew heavy. "I should-"

"Go to sleep, Sunshine. I've got you."

It'd been so long since I'd been wrapped up in male arms. There was no resisting the urge. Trusting that he wouldn't let anything happen to me, I closed my eyes and fell asleep with him holding me.

CHAPTER 21

Jordan

Stretching, I yawned and opened my eyes. The unfamiliar wall staring back at me brought back everything that'd happened last night. It made me aware of the heavy arm that was flung over my hips, and the furnace of muscle that was spooned up behind me.

I bit the insides of my lips, eyes closing again as I ran through everything I'd done and said last night. There was no fog of forgetfulness to help tame some of the words I'd used while I'd begged Ricochet to make me orgasm.

"Quit it."

Jumping as his deep voice pierced the silence around us, I twisted and shot him a quick look. His hair was tousled and the heat in his eyes told me in no uncertain terms that he was ready for round two of what we did last night. Though for him it would still be round one.

"Quit what?"

"If you worry any more you're going to break something." There was amusement in his voice.

With a huff, I laid back down. "I'm so sorry."

"For what?"

"For jerking you around like that. It wasn't fair to ask you to wait and then…that."

"I didn't mind. Just in case you don't remember, we didn't have sex."

Just oral. And it was the most amazing thing I'd ever felt. I'd never come so hard, or so many times before. And I'd begged him to fuck me. To get me off. "I know. And I'm not upset." I'd been wondering what it would be like to be with him for a while now.

He shifted, rolling me until he was over top me again. It reminded me of our positions last night and heat swept through me. I'd like to claim it was only embarrassment, but my core throbbed to life between my thighs as he stared down at me.

"I agreed to give you time to get to know me, Jordan, but I've also told you that you're mine. I mean that. The minute you give me the go ahead, when you're sober, I'm going to fuck you until you're writhing beneath me and coming all over my dick."

My jaw dropped open. I'd never really heard anyone speak this way. It was…sexy, for some reason, but a little overwhelming. Mostly because now I knew he would keep that promise. If the man could make my whole body combust like he had with just his mouth and fingers, I could only imagine what he'd do when he had free rein.

His eyes narrowed on my face. "You lived with Dan the Douche," I laughed as he took up my nickname for my ex, "I assume that means you aren't a virgin."

"Oh! No, I'm not." Now the blush was pure embarrassment. "But, I haven't…um…"

"He's the only man you've had sex with?" His eyes were a blazing blue.

I wasn't sure if he was angry, or feeling possessive, or what the intense emotions were that were sparking there in his gaze. All I could do was nod.

"Good. And I'll be the last man you'll be with," he declared. "That's why I'm in no hurry. I'm not going anywhere, Sunshine."

My hands went to his chest and I had to fight the urge to squeeze the bare muscle. My brain stuttered as I realized he'd taken off everything but his boxer briefs sometime last night. My eyes roved over tanned skin. He had ink from his shoulders down to his forearms and all down the left side of his ribs. There was a set of dog tags inked there at the top of his ribs. In the middle of his chest was a huge snake. My fingers trailed over the dog tag tattoo.

His eyes fluttered closed, and he caught my wrist, but didn't pull my hand away. He pressed my palm over the tattoo. "You aren't the only one with a painful past," he croaked out, voice oozing sadness. "I have a lot I need to tell you, as well."

"I want to hear it, but Ricochet… I don't know about all this," I admitted. "It's scary that you just somehow seem to know that you want to be with me."

"You're telling me you don't feel the connection between us?"

Sighing, I shook my head. "No. I mean, yes, I feel the connection. Who could miss it? But that's my point. That isn't enough for us to jump blindly into something together. We need to make sure we're compatible. That we want the same things. We have very…different lifestyles. I still don't know much about you, or the way you live."

"Are we that different?" He arched a brow. "I think I remember Gwen saying something about you spending time with your family every Sunday."

"I do," I hedged, unsure of where he was going with that.

"We spend time together as much as possible, too. My family just happens to be a bit larger. More extended. And not blood related." He gave me a coaxing grin.

I couldn't help but mirror his smile. "True. But we don't throw wild parties that last until who knows when."

"You might if you had multiple single brothers," he countered.

Getting back on track, I pointed out, "We still don't really know anything about each other."

"Then we'll start today. Now."

His big, warm body rolled off me so quickly, I shivered as he let the morning air dance over my exposed skin. Gasping, I snatched the blankets up to my chin. How hadn't I realized I was naked?

His laughter was low and bounced around the room. "I saw it all last night. Don't hide from me. You're fucking gorgeous." His eyes swept over the blanket as though he could see through it.

"That was then, this is now," I told him. "Could you please hand me my clothes?" I watched as he bent at the waist. He'd only managed to tug his jeans on. My mouth all but watered as I finally got a good look at him shirtless, up close and personal. "Could you turn?" My words were shy, but I couldn't hold them in.

His head snapped up as he picked up my panties. He straightened up and turned. His entire back was covered in black ink, too. I'd never seen so many tattoos on a guy before, but I was sure his brothers had just as many. They seemed to be a way for these guys to express themselves. I saw a military tattoo that said US Navy. It covered his right shoulder. One image bled into another and my eyes roved over them all.

"They're beautiful," I breathed. "The one on your side-"

"Not now," he said, interrupting me. "I'll tell you about it, but not here. Not now." He moved forward and grabbed my jeans and top, then handed them all to me.

I found my bra tangled in the sheets, so I started dressing while he finished getting his own clothes from a dresser. He motioned for me to follow him into the bathroom and handed me a new toothbrush. It was all so normal as we stood, side by side, brushing our teeth. I almost smiled at how easy it was. If only I wasn't who I was, then maybe it *could* be this simple. But my trust had been broken and I didn't give it out freely anymore. Doing so ensured that those I loved would be hurt. I couldn't allow that to happen. Then there was the matter of protecting my own heart.

We headed downstairs, and even though it was ten o'clock in the morning we were being quiet. I'd been drunk, and tired enough, that the pounding music from last night hadn't kept me awake, but Ricochet had mentioned it'd been a late one for his brothers.

I'd just stepped off the last stair when Ricochet cursed. Peering around him, I gasped and then tried to smother my laughter. My hands were pressed tightly to my lips and still the giggles spilled around my fingers.

One of his brothers was face down on the bar, snoring so loudly I was sure it could be heard outside. That wasn't the funny part. He was bare ass naked. And that bare ass was sporting a tattoo on his left butt cheek. It was a bright red heart with something written in the middle. I couldn't read it from here and I had a feeling that Ricochet wouldn't appreciate me getting a closer look.

"Butcher!" he called out, casting me a smirk as I continued to laugh. He walked over and shook the man's shoulder. A chorus of snorts and grunts escaped from his mouth.

"Yeah, I know," Ricochet said as if the sounds had been some sort of words. "But you're fucking rubbing your cock all over our bar top. Go to bed."

More grunts.

"I don't give a shit. Wait… What?" He leaned over the bar and looked down, then sighed loudly. "Goddamn it. We're going to have to throw all that out, Toxic. It's going to take a power washer to clean this," he said, as though to himself more than anything.

Creeping closer forward, I peered over the bar and bit the insides of my lips. These guys were something else, and it looked like they'd had more than their fair share of fun last night. Toxic was lying on his back, as naked as Butcher, with three women curled around him on the tiled floor. There were various liquids on the floor that I didn't want to examine too closely, but it looked like most of it was coming from the bottles of liquor that were spread around them. Some were upended, others on their sides, while more than a few were lying in glass shards in the corner. What in the world had they done last night?

Toxic was older than we were, I'd guess somewhere in his late thirties, but he was in impressive shape. Butcher was a bit younger, but just as fit, if his tight ass and back muscles were anything to go off of. Thankfully, one of Toxic's naked women had her thigh thrown over his hips, hiding his dick. Not that it didn't give me an entirely too intimate look at her parts. I hadn't been prepared to see so much nakedness this early in the morning.

"I swear to Christ if you don't stop ogling my brothers I'm going to have to kill them, Sunshine," Ricochet growled. He was busy hauling Butcher down off the bar.

Taking a step back, I cleared my throat. "I wasn't. I just wanted to see what was going on."

He gave me an unamused look as he tried to deal with the man leaning on him. He scowled at me when my jaw dropped and my eyes widened. "Out!"

Butcher was standing in front of me in all his glory. Even with the alcoholic coma he was in, his glory wasn't too shabby.

"Jordan," Ricochet snarled and my eyes snapped up to his. "Outside. Now. I'll finish up here and come find you."

He didn't have to tell me twice. Okay, he had. All of these men were handsome, huge, and had a dangerous edge, but it didn't mean I needed to see all their bits and bobs. I'd already seen far too much of Butcher. Besides, no one could outshine Ricochet in my eyes. Not that I'd gotten to see all of him yet. Though I'd gotten to feel quite a bit from the night before.

I hurried outside and took a deep breath of fresh air as the door closed behind me.

"Where's the fire?" Hush asked as he walked up.

Smiling, I said good morning, then pointed over my shoulder. "Butcher and Toxic-"

"Say no more darlin'. I'll go give Ricochet a hand."

He squeezed my shoulder as he went past and disappeared into the clubhouse.

I laughed to myself and shook my head. Here I was, a boring, self-proclaimed stick in the mud, and I'd just spent the night with a biker at his clubhouse. The things we'd done made my toes curl in my shoes at the memory. Then the antics of his brothers just made it that much better.

"That's a beautiful sound early in the morning."

This time it was Lockout walking toward me. I stiffened slightly, unsure of what to do. Ricochet's president was standing in front of me and he was nowhere around. He still hadn't fully explained what all the rules were here, and while the girls had told me about a few, I didn't want to do something to mess things up for him.

"What's wrong?" Lockout asked, a frown forming on his face.

"Nothing. Sorry, I just…" I licked my lips then gave him a weak smile. "No one has exactly explained *all* your rules. I don't want to accidentally do something to get Ricochet in trouble." The girls had definitely mentioned that a brother could get kicked out if his old lady made too much trouble for the club. I remembered that vividly despite the alcohol.

Lockout stood staring at me for a few heartbeats, then a large smile spread over his face. "Trust me, Jordan. If you're that worried about it, you likely won't ever have anything to worry about."

It was my turn to frown. "What do you mean?"

"The biggest rule for the old ladies is to remember that this is your old man's club and not to make trouble for him. You're already following that rule." He folded his arms over his chest. "Something tells me you won't have an issue."

I smiled at him, relaxing a little. "Thanks. I-"

The door burst open behind us and my eyes widened as a naked Toxic bolted down the stairs toward us. He was on a collision course with me, but was looking over his shoulder at a pissed off Hush and Ricochet as they chased him.

"Get back here, Asshole!" Hush bellowed.

Something slammed into me from the side, knocking me out of the way. Strong arms were around me, preventing me from falling as Lockout picked me up off my feet in a form of a tackle in order to keep Toxic from slamming into me.

My feet hit the ground about the time Hush took Toxic down into the dirt and gravel. I winced as they skidded to a halt. That wasn't going to feel good, picking the gravel out of all the naked flesh later.

"You okay?" Lockout asked, setting me aside and snatching his hands back as soon as I was steady.

"Yes, thank you." I was stunned and all I could do was laugh at the shenanigans. "Is it always like this?"

Lockout gave me a wry grin. "No. This was a tame party."

"I can see why you guys like it. All freedom and fun," I replied.

Lockout's smile dimmed, but didn't disappear. "Not always, but we do our best to enjoy our down time." He nodded toward me, then went to help the others with a still struggling Toxic.

Angry blue eyes met mine and I looked away as they wrestled Toxic to his feet. I'd now had an up close look at two of Ricochet's brothers naked. It was two too many if his scowl was any indication.

"There's ladies around," Lockout barked at Toxic. A quick glance showed the drunk man hanging his head in shame. "You're going to go sleep it off in your room. Get your shit together and walk, Toxic."

Lockout and Hush were helping the man to his feet, supporting him as they all hobbled toward the clubhouse. Lockout reminded me a lot of Ricochet. He was older, and his hair was a darker brown, and his eyes were hazel rather than blue, but despite those differences, I might have wondered if they were brothers if I didn't know that Gwen only had the one.

"Fuck, are you okay? I'm sorry about that." Ricochet was wrapping me up in his arms before I had the chance to respond. "Glad Lock was there to get you out of the way."

"Toxic is a lot faster than he looks."

Ricochet chuckled. "He's a lot of things. Both him and Butcher."

"Why was he running?"

"Had this idea he was going to find himself some new playmates, since he woke up and realized we'd put his others to bed."

"All of those women were…with him?" I asked, eyes wide.

Ricochet led me across the parking lot and started fitting my helmet on my head. "Who knows. Could've all been his. Or Butcher's. Or they split them up between them. Or… You get it," he said when he realized the look of shock on my face was growing with each word.

This really was a whole different world. Was I ready for it?

CHAPTER 22

Ricochet

I stopped my bike in the parking lot of the little restaurant I liked to eat breakfast at. That was all it served and it was a little Mom and Pop shop where they knew all their regulars by name. It was always busy, but the owners were friends and Sue always made room for us.

The last thing I'd meant to happen this morning was to give Jordan that much of a look into club life. I let out a humorless laugh and wondered what she must think. Butcher and Toxic were a lot for those of us who were used to this life. There were times Lock swore they'd never settle down. We were all expecting them to be this crazy until the day they died. Some of the guys were starting to get married and have kids. I wondered if Butcher and Toxic were going to be our resident bachelors forever. I tried to imagine them settling down with wives and kids, but the image just stood up and ran screaming from my mind.

I twisted and held out a hand to help Jordan off the bike. She wasn't used to climbing on and off and I didn't want her falling. The smile she shot me made me want to do whatever I needed to in order to see it again. I wanted to go my whole life seeing that smile every day.

Throwing my arm over Jordan's shoulders, I led her into the restaurant. Sue's head popped up from where she was doing something in the back. With a little crow of pleasure, she came bustling over.

"I haven't seen you in a while! Come, come, there's a seat in the back for you." She motioned for us to follow her as she showed us where to sit.

"How's the family, Sue?"

"Good! Added a new grandbaby to the mix."

"Congratulations," I told her with a smile. My chuckle was instantaneous when she reached up and patted my cheek. She had to stand on her tiptoes to reach. Sue was the epitome of a grandma.

"I'll send your waiter right over," she promised. She paused and gave me a sharp look. "You'll be coming back more often now, huh?"

"Yes Ma'am," I told her. With my sunshine by my side, I was hoping to be able to do a lot of things that had seemed impossible before.

"Good, good. Joey!" Sue hustled away, bellowing for the server.

Jordan laughed. "She's...exuberant."

"To say the least."

"Jordan?"

Snapping my head to the side, I saw a young woman standing beside us. She'd been on her way to the bathroom and now she was just staring at us with her mouth hanging open.

"Hi, Mallory," Jordan said with a grimace. She looked behind the cute petite blonde as though she was expecting someone else. "Is Noah with you?"

Recognizing her brother's name, my muscles relaxed and I sat back in the booth. Mallory's gaze kept flicking between us and there was a storm of curiosity there.

"He's still in the booth," Mallory motioned across the restaurant. "He's-"

"Jord?"

My sunshine groaned and gave me an apologetic glance before she focused on her brother as he approached. "Hey, Noah."

Noah wasn't paying attention to her because he was staring at me. "Who's this?"

"Noah."

I ignored Jordan's warning tone and stood up, holding out my hand. "I'm Ricochet."

Jordan scrambled out of the booth too, she and Mallory casting each other uneasy glances.

"Noah, Jordan's brother."

"Heard a lot about you."

"Haven't heard much about you," Noah said, taking a small step back so he didn't have to tip his head back as far to look up at me. He was about five-ten and had the same dark hair as his sister. Instead of her green eyes, his were a dark brown.

At six-three, standing this close, I towered over him. Folding my arms over my chest, I waited. I didn't mind the attitude. In fact, I respected it. I liked seeing my woman's family stand up for her so fiercely. It was a good indicator that I would be able to trust him.

"Noah!" Jordan and Mallory snapped at him in unison for his rudeness.

"I told you guys about him a few weeks ago," Jordan said, her cheeks pinkening. She gave me a wan smile, embarrassed to admit she'd been talking about me to her family.

Satisfaction at that knowledge was paramount as I watched the siblings wage a silent war with angry gazes. Gwen and I had done it plenty enough times to be able to read the subtle clues. Jordan was telling him to back off. Noah was telling her no way. Mallory gave me an apologetic smile.

"He's not what I was expecting," Noah claimed, not caring that I was standing there listening.

Both women goggled at him, unable to believe he was being this rude. I just chuckled. I fully understood that my look was a bit rough. The leather cut with a huge Viking's head on it, the dirty jeans, the combat boots, the tattoos. Most people judged a book by its cover. Noah wasn't completely wrong about me. I was what most people would think of as a criminal. We considered ourselves vigilantes, but most of society didn't make that distinction.

"Just letting you know, *nothing* will happen to your sister while she's under my protection," I told him.

Noah's stiff posture relaxed a little. "I actually believe that. But how am I supposed to know that *you* won't hurt her?" He must have seen how much the question pissed me off. I'd never hurt my sunshine, but he didn't back down.

"You'll just have to take my word for it until I can prove it to you."

"Noah," Jordan growled his name. "Are we still on for that *thing* tomorrow?" she asked.

Noah's eyes widened. "You wouldn't." He cast a quick glance at Mallory, before looking back at his sister with a pleading look. Gone was the man who was willing to grill me to make sure I was good enough for his sister.

"I absolutely will if you don't stop being a complete asshole to my date." She stuck her hands on her hips. It was a classic, pissed off woman move.

"I'm just looking out for you."

"And I appreciate that," I told him. All three of their shocked gazes fell on me. "I like knowing that if I'm not around she has men in her life that will watch over her."

A slow smile spread over Noah's face. "Oh, Mom is going to love him," he said with a laugh. "You might not be so bad, Ricochet," he admitted.

"Go *away*, Noah," Jordan said, giving him a perturbed look. She gave Mallory a hug, ensuring the other woman knew she had been glad to see her, just not her brother.

Noah ruffled her hair, only laughing and dancing out of the way when she tried to smack at him. "See you later, Sis," he called.

We watched as they walked back to their table and could hear

Mallory asking, "What are you two doing tomorrow?" Noah shot Jordan a glare over his shoulder.

"I'm so sorry about him," Jordan apologized as we sat back down. People around us were watching us with varying degrees of curiosity.

Ignoring them, I sat across from her. "I meant it. I like how protective he is."

"He was rude. Mom is going to snatch his hair off his head, talking about how she hadn't raised him that way." Amusement sparkled in her eyes.

"So what are you planning with him tomorrow?" I asked, curious what finally made him back down.

"Oh, I'm going ring shopping with him," she said with a devious smile. "I wouldn't have really outed him, because that would have ruined the surprise for Mallory. They've been together for three years now and we're all completely in love with her, including him."

I nodded in understanding. She'd seemed like a sweet girl. Nowhere near as gorgeous as my sunshine, but pretty enough.

We ordered and I sat back in the booth, studying Jordan. "Sorry about this morning. That was a bit more than I planned to expose you to."

"I think it was Butcher and Toxic who did the exposing," she quipped.

We both laughed, though I wanted to rip their balls off. They hadn't meant for my old lady to see their junk, but she'd gotten a firsthand look, and I didn't care much for that.

We made small talk until the waiter put our plates of food down in front of us. By the time he dropped everything off, my muscles were rigid and I was wound tight.

Jordan frowned as she picked up her fork, sensing the shift in my mood. "What's wrong?"

"I promised you I'd tell you about myself." Glancing around to make sure that no one was paying attention, I started in on the last subject I ever wanted to speak about. "I can't tell you all of it. Not yet. Not because I don't want to, but because…it's hard for me to talk about."

Shoving a bite of eggs into my mouth, I almost wished I'd waited until after we ate to tell her. The food was like ash in my mouth. Setting my fork down, I balled my hands into fists on the bench on either side of my legs. "I was in the military. A Navy Seal."

Surprise filtered over her face, but she didn't say anything. Didn't interrupt. It was like she knew I was barely hanging on and one interruption would cause me to clam up.

"Our team had six guys on it, but Jack and I had grown close. We were brothers. Every mission we watched each other's backs. We were on deployment to Afghanistan. We were tasked with finding and capturing a warlord in the northern province. We were responsible for getting weapons and new recruits to the insurgent fighters in that region."

She was watching me with a solemn look on her face, already understanding where this story was going.

"Anyway. We spent a few months kicking down doors and taking prisoners. The intel guys would interrogate them, give us new names and locations, and we'd go out and do it again."

I ran a hand through my hair, staring down at my plate. The further I got into this, the less I wanted to watch her reactions.

"This warlord was a real snake. We'd always arrive a day or even an hour behind. We must have kicked in two or three dozen doors. It was becoming a normal routine for us. That is, until we finally caught up with the bastard. That's when it was anything but routine.

You see, this guy wasn't just a weapons smuggler, he was in charge of recruiting. After a decade plus of us being there, it gets hard to get adult recruits. He'd started recruiting younger and younger. It was getting normal to find teenagers out fighting."

Swallowing hard as a series of faces flashed through my mind, I shook my head to clear it. There were so many fucked up things we'd seen on that deployment.

"I'm getting ahead of myself. We didn't know this going in. Intel had somehow completely missed that. We got to his hideout, and as usual we kicked in the door and began clearing the building.

"That's...when everything went to shit. I was the point man, the one leading us through the building. I rounded a corner and found a room full of children. They began screaming and reaching for their guns. I…I just…I froze. Couldn't move. Just stood there staring at them in shock. These were children, some of them only about eight years old. I had no idea what to do or how to process what I was seeing.

"Jack didn't freeze. He grabbed me by the shoulder and pulled me out of the way, throwing me to the side and placing himself between the kids and me. Then the gunshots rang out. They'd shot Jack. Shot him in the back as he was pushing me out of the way. The rifle rounds ripped through his protective gear, shredding his insides. He saved my life and came home in a pine box because I fucking froze."

My voice was low, but even I could hear that I sounded more like a wounded animal than a man. My body jerked when her hand covered mine. I hadn't even realized I'd put them on the table. That I was holding the knife that'd been lying there. Forcing my fingers to release it, I left it there, taking the comfort she was offering. I didn't intertwine our fingers because I didn't want to inadvertently hurt her, but I let her fingers squeeze around the top of my hand. Used the sensation to keep me grounded to the present. I didn't want to slip fully into the past in the middle of a restaurant.

"I broke right there. I didn't just unfreeze, but completely lost control. I was holding Jack as the bullets slammed into him, killing him almost instantly. I saw the life leave his eyes and I flew into a blind rage. I dropped his body and brought my rifle up, I didn't stop firing until everyone in the room was dead. I killed a child Sean's age. Most of them had taken off out the back before I started shooting. I cost Jack his life. It set a pattern in motion. If I hesitate, my friends are killed. If I act, children die. It's why I was ultimately discharged. I'm broken goods."

"Coming home and having to explain to Mary why her husband was dead was hell. Having to watch their two boys go through his funeral nearly broke me again." I shook my head again, trying to rid myself of the guilt. It would never leave me. I was able to go on living because he'd given up his life for me. There was nothing I could do to atone for that. The money I sent to his family every month was the only way I could help without being a burden to them. I hadn't seen them since the funeral, just couldn't bear to see the sadness and disappointment.

Tears were sliding down Jordan's face by the time I looked back up. She'd long since set her fork down, but I hadn't realized the way my story was affecting her because I'd been in and out of the memories. I hated how unaware of the present I was when that shit happened.

"I'm sorry," I told her. Reaching forward, I brushed one of the tears from her cheek. That this woman would cry for me shook me to my core. "That was a lot." And I hadn't even told her everything. Like the pleasure I felt when I had embraced my rage. That I often used fighting as a coping mechanism. That I sought out battles now in order to numb myself again.

I took on any and all enemies, whether it was for the club or just for myself. It didn't matter who that threat was. I used it as a way to go back to the day Jack had died and redeem myself. If I hadn't done my job and killed everyone in that room, more men in my team would have died. Hell, I might have died. I didn't tell her how all of this, plus what happened a couple months ago when we'd attacked that cult, affected me. I couldn't. This was all I could get out for now. I'd tell her more at some point. She'd know all of it eventually.

"I-" She swallowed and wiped the tears from her cheeks. "I don't know what to say. I'm sorry…it just seems so insignificant," she told me. "I can't imagine how horrible that was. Losing your friend. Having to do what you did in order to save everyone else…"

The knots clenching in my gut loosened the slightest bit. There was no judgment in her tone. She probably didn't realize the full extent of what I'd had to do to get my team out of that situation. And that was fine. But for now, there wasn't any accusation or pity when she looked at me.

"What helps you the most to hear?"

My brows shot up. Most people just told me how sorry they were.

Only my brothers had ever asked what I needed. Well, them and one other man. The man who was responsible for me even still being here.

"Come here." I scooted closer to the little half wall so she could sit next to me. As soon as her body settled on the bench seat, I wrapped an arm around her and pulled her into my side. "Don't cry for me. I don't deserve it."

"I doubt that's true," she argued.

Leaning forward, I brushed my thumbs over her cheeks again. "There's still a lot to know about me, but that's all I have in me to tell for now."

"I understand." She leaned her head on my chest, content to let me hold her.

My body began to unwind, to relax as my mind let go of the past. Not forever. These memories were never truly gone, they always popped back up. But I would get a reprieve for now. I was grateful for the woman I was holding and her part in that.

CHAPTER 23

Ricochet

"What the fuck?" I muttered as I got off my bike. My crew was standing around, not prepping for the full day of work we had ahead of us. Meanwhile, a good portion of my brothers were standing around, talking.

It'd been a month since Jordan had stayed with me at the clubhouse and things were going smoothly. We saw each other every day, thanks to Gwen living next door to her. Plus, we texted throughout the day. Everything was going to plan and she was dropping her guard around me.

Static and his friend, who he only called the man from Idaho, had managed to work their magic and had gotten the permitting for the school approved in that short amount of time. When I'd asked how they'd managed to get an architect to sign off on everything so quickly, Static had mentioned that the man from Idaho had one on retainer. That when he called, everything had been dropped to get the plans done and signed off. Apparently, he knew people in the permitting office. It should have been impossible to do everything in three weeks, but according to Static, this guy had people for everything because he didn't like waiting.

Lockout had just scowled while we'd marveled over the man's ability to get things done so quickly. We'd been working here for a little less than a week now. It was nice to be back into a routine again.

I'd needed the break that had sent me back home and still had me living with my sister, but I was slowly starting to feel like myself again. Sticking close to Jordan seemed to be helping with that, and I didn't plan on letting her go, so it was working well for me.

Walking over, I rested a hand on Hellfire's uninjured shoulder in greeting. Smokehouse was standing on the other side of him while the rest of my brothers formed a circle. "What are all of you doing here?"

Lock looked over at me, frustration etched into his face. "We've hit a snag."

"What kind of snag?" I asked.

"Permitting got pulled," Static told me, cursing low under his breath.

I frowned looking back and forth amongst the faces of the men I knew so well. "How the hell did that happen?"

"No idea," Static said with a sigh. "I've got my guy on it. If anyone can work it out, he can."

"Who *is* this guy?" Toxic asked, looking tired and grumpy as hell. It was a bit early for him, though he'd never complain since this was club business.

"Nevermind who he is," Lockout told him. His eyes fell on me. "This is unusual, to have the permits pulled after we've already started construction. Especially with Idaho having filed the shit."

My brows rose. "You know him?"

Static chuckled. "Idaho. He'll like that."

"Any ideas what might have happened?" Lock asked the group, looking specifically at Static, ignoring my question completely.

Hellfire and I shared a look. He'd caught on to Lockout's dislike of this 'Idaho'. "It is really weird for permits to have been pulled," I said in agreement, getting the conversation back in line. One of the perks of being the boss was Lock didn't have to tell us shit until he was ready. I wasn't going to press him about whatever was going on unless he needed it. For now, he seemed to be fine as long as we weren't talking about the man from Idaho.

"Do you know anyone in the mayor's office?" Riptide asked Lockout. "Dash and I did a little poking around. The request came directly from the mayor himself," Rip explained.

"Why the hell would the mayor of Tucson care about a charter school?" Hush asked before I could answer.

I closed my eyes and rubbed the spot between my brows as a tension headache began to brew. "I know what it's about."

Every eye was on me now. My shoulders tensed as I realized the consequences of antagonizing Trent before were coming back to bite me in the ass. I'd like to believe that he wasn't so petty he'd hold what was said at Gwen's dinner against me. It'd been weeks. But that was the only explanation that made sense.

"It has to be Trent." Anger flowed through me like a raging river as I realized he was only doing this to fuck with me. What other reason would he have? If I hadn't hated the man before, this would have definitely sealed his fate.

"Your sister's ex?" Lockout asked. He raised a brow. "Why would he be fucking with our permitting?"

"We got into it a while back at my sister's house. I may have said some shit to him," I admitted.

Lock let out a gusty breath, giving me an irritated look. "Some shit?"

"It was pretty reasonable considering what the asshole was saying," Smoke told him. Hell nodded in agreement.

"You two knew about this?"

"Oh look, the sky," Smokehouse mumbled, staring straight up. They went back to avoiding their president's gaze. If this wasn't so damn serious, and I didn't want to rip Trent's head off, I would have laughed.

"He was talking shit. I lost my temper and words were exchanged. He left of his own free will, though, and for once I didn't hit the fucker," I explained. Really, it had ended as nicely as it could have. Things would have been a whole lot worse, for Trent, if I hadn't kept my cool as much as I had. "Can't believe he's fucking around because of that. And so long after it happened."

Lockout folded his arms over his chest with a pensive look on his face. "What does Trent have to do with the mayor's office?"

"No idea, he works with the DA," I told him. "My guess is it was the only way he could think to get the permits pulled. The DA wouldn't have any sway over that. Not directly. But they are all chummy with each other. It's not a far stretch."

Priest frowned. "Makes me wonder what Trent promised the mayor." When everyone looked at him, he shrugged. "No way the mayor is doing this guy a favor out of the goodness of his heart. If he's helping Trent out, there will be a price to pay."

"Good point," Butcher muttered.

"Could be trouble for us," Hush added.

"Well, it's too late now," Riptide said. "We'll keep looking into the mayor, and we'll add Trent, and even the DA to the list. See how they're all connected. See if it's going to be an issue in the future."

"In the meantime, no one mentions this to anybody," Lock warned. "Not even your old ladies. Not until we know what that connection is. See if we can figure out what kind of use the mayor would have with Trent." He looked over at me. "And you. *Stay* away from him. I know what you're thinking, but it won't work. We don't need you getting into it with Gwen's ex. If you get arrested assaulting the DA's assistant, or whatever the fuck he is, it's not going to be easy to keep you out of jail."

"Got it," I replied. I was already trying to tamp down the rage. The fact that Lock knew I had already been planning to pay Trent a visit wasn't all that surprising. That I was willing to listen and planned to let this go and let him and the others deal with the permitting the proper way was what was shocking. Maybe some of Lock's good sense was rubbing off on me. Or maybe being with Jordan had me just relaxed enough that I realized it just wasn't worth the fight and the fallout that would come after. Either way, I seemed to be evolving.

"Static. I know you said your guy was on this. Does the paperwork need to be redone?"

"Fuck no. Paperwork is solid, Lock," Static responded with a smirk. "This isn't about paperwork, it's about influence. Right now, he's talking to someone who has a bit of pull within the Arizona Charter School Committee. He's thinking if they put a bit of weight on the permitting office about needing this school up and going, they'll cave faster."

"You guys need to remember," Lock said. "This school doesn't benefit us. It's for the women and kids we pulled from the cult. They need this. For once in our lives, this needs to be by the books." He shot me another warning look.

Guilt ate away at me as I listened to him explain the ways it was going to benefit the women and kids. They'd been through so much already, the last thing I wanted was to fuck this up for them. They deserved the best we could give them.

"Shit, it might even benefit us in the future as well," Rip added. "It's a school, just down the road from our club, built and run by us. Our kids will go to this place. They'll be in a safe environment that we can control."

Everyone nodded in agreement. No one was doubting or arguing the benefits of having this school. I sure as hell didn't want to take it away from the kids. It had just been one momentary loss of control because Trent couldn't keep his mouth shut. I was doing my best to put him out of my mind now that Gwen had kicked him to the curb again. He was just a shit stain on the sidewalk and didn't matter anymore. I could figure this out.

"Good. Then we stay the course. We'll have to wait until the permits are reissued and then we can get started again." Lock gave me a warning look. He didn't need to hammer it home. I'd behave. He must have seen that from my expression, because he let it drop.

"So…" Butcher said, letting the word hang there in the morning air. When I looked over at him he shot me a smile. "How's your old lady?"

Narrowing my eyes, I scowled at him. "She's fine."

Lock cleared his throat. It was a less than subtle nudge from our president.

"We're supposed to apologize," Toxic said, speaking up. "Sorry about the other day…" He trailed off, shooting Lock a quick look, then grinned at me. "Did she like the view?"

"You fucking-" A hand landed on my shoulder. It was Hush holding me back from going after my brothers as they hooted with laughter.

"Sorry," Toxic said again. "Never meant for your lady to see my junk, but anytime a woman does, I need to know what she thought." He shrugged as though that were a completely normal thing.

A grin tugged at my mouth while the others laughed. It was hard to stay mad at these two.

"She probably thought it looked like a disease riddled snake," Hellfire said with a snort of derision. Smokehouse barked out a laugh.

Toxic tilted his head. "As long as we're talking a python or an anaconda, I'm good with that. It's *not* diseased," he added.

Shaking his head, Lockout motioned for me to follow him. We left the others behind, continuing to compare Toxic's dick to everything they could think of that would curdle your gut.

"I'll watch myself from now on," I promised him as soon as we were out of earshot.

"I believe you. And trust me, Ricochet, I appreciate it. That's not why I pulled you to the side, though."

The fact that all it took was my promise to shape up and Lock was on board was part of the reason I loved this man and this club so much. You could fuck up, but ultimately we were each other's brothers and we'd always have each other's backs.

He was studying me, looking for any clues about my state of mind. I was used to it by now. "How are things going?"

"Decent," I admitted.

"You look good."

I chuckled and ran a hand through my hair. "Thanks." Without Butcher or Toxic listening in there was no joke tossed my way that I'd have to deflect. Lock kept a close eye on me and it was no surprise that he noticed the change.

"She's good for you." He was watching every move I made, determining if I was faking it for his benefit. He didn't need to bother. I wasn't that good of an actor.

"She is. I plan to keep her around."

"Good. Offer's still on the table to find you someone to talk to," he told me. "There are supposed to be a few good psychiatrists here that deal with PTSD-"

"No." I cleared my throat and shifted my weight from one foot to the other. "Sorry," I hadn't meant to bark the word at him, but that's how it'd come out, "but I think I'm good for now."

"For now. Anything changes, Ricochet, and it won't be a question anymore. I'll do whatever it takes to keep you in the right mindset. To keep you here with us." His tone didn't allow for argument.

"Sure thing."

"You really should find someone to talk to. Even if it's not a counselor. Someone who you can go to whenever you need to let off steam."

I met his gaze, one corner of my mouth lifting in a lopsided smile. There was no way for me to explain to him the emotion that was unraveling inside of me. "I've always had someone for that. You have no idea how many times you talked me off the ledge, do you?"

Between him and my other brothers—especially Smoke and Hell—they'd helped me keep my sanity long enough to stay grounded. To realize that ending things came with too much finality. I wasn't ready to leave this world behind and all those I loved with it. It was my extreme hope that it would never come to that, but one thing I'd learned about myself and the situations I'd found myself in was to never say never.

Shock entered his eyes, confirming my suspicion, but I didn't want to talk about it anymore. Giving him a respectful nod, I left him standing there and went to talk to my crew.

It didn't take long for them to clear out, leaving me to go back and shoot the shit with my brothers. It was damn nice to be able to put everything aside and just hang out without the memories battering at me. To reconnect with the men who were family.

Pulling out my phone, I stared down at the last text from my sunshine. She and my sister had planned a sleepover tonight with the old ladies from the club. I grinned, wondering what kind of trouble they were going to get into. The plan was for me to babysit my niece and nephew at Gwen's house while the girls had their fun next door. It meant I was close enough to keep an eye on them, while still giving them the illusion of freedom. As long as they were safe, I was glad that both Gwen and Jordan were making new friends.

* * *

"Can we watch a horror movie?" Sean asked, a hopeful look in his eyes.

Grace's eyes widened and she shook her head slightly. Her lower lip trembled a little as she thought about what her older brother might pick out.

"No way," I told him. "I don't want to deal with nightmares tonight."

"I won't get nightmares," he said, puffing out his chest.

"Who said anything about you?" I asked with a grin. "I meant my own. Those movies are scary."

"Yeah they are," Grace said, sidling up to me on the couch. The bowl of popcorn in her lap tipped precariously.

"How about an action movie?" I suggested and tossed the remote to Sean.

"Okay!" He started flipping through one of the streaming services looking for one that we'd enjoy.

"Where have you seen horror movies?" I asked.

"Bobbie's house. His dad doesn't care what we watch."

Dropping my arm down over Grace's shoulders, I met Sean's gaze over her head. "No watching that stuff in front of your sister," I warned.

He nodded in agreement, then chose a movie. It was my favorite movie, the one where Liam Neeson is an old man kicking the crap out of everyone. I spent the whole time Liam Neeson was beating up bad guys texting Jordan. I wasn't checking in on them so much as just getting my fix of her for the day. Gwen had shooed me off her porch so fast, I'd barely gotten a glimpse of her as the other women had started showing up.

I had plans with her for tomorrow and I couldn't wait to get her all to myself again. Static had texted, letting me know that the permits should be reissued by the beginning of next week. Until then, I was fixing things around Gwen and Jordan's houses. My sister was good at many things, but upkeep on her home wasn't one of them. Seemed Jordan was the same. I'd already replaced some rotted aphasia at the back of Gwen's house and replaced some shingles on Jordan's roof.

It was keeping me busy during the days. What I wanted to do was go straight to Trent's office and unscrew his head. But Lockout was right, I had to stay out of it. I was both shocked and impressed at my own self-control. A few months ago, before Jordan, I would have fallen into a blind rage. And we all knew that would just end with my ass in a jail cell. Maybe this was the start of a newer, better me. I snorted in disbelief at that idea. I might be reining in my temper for now, but I was who I was. I'd do my damndest to keep my cool, but at some point my rage would rear its ugly head and I'd be right back in the thick of it. I was sure of it.

There wasn't a lot going on with the club right now. Lock was giving us all a break after dealing with the cult. Something would come up eventually. Things always did. Until then it was better when I had things to keep my hands and mind busy.

"Whoa!" Sean crowed, then cackled as something blew up on the screen.

Shoving thoughts of the club and the women next door out of my mind, I settled in to enjoy the evening with the kids.

CHAPTER 24

Jordan

"A round of margaritas for us," I said, setting the pitcher on the coffee table, "and a virgin Shirley Temple for the mama." This was my first time meeting Sloane, but I was so excited to get to know another old lady.

Seek grinned as she took the drink. "Thanks."

"So Gwen," Tori said as she poured a large glass from the frosty pitcher. "Ricochet is your brother?"

"Her twin," Kit replied instead.

"Your kids are so adorable," Jenny said, struggling with the pitcher now that Tori was filling her glass to the brim. "That's too much, Tori," she laughed.

"There's plenty more where that came from," I told them. "Drink up."

"Thank you," Gwen said, drinking from her glass. She made a face, then looked over at me. "Jeez, did you put anything other than tequila in here?"

"Hey, it's our day off tomorrow and we're going to have fun tonight. No more sticks in the mud," I declared.

"Sticks?" Daisha asked.

"Mud?" Suzie followed up.

Sloane eyes lit up with a smile. "You don't seem like sticks in the mud to me." She and Riptide had gotten home a while ago from their wedding. That was why I hadn't met her before now, they hadn't been at the barbecue.

"We've been single and holed up out here for a few years now," I told them. "We decided we were better off without men."

"Just working and living," Gwen said with a sigh. "No dates, no girls' nights, nothing."

"That's depressing," Kit replied, horror on her face. "Why no girls' nights? At the very least you deserve that."

"Girls' nights," I told her, pointing my straw at her, "lead to handsome men hitting on you. We have terrible taste in men."

"Hey!" Gwen tossed her straw my way. She wasn't offended on Trent's behalf; she just didn't like hearing her brother was terrible. She was right. He wasn't.

"Well, I might have found a good one," I admitted with a sheepish look.

"Are you two finally dating?" Jenny asked. "Are you admitting that you're a couple now?"

"They're getting to knooow each other," Gwen sang out.

The women all laughed. Even Sloane seemed to be settling in. She was a quiet woman, but absolutely gorgeous. She let the others do most of the talking, but I could see she was absorbing everything. I looked forward to a time where she'd be comfortable enough to talk with me openly. The others had just explained that she'd been through a lot lately and was slow to trust. I understood that completely.

We all know what 'getting to knooow' a biker means," Jenny laughed, then snorted. She immediately brought her hands up to cover her nose. "Ooops."

The sound was so cute we all let out peals of laughter. There was just something about someone who snorted when they laughed that made you just laugh more.

"Sexually?" Seek asked. "Please tell me you're getting freaky in the sheets?"

I groaned and covered my face with one hand.

"They are!" Kit crowed.

"Not really," I confessed. "And I can't talk about this in front of his sister."

"Oh you can," Gwen responded, tucking her feet up underneath her so she was sitting on my recliner legs akimbo. "I'm not Gage's sister tonight, just a friend."

"We…did a few things," I admitted, face heating up.

"What about the rest?" Daisha asked in disappointment.

"I don't really trust myself anymore." I stared down into the alcohol in my glass. "I thought I was a good judge of character, but then someone completely took me for a ride." I hadn't really told them much before at the bar, and I wasn't sure I wanted to get into it all tonight.

They were all wearing sad expressions now. "I hate when that happens," Kit commiserated. "I swear we all know at least one guy like that."

Everyone nodded.

"So now I'm making Ricochet wait. It's not really fair. He hasn't done anything wrong. In fact, he's almost too perfect. For me, I mean." My sigh came out as a happy little sound.

"Aw, she's in love!" Seek said, her eyes filling with tears. "Sorry, damn hormones," she sniffed.

Sloane handed her a tissue box she'd dug out of her purse.

I blinked in surprise. "Do you always have whole boxes of tissues on hand?"

Sloane flushed, but gave me a shy smile. "I'm pregnant, too, and I cry at the drop of a hat, so I like to be prepared."

"Congratulations!" I told her. "That explains why you haven't touched your drink. I'll make you a virgin, just like Seek's."

"Thank you," she replied. "I'd like that."

"Back to-"

"Enough," I said, waving my hand in the air, interrupting Kit before she could get the conversation back onto me. "Someone else's turn." I hurried into the kitchen, listening in while I made Sloane's drink.

"Gwen," Susie declared. "Tell us about you."

"Oh." Her gaze shot over to me, nerves easy to see. "Well, I'm a mom…" She gave us a weak smile. "That's about all I got."

"What do you do for work?" Kit asked.

Sitting back down, I passed the glass to Sloane and took the one she'd been holding.

"I'm a vet tech," she replied. "I love being able to help people and their pets."

"That's cool," Seek said. "Which office do you work at? I've been looking for a new place to bring my dogs."

"Pets and Friends, off Oracle."

"Next to the Fry's?" Seek asked.

"That's it!"

"I was looking into that place already. You guys have a lot of great reviews."

"Yeah, the vets are fantastic and everyone is really great. We're all really happy to be working there," Gwen said. "And it's close to Grace's pre-school."

"Long drive into work from all the way out here," Tori said. "About an hour?"

"Yeah, sometimes an hour and twenty with morning traffic, but it's worth it to live out here where my kids can play outside without me having to worry about them."

"I get that," Susie said. "That's why we like living in Marana. It doesn't have the same city feel."

"That's not going to last long the way they keep building everything up," Kit muttered.

I stood up, noticing that the pitcher was already empty and went to the fridge to grab the second. There were four in there and judging by the slight waver to my vision we weren't going to make it through them all.

Listening to the women in the next room laughing together, I made up second drinks for Seek and Sloane. By the time I came back, the room had taken on a more serious note.

"Have you told Ricochet?" Seek asked.

"Told Ricochet what?" I asked, setting the drinks down on the coffee table again then settling onto my spot on the couch.

"Gwen thinks someone's been hanging around the house."

My eyes flashed over to her, concern for her and the children's safety settling in my chest. "What?"

"No, I said there was a car that was parked at the end of the road," Gwen corrected.

"No one ever comes out here," I told the others. To Gwen I said, "Did you see who was driving it?"

"That's the thing. No one was inside."

"Weird," I mumbled. "Maybe it was just somebody who was tired or drunk and decided to pull over."

"That's what I thought," Gwen offered, "but I saw it again yesterday near dusk. You were already home from work. Did you see it driving in? It's a gray Corolla."

"I didn't."

The others' heads were turning back and forth as they followed our conversation.

"Definitely tell Ricochet," Kit told us.

"Agreed," the others parroted.

"I don't want to worry him," Gwen replied, sounding hesitant.

"He'll be pissed if he finds out you didn't tell him," Seek argued. "These guys are all super protective. If you saw something out of the ordinary they'd want to know about it."

"I know," Gwen said in an amused tone. "That's what I'm worried about. I don't want your men out here guarding us anytime Ricochet can't be here. That's not fair to any of them. Not for a car that's been parked here twice. For all we know it's a pair of teenagers sneaking off into a wash to smoke a joint."

Everyone wore matching frowns. They weren't convinced. Gwen laughed and shook her head, holding her hands up in defeat. "Okay, I'll tell him."

There were sighs of relief. "You never know," Susie told us. "The club has enemies. It's better to be safe than sorry."

"Enemies?" I asked. Even though the girls had told me a bit about club life, there was still so much I needed to learn. Ricochet hadn't brought anything up and I hadn't wanted to force him into it. But I was so curious to know about this part of his life.

They all gave each other looks. Even Gwen seemed to know what Susie meant.

"Has Ricochet told you yet about some of the things the club does?" Kit asked.

I shook my head in answer.

"He's taking too long. She needs to know this stuff," Kit sighed.

"I think he was waiting on the go ahead from Lockout," Seek replied.

"No. Smokehouse told me Lock approves. He's just trying not to scare Jordan off," Kit told her.

"Well, now you have to tell me," I commented, a feeling of dread curling in my stomach.

"We can't tell you everything," Daisha answered. "That's for Ricochet to do, but the guys are..." She looked around for help.

"A lot of people would consider them criminals," Gwen spoke up. "But they help people. Sometimes in a...borderline criminal way."

"You knew about this?" I asked.

She nodded. "When Gage first joined he asked Lockout if he could let me in on things. Not everything, I'm sure," she said with a wry smile, "but just enough that I took it seriously if there was ever any kind of threat made against them. He said it was the only way to keep me and the kids safe."

That made sense. I looked around at them all. "What kinds of things do they do?"

"They step in and help out when the cops' hands are tied," Seek replied. "Of course, the cops don't know about it."

"They take care of bad people," Tori said.

"Permanently," Daisha piped in.

My jaw dropped. "They kill people?"

"If necessary," Kit said. "But they don't hurt innocents. They only go after someone if it's brought to their attention. If they're hurting people, or doing other bad things."

"They help people," Sloane said, her voice soft. She was looking directly at me, almost as though she were pleading with me to understand.

"I'm glad to hear that," I told her, meaning it.

"I know it's a lot to take in. It took me a while to come to grips with it. To understand that they put themselves in harm's way so that others are safe," Gwen said.

Nodding, I took a drink of my margarita to ease the sudden dryness in my mouth. "I'm not judging them," I told the room. Tensions eased after I said that. "It's just... I'm not used to anything like this. Stick in the mud, remember?"

That made them all laugh.

"Ricochet will explain more to you," Kit assured me. "He'll be able to answer any questions you have. I'll have Smoke talk to him about having that chat with you sooner rather than later."

I nodded and thankfully Daisha changed the subject by asking Seek and Sloane about the double baby shower they were all planning. My thoughts drifted as I remembered what Ricochet had told me about his time on deployment. The thought of him being in dangerous situations here at home, with his club, made my belly clench with fear. I didn't want him to get hurt. And even though it made me feel guilty, I didn't want my family to get hurt because of my association with him. The picture of my dad lying on a hospital gurney flashed through my mind. Never again did I want the choices I made to affect those I loved.

The last thing I wanted was to make the women around me feel badly about telling me what they had, so I kept my mouth shut. I wanted to hear all this from Ricochet anyway, before I made any kind of decision about us being in each other's lives permanently.

I *needed* to hear it from him. I wasn't sure how to take it that he was some kind of Punisher-like vigilante. Or how to process the fact that I wasn't alarmed and running away. That I was almost accepting of this. What did it say about me?

The hours passed quickly and we were all—except Seek and Sloane—buzzed, well, drunk, and enjoying ourselves by the time their men started arriving to pick them up.

I walked each of them out and hugged them goodnight. "Thanks so much for coming," I told Kit. I waved at Smokehouse, who was waiting in his car. He grinned and gave me a nod in acknowledgment. All of the men had shown up in cars. It made sense. The idea of a drunk woman hanging on to the back of a motorcycle was downright terrifying to think about.

"You'll both come to the baby shower, right?" she asked.

"Wouldn't miss it," I promised.

Watching as they left, I waited until the tail lights went around the corner at the end of the street. I walked around to my backyard, peeking in on Haze to make sure she was settled for the night before going inside.

Smiling down at my best friend, who was passed out on the couch, I covered her with a blanket, then kicked back on the recliner with my own blanket that my grandma had knitted for me. I'd just had a wonderful time tonight with these women and was starting to see the way my life would unfold with Ricochet. The things they'd told me worried me, but not nearly as much as I would have expected. I wasn't going to jump to any conclusions until I got to speak to him directly. Closing my eyes, I pictured him in my mind and fell asleep with a smile on my lips.

CHAPTER 25

Jordan

The motorcycle came to a stop and Ricochet reached around to help me off the bike. I smiled as he unstrapped my helmet, then stowed it in one of his saddle bags. The way he always looked out for me made my heart warm. Who was I kidding? He'd had me giddy as a school girl for the last few weeks. Just speaking with him each day was enough to have me singing in the shower each morning. Badly. It was not a skill I possessed. And yet I'd wailed along with my playlist this morning as I'd gotten ready.

My smile had been permanently affixed to my face since I woke up. And now here I was. My heart skipped a beat as Ricochet ran a hand through his hair, looking between me and the sign welcoming us to the Tucson Zoo.

"I figured you liked animals, so…" he trailed off, uncertainty coloring his tone. "Then again, you sort of work at one."

"I love the zoo!" I told him, grabbing his hand and yanking him toward the entrance. Seriously, how was someone so rough around the edges so sweet? He always seemed to take the time to think of what would please me and then made it happen.

His chuckle was fast becoming one of my favorite sounds. He wound our fingers together as we walked. We checked in on some of my favorite animals and walked the entire grounds twice since it was a cool day. There were times, even though we were at the end of March, where temperatures could spike into the low nineties, but the cloud cover that had rolled in overnight gave the air a slight chill.

We spent the majority of our time with the river otters. They were some of my favorite animals and I loved to watch them dance and play. It didn't surprise me that he liked the huge powerful animals like the bears and big cats. They were a lot like him.

"Where do you want to get dinner?" he asked as we were heading toward the exit.

"Do you trust me?" I asked, giving him a mischievous look.

His brows shot up and he gave me the sexy little smirk I was becoming used to. "Sure."

I glanced around, then hung a right, down the path that would bring us over toward the big cats again. "Hopefully it's here. Ah! There it is." I hadn't seen it the first time through because we'd been so intent on the animals.

"Shit, seriously?" Ricochet asked when he saw the small building sitting off to the side of the path. "I haven't had Sonoran hot dogs in a long time."

"How long?" I asked while we got into line.

"Years, at least six."

"Well you're overdue. They're so good." I licked my lips in anticipation of the treat that I loved to eat every few months or so. You could order them however you liked, but they typically came with a thin layer of beans laid across a thick roll type bun with a bacon wrapped hot dog on top. The toppings included avocados, tomatoes, onions, jalapeños, and zesty mayo. "What do you like on them?" I asked, bouncing on my toes a little while I tried not to drool at the aroma in the air.

Ricochet laughed at my exuberance. "Tomatoes, jalapeños, and mayo."

Giving him an affronted look, I asked, "No onions?"

"Not when I'm on a date," he teased.

"Psft," I scoffed. "Date, schmate. You're not being spared the onions, my friend." I rubbed my hands together as though I were a villain plotting her next scheme.

"I guess I can live with your selfishness."

My jaw dropped and I shoved him lightly. "I am *not* selfish," I replied in a haughty manner. "I just don't think a person should have to give up a key ingredient of a Sonoran Dog."

"Whatever you say, Sunshine. If Princess wants onions, that's what she'll get. Besides, there are plenty of places to kiss you other than your mouth."

The man could make a girl swallow her tongue with words like that. A blush worked its way over my cheeks and I just shook my head at him while he laughed at how nervous he'd just made me.

How long had it been? How long since I stood in the sunshine on a simple date, about to eat hotdogs, with a man who made butterflies appear in my belly? Far too long, if at all. I couldn't remember ever being this excited to be with a man. After everything Dan had put me through, I'd shut myself away, too afraid of being hurt.

Ricochet had taken the time to pull me from my shell, allowed me to take things at my pace, and now here I was…falling in love. Remembering the conversation from last night, I tried to shove all the feelings swarming me back down, but the damage was done. This man had me standing on the precipice. I really needed to find out if my heart was safe with him before I did something stupid, like hand it over on a silver platter.

We took our hotdogs, churros, and drinks over to one of the metal tables and sat under an umbrella. The days were warming back up and soon enough we'd be heading into the summer months. As someone who enjoyed the heat, I was looking forward to it. I was used to the mild winters and scorching summers. I wouldn't want to live anywhere else.

I took a massive bite of my dog and groaned in pleasure as all the flavors mixed on my tongue. When my eyes opened, I found Ricochet, hotdog halfway to his lips, just staring at me with hunger churning in his gaze.

"Sorry," I said, a little embarrassed. "This is one of my favorite things to eat. If I let myself, I could eat them every day for the rest of my life."

"I like watching you enjoy yourself," he replied, then did me the favor of taking his eyes off me.

It was hard to swallow when a man was staring at you like he had been. We were only about halfway through our meal when I decided to bite the metaphorical bullet. "Ricochet?"

"Hmmm," he responded, wiping his chin with a napkin.

I wanted to lick the juice from the jalapeño straight off his skin. Oh boy, was I in trouble. Heat zipped through my system. Never had I felt for a man the way I was feeling now. "I want to be honest with you."

Now I had his attention. He'd set his hotdog down and was watching me with a wary gaze.

"I really like you."

The smirk was back. "I like you, too, Sunshine."

His nickname for me made me all tingly. *He* made me tingle. "I need to know that I can trust you."

His eyes narrowed, all semblance of a smile gone from his lips. "Of course you can."

"I…I'm not trying to be insulting," I added. "I just need to know what I'm in for if I decide to take you up on your offer."

"My offer?"

"To be your old lady."

He sat back in the chair, it groaned under the movement and his weight. He was a big man and these small metal chairs were old and sun worn. "It's not an offer, Jordan."

I frowned. "Oh. I thought… Have you changed your mind?" Embarrassment was starting to creep over me. "What has all this been for the last few weeks if-"

"No. I haven't changed my mind. It's not an offer because you already belong to me." He shook his head. "Not sure how many times I have to tell you before you'll believe me. I know this lifestyle is new to you. I'm…probably not the sort of man you're used to."

"You've got that right," I told him, a little irritated, but also secretly thrilled that he was still pulling the caveman routine. I shouldn't like something so blatant and unforgiving as him just claiming that I was his, but I did. How was a girl supposed to figure out her feelings when he kept saying things that elicited such gut wrenching responses from me? I wanted to toss it in his face that I wasn't his…yet. But that was stupid. I wanted to be. Shoving the conflicting thoughts to the side, I waited.

"This is the way I am. I'll probably piss you off sometimes." At my snort he lifted his brows and grinned. "Fine, most of the time. But I'll always protect you. You won't be safer with anyone else than you will be with me."

"I want to believe that, but…" I used a napkin to wipe off my fingers. It was more to give my nerves a chance to settle than anything. "We were talking last night and the girls mentioned a few things. About the club."

He nodded, as though he was expecting this. "I planned to tell you myself. It just seemed important to give you a chance to get to know me before I told you about that. I wasn't trying to be misleading or secretive, I just couldn't have you running off." He was throwing a little teasing in to ease the tension—at least that's what I thought it was, but he could be serious, knowing him.

"My club is complicated. We're not your typical weekend kind of club. We have chapters all over the country and each has a little bit of a different *vibe* to it."

"And what's your…vibe?"

He tapped a finger on the table in front of us, watching me like my hawk liked to watch a rabbit. "We're vigilantes. We help keep the crime down in our city."

"Your city."

"That's right. Tucson and all its surrounding towns belong to us. We help watch over it." A blank mask had fallen over his face. He was waiting to see my reaction.

"And by helping you mean?"

"Whatever we have to do."

"Is it dangerous?"

"Yes."

I swallowed hard and looked down at my plate. The meal I'd been so eager to eat was churning in my stomach. "That scares me."

"Why?" He reached across the table and took my hand. "I wouldn't let anything happen to you."

My laugh was a little hoarse. "I don't care about myself, Ricochet. You may not know me well enough to realize that yet. I'd rather something happen to me than those I care about."

A muscle ticked in his jaw. "I get that. I'm the same way."

"Then you can understand how getting involved with a man who actively goes looking for trouble isn't something-"

"I'm not your ex," he snapped, eyes blazing.

"How do I know that? You and your brothers-"

"It's not so much that we look for trouble, we just take care of it when it shows up. We do what we have to in order to help people. Sure, we get drunk. We take risks. We live life in the fast lane, but I would never put my girl and her elderly father in the line of fire. I take care of what belongs to me."

He was biting off every word. I hadn't meant to offend him, or call his honor into question. I was just worried about history repeating itself. The air around us was charged and the only couple that had been sitting nearby gave us wary looks as they walked away.

Needing to break the tension, I let out a small laugh. "Don't you dare let my dad hear you call him elderly. He's only sixty."

Ricochet took a few deep breaths and slowly his shoulders relaxed and he loosened the death grip he'd had on my hand. "Sorry. Look. I know this is a lot to take in. It was years before Gwen truly understood why I chose to be in this club."

"I think I understand that part," I told him. When he gave me a questioning look, I continued. "They're your family. And they understand what you went through in the military. What you need now that you're out. They get you." The girls had mentioned that all the men in the club had been former military, not just Ricochet.

"Pretty damn close," he admitted. "It's hard to put into words, but you got it. Give it a chance." Our eyes locked. "Give *me* a chance. I can show you how good it feels to be a part of this group of people. How good it'll be to belong to me."

"I want that," I whispered.

"Then say yes, and put me out of my fucking misery."

"Yes." I squealed when he leapt out of his seat and swung me up into a bear hug.

His lips crashed into mine and suddenly nothing mattered anymore. Not the people at the zoo. Not my many worries. It was just him and me, and this thing that had been simmering between us for too long. It wasn't a slow flame any longer, it was a raging inferno.

He growled in frustration after he broke the kiss. My dizzy mind tried to make sense of it. "What's wrong?"

"Everything is too fucking far away."

"Huh?"

"Your house. My clubhouse." He gave me a considering look. "A hotel would-"

I made a face, understanding he was thinking of taking me to a nearby hotel for our first time together. I'd just consented to being his old lady. My body was on fire for him, but that didn't mean I wanted to make love to him for the first time in a place where who knew how many other people had done similar things. Bleh.

He sighed. "Fine. My place it is."

"Mine is just as close," I offered.

"I don't want my sister crashing our party," he told me, grabbing my hand. He was walking so fast toward the parking lot I could hardly keep up with his long legs.

"Slow down," I called out.

He stopped in his tracks and did something that had me shouting and laughing at him in the same breath. He hauled me up over his shoulder. "Can't slow me down now."

"Ricochet!" My insides clenched, ready for what was coming next. I somehow already knew he was going to upend my world. I couldn't wait.

CHAPTER 26

Ricochet

She'd only held out for a few weeks, months if you counted from the moment we met, but I'd been waiting for this girl all my life. Sunshine wasn't just what she brought to my world, or my pet name for her. It was going to be her official club name. Each of the guys' old ladies had one. Seek, Taz, Angel, and now my Sunshine. It fit her to a T.

She always had a warm smile and a kind word for those around her. She thought she had turned herself into a stick in the mud, but really she'd just been protecting her heart. She gave it freely and fully and I already knew it belonged to me. I still had every intention of letting her tell me herself, but she was as caught up in me as I was in her. There was no denying this.

I weaved in and out of traffic, enjoying the way her curves pressed against me as we rode down the highway. Knowing my hands were going to be all over them soon had me pouring on more speed.

Her laughter reached my ears before the wind ripped it away. She loved riding on my bike. She was made to be an old lady. She'd just never known it. It was my job to show her.

There wasn't anyone around when I carried her through the clubhouse. She was back over my shoulder and calling me names as she pounded on my back. Even now, when she was irritated with me for hauling her around like I was, she didn't land any of her blows with any force. She didn't want to hurt me. As if she could. Not physically anyway. The only way she could injure me was if she took herself from me.

I had her pressed back against my closed door before I even realized we were in my room. There were no more insults, just moans and gasping little breaths. I drank in every sound she made, wanting more, needing to make her mine in every sense of the word.

Now that we were here, I found the control I needed in order to take my time with her. I placed my cut on top of the dresser. Laying her back on the bed, I kissed each spot of her gorgeous body as I stripped her clothes off. I tossed her shirt over my shoulder, my tongue following the sweep of her collar bone.

"Ricochet," she moaned. Her hands pulled at me, wanting more, needing it faster.

This is where self-control became easy. There was no rushing me. Not now. Revving her up was so much hotter than immediately satisfying myself. Reaching under her body I flicked open her bra and tugged it off. I drank in the sight of her, naked from the waist up. There would be no getting used to this. The way she was watching me with heavy lidded eyes filled with desire.

I cupped her breast as I leaned down to take her mouth in a long, drugging kiss. Her tongue brushed mine and I had to fight back the urge to shuck off our clothes and thrust into her. My cock ached behind my jeans, but I wanted her crazy with lust.

"I can't wait to fill you up," I told her, nipping her jaw with my teeth.

The little hitch in her breathing told me she enjoyed the thought of that as well. Her legs moved restlessly as she rubbed her thighs together, so I pinned them with my own.

"Naughty girl," I growled into her ear. "You don't get to get yourself off. That's my job."

"Then how about you do your job?" she gasped.

I chuckled. "Is someone ready to get fucked?"

She nodded, her dark hair spread around her like a halo. Her hands were under my shirt, sliding along my ab muscles and damn did it feel good to finally have her touching me. To have a green light for both of us to enjoy each other's bodies to the fullest. "Please. I need you," she begged.

"Don't worry, Sunshine. I'll give you exactly what you need." I plucked her nipple, watching as it beaded into a tight little nub. "When I'm ready." Sucking it into my mouth, I used her sighs and groans as a roadmap as I explored her pleasure. Her nipples were sensitive and a direct line down to her pussy, I opened her jeans and dipped my hand beneath her panties.

My fingers slid through her wetness and I groaned as I slid two into her pussy. She pulsed around me and cried out, lifting her hips, asking for more.

"Fuck, Baby, you're soaking wet. I can't wait to feel you wrapped around me."

She gasped as I pulled out of her and licked my fingers that were coated with her sweet juices. Her eyes were wide as she watched my tongue lap over them.

"You want a taste?" I brought my fingers and smeared her wetness over her lips. As soon as her tongue peeked out, I pressed them inside of her mouth. "Suck on them for me." The rhythmic pull of her mouth had me hardening even more. "Such a dirty little girl."

Her eyes flashed to mine, heat and confusion warred in her gaze. She wasn't sure if she was supposed to be liking the things I said to her, but she did.

"You're *my* dirty little girl. Anything we do here together is right and perfect."

Her rigid muscles relaxed and she made a little distraught noise as I pulled my fingers away.

"You want something else to suck on, Sunshine?"

"I...I'm not very good at it," she admitted in a small voice.

My eyes narrowed as I tried to hold onto my temper. It was clear that was what her ex, Dan the Douche, had told her since she'd never slept with anyone else. "I'm willing to bet that's not true. How about you let me be the judge of that."

I rolled off her, then pulled her to her feet next to the bed. Pulling off my boots and jeans, I tossed them over into the corner, along with my shirt, baring my body to her. I hadn't bothered with my boxer briefs today.

Her mouth made a little 'o' of surprise as she stared down at me. She reached her hand out, fingers twitching as though she couldn't wait to touch me. "Not yet. You first."

I sat back on the bed. Slowly stripping her jeans down her legs, I revealed the pretty lacy panties she was wearing. "We'll leave those on while you do this," I told her, grasping her wrists to keep her from taking them off. "I like them." My thumb brushed between her thighs, rubbing over her clit and I grinned as she swayed a little. "You're so fucking responsive. You going to scream for me again tonight?"

"Yes." Her blush stained her cheeks red as she nibbled on her bottom lip.

Her shyness didn't bother me. In fact, I liked it. She was mine to corrupt and I planned to show her every wicked thing I wanted to do to her.

I couldn't resist cupping the back of her neck and pulling her down for a kiss. I was still sitting on the bed, but with my height she didn't have to bend far for our lips to press together.

By the time I released her, she was breathing harder, her tits bouncing with each breath. "On your knees, dirty girl." I tossed one of my extra pillows down onto the hardwood floor between my feet. Holding out my hand, I steadied her as she knelt down.

"Fuck that's a pretty picture. Look up at me."

Her chin lifted as she obeyed my command, making my dick bob in anticipation. I couldn't wait to see her watching me while she had my cock stuffed inside her mouth. Swallowing hard, I tried to stomp down some of my excitement, otherwise she was going to be disappointed before the night was over. I'd be damned if I'd take my pleasure and leave her feeling unsatisfied.

"You'll tell me what…you like?" she asked, her hands reaching out. She wrapped both sets of fingers around my dick and squeezed in a light, testing way.

My head dropped back. Fuck. She was going to have me blowing my load just from that light touch. I'd been waiting so long for her to touch me, I wasn't sure I could hold back. Gathering my remaining willpower, I looked back down at her.

Pre-cum was gathered on the tip of my cock and she was looking down at it, licking her lips in that nervous way of hers. "Taste it."

Her eyes flashed up to mine briefly, but then she lowered them again as she leaned forward. She wrapped her lips around the head of my dick and swirled her tongue over the slit.

"Fuuuck, yeah. Do that again," I told her. My eyes nearly crossed as she did.

She scooted a little closer, never taking her mouth off me and let my length slip further into her wet heat. One hand went to my thigh, to steady herself, while the other continued holding me. She lined me up in a way that was comfortable for her and dropped her head even more.

I sucked in a breath as she took more than half my shaft into her mouth. Her tongue swept along the back and she hummed a little. The noise was a mixture of surprise and interest.

"You enjoying this too, Jordan?" Her eyes lifting to mine nearly had me coming in her mouth. She was on her knees, staring up at me as she sucked my cock. This was going to be the object of every sexual dream I had for the rest of my life. "Because I fucking love having your mouth on me."

Her lips stretched around my length into a small smile and there was pleasure there in her gaze. She liked pleasing me.

My hands went to her long straight hair and I wrapped the tresses around my fists. I wasn't going to last long like this, but I wanted to enjoy her attention as much as I could. I didn't yank on her hair, just fisted it up and held it out of her way. My balls were tingling as she licked and sucked on me. She was inexperienced, but it didn't matter, she still had me at the edge.

She bobbed up and down on my dick, getting more brave as she went. She must have gone a little further than she meant to because she jerked her head back, my dick popping from between her lips.

Using her hair, I prevented her from going back down on me. As much as I was enjoying this, I was ready to fuck her into a coma. "One day I'll teach you to deep throat me," I promised her. There was a spark of interest in her eyes. "But not today."

Releasing her hair, I grabbed her by the waist and twisted, tossing her onto the bed behind me. Her laughter filled the air as she bounced on the mattress. I was over top of her before she could move, sucking as much of one breast into my mouth as I could.

Her breath whined out as she arched into my touch. Her nails raked down my back, a physical plea to give her what she wanted. She was moving beneath my weight, trying to rub herself against me as much as she could.

I scraped my teeth over her nipple in warning to be a good girl. Her squeal of surprise turned into a moan of pleasure as my tongue laved the spot I'd tortured. I repeated the move to her other breast before I began kissing my way down her body.

Settling between her legs, I licked her clit through the lace. When she reached her hands down to shove off her panties, I caught her wrists and pinned them to her sides. Sealing my mouth over her, lace and all, I sucked hard. Her cries echoed through my room as I continued to torment her.

Finally, when I'd had enough, I released one of her wrists and, meeting her eyes, tore the panties off her body. Her gasp of shock was replaced by incoherent words as I pressed my finger inside her. She was dripping for me.

Pulling my digit out, I sucked on it as I lined my body up with hers. I picked up one of her thighs and spread her legs apart, adjusting until I was settled between them. Her eyes rolled back into her head as I pressed into her body. "How does it feel, Sunshine?"

"So good," she moaned.

"Tell me more," I demanded through gritted teeth.

Her pussy was so fucking tight, I was having to shove a little to get my entire length into her. Ecstasy was fire in my veins as her little cunt rippled around me, squeezing and massaging. Holding back was fucking killing me. But if I died, what a damn way to go.

"You're stretching me so much," she breathed out. "I feel so full."

I shoved in the last inch and held still. Buried in her body, I closed my eyes and forced myself not to move. I wanted to give her time. My elbows held my weight off her. The last thing I wanted to do was crush her beneath me. My lips trailed along the shell of her ear. "You ready for me to fuck you, Jordan? To make you my old lady?"

"Yes. Please," she begged. Her legs were wrapped around my hips, but my lower body kept her from being able to rock against me.

I was in control here. Sliding out of her was torture, but just as quickly, I was thrusting back in. The ebb and flow of friction was building our pleasure at a rapid pace. I wanted to fuck her all night long, but feeling her sweet, wet tightness gripping me, I wasn't going to last on this round. There was always round two, or three.

The headboard thumped against the wall as I set a brutal pace. There was no more holding back, my control was gone. Burying my dick in her sexy body as many times as I could was the new goal. Well, one of them.

"Come all over my cock, Sunshine. I want you to come so hard you cream."

She blinked up at me. "I don't even know what that means."

I chuckled. "I'll show you what it means once you come for me." I wrapped my hand around her throat, not allowing her to turn her head. "Eyes on me." I adjusted my movements to a thrust and grind so that I was pushing down on her clit with each forward motion. The way her eyes widened told me how good it was.

Rolling my hips, I focused solely on her, holding back my own orgasm until she was panting beneath me. Building her up until she was crying out in bliss. I didn't stop as she clenched and spasmed around me. I wanted her to ride that wave until it was done. Her body trembled and I could see the moment she relaxed, so I slowed down.

I pulled out of her, and knelt on the bed, straddling her hips. Cupping her cheeks, I kissed her, enjoying the way our tongues rubbed together. Releasing her, I smirked down at my dick. "That, Sunshine, is cream."

She looked down and saw that she'd coated my cock in her orgasm. Pink bled into her cheeks as surprise and embarrassment took over.

I grabbed a fist full of her hair and gently turned her face up until she was looking at me. "None of that. I fucking love that you were so aroused and came so hard that you did this. It'll be my mission to get you to do it every time."

The tension left her face. She would soon learn there wouldn't be anything to be embarrassed about between us.

"Lick it off."

Shock filtered over her expression. "Oh, I-"

I laid down next to her. "Do it."

She licked her lips, then rolled onto her side. The look she gave me was questioning, but she swiped her tongue up my length from balls to tip, collecting the wetness she'd left there.

I groaned as she worked my sensitive flesh, watching as her pink tongue lapped at me. Before long, I couldn't take it anymore. I grabbed her, shoving her onto her stomach, so I could enter her from behind.

She huffed out a breath as I pushed on her hips, rocking against her sweet ass. I watched as my dick disappeared inside her body. Her breathing was picking back up again. "You going to come again, Jordan?" I teased.

That was the last thing I'd expected. It meant she'd gotten turned on again sucking on my cock. Shoving a hand between her and the mattress I found her clit and started rubbing in circular motions.

"I can't!" she cried.

"Doesn't matter," I told her. "This pussy belongs to me. Come for me again." My thrusts were measured so I could hit her G-spot tucked up inside of her. Between that and stimulating her clit, she couldn't hold out.

She turned her face into the mattress and screamed as she came a second time. Her ass jiggled as her orgasm overtook her body, making it quake with pleasure.

"Good fucking girl," I groaned. Pulling my hand out, I grabbed her hips and set a rhythm that had me coming not long after her. My hand gripped tightly onto her hips as I lodged myself far into her body, as deep as I could get, filling her with my cum.

I rolled to the side, taking her with me and spooning up behind her body while we waited for our heart rates to return to normal. My eyes were closed as I basked in the aftermath, so I didn't see her glare at first. She shifted in my arms, and I looked down at her.

Her beautiful face was set into a scowl. I frowned because it wasn't the reaction I was expecting.

"You didn't use a condom." Her tone was accusatory.

"Mmmm," it was the only sound I could make at the moment, but it was one of agreement. I closed my eyes again, determined to enjoy the euphoric feeling I hadn't experienced in a long damn time.

Her hand smacked against my chest. Sighing, I opened my eyes again and looked down at her. She looked like a pissed off little kitten. My lips twitched.

"This isn't funny, Ricochet," she said. "If I wasn't on birth control we'd have a problem."

That made me frown. "Why are you on birth control?"

"It helps with things other than getting pregnant," she informed me.

"So what's the problem?" I asked, though disappointment filled me. For a moment, I'd been imagining her round with my baby.

"You could have gotten me pregnant!"

"You don't want kids?"

That made her stop short and think about what I was asking her. "Well...yeah, but-"

"No buts," I told her. "I can't wait to get you pregnant and start a family with you."

Her mouth dropped open and she was finally stunned into silence.

"If that's tomorrow, I'll be fucking ecstatic. If it's years from now, that's fine too. I'll leave it up to you to decide when to come off birth control, but just know I'm ready when you are." I shifted onto my back, shoving one arm beneath my head like a pillow. I used the other to gather her up and situate her against my body.

She gave in and laid her head on my chest. "Really?"

"Mmmhhmmm."

"It's impossible to stay mad at you," she declared.

"Good. I don't want you mad. I knew you hadn't been with anyone but your ex," I refused to say his name and ruin the moment, "and I haven't slept with anyone in years. I didn't want anything between us. Figured after this we could have the preventative talk."

"And if this was all it took to get me pregnant?" she asked, but there was amusement in her tone now instead of anger.

"Like I said, I'd be thrilled. I want kids. Want them with you. I'm willing to wait for now, but at some point, I'm going to knock you up, Sunshine."

Her laughter warmed my insides as I closed my eyes again and relaxed. When was the last time I'd been this loose? This calm? I was actually looking forward to sleep for once. With my sunshine next to me to chase the dreams away, I might get some decent rest.

CHAPTER 27

Ricochet

It'd been another few weeks since Jordan had agreed to be my old lady and somehow everything had clicked into place. I couldn't remember a time when I was so damn happy. When I felt more myself.

We walked down the sidewalk, holding hands, and I grinned over at her as she devoured her ice cream cone. She was this interesting mix of cute and sexy. She made me laugh more than I had in the past four years, but I also wanted to toss her down on the nearest flat surface and pound into her body until she was screaming in ecstasy.

"Why are you looking at me like that?" she asked, licking between her fingers where some of the ice cream had dripped.

My cock hardened in an instant as I thought about her licking the sweet substance from it. "Just enjoying the view."

She shook her head and knocked her shoulder into mine. She'd dropped her guard, letting me in fully over the past few weeks and it was giving both of us an idea of what our life together would look like.

I had to admit it was everything I wanted. She was all I needed. Wrapping an arm around her, I tucked her up close to my body while we strolled. We were just killing time before a movie. It was all so damn normal.

After a few more delays we'd finally gotten word that construction on the school should be good to start up by next week. I was beginning to connect more with my MC brothers. Even though I was still living out with Gwen and the kids, I was at the clubhouse each day for a few hours. It was like I was slowly emerging from the depression I'd been living in for the last few years. It wasn't completely gone. I wasn't an idiot. I'd still have to deal with my PTSD, probably for the rest of my life. But somehow Jordan made it all a little easier.

I'd said something like that the other day when I was sitting around, having a beer with some of the guys. It was my olive branch. Admitting that I knew I had an issue, but that I was working on it.

Butcher had looked over and shocked the shit out of all of us. "She gives you something to look forward to. Knowledge that life can and will move on. And that you can look forward to tomorrow."

It'd been so damn insightful we'd all just stared at him in silence. At least until Toxic had asked him when he'd become Dr. Phil and made everyone laugh.

I was caught up in my own thoughts as we walked, so much so that we almost ran into the man standing in our path. My groan was only loud enough for Jordan to hear as I recognized him. This was the last fucking thing I needed tonight.

Before I could say anything, Trent stepped closer toward me and shoved a finger into my chest. My eyes narrowed on the smaller man. "You're going to lose that fucking finger if you don't get away from us."

Jordan's hand squeezed mine, silently asking for me to behave. That was easier said than done, especially with my sister's piece of shit ex in my face. Knowing what he'd done with the permitting, but not being able to confront him on it was a burning ache in my gut.

Taking a deep breath, I tried to relax. *This shit stain isn't worth losing my temper over.* That thought right there was a sign that I was evolving. The rage that lived inside of me for so long was finally dying down.

Trent had other plans.

"I heard you were trying to get the permits for your little school re-issued," he told me with a smarmy smile. "I'm just going to keep getting them pulled," he taunted. His eyes were wide and blood shot. He was just a little too excited for this conversation.

"Why do you care about a random charter school?" It was the one thing none of us had been able to figure out.

"Because you care about it," he replied.

Of course that would be it. Being associated with me would come at a price for all of my brothers.

"Why are you being such a dick?" Jordan asked, making me snort out a laugh.

His eyes drifted over her and the smile he gave her made my free hand clench up into a fist.

"You're hot. Way hotter than Gwen. Better than this piece of shit deserves. Why don't you come with me and I'll show you a good time?" He flashed straight white teeth at her in a smile that he thought was charming.

Jordan just had a look of disgust on her face. "Gross. Not happening."

The pounding she was giving Trent's ego was stroking my own and making it a little easier to keep my temper in check. But as usual, Trent couldn't shut the fuck up.

"You'd look way better with me than this loser," he said, shooting me a look.

"My sister was always too good for you."

"So it was you who told her to stop letting me come around." He looked pissed. That was when it clicked. He blamed me for Gwen cutting him out of her and the kids' lives again.

If that's what he thought, I'd let him. Better he was pissed and retaliating against me, than my sister. I shrugged my shoulders and pasted a bored look on my face. "You're not worth her time. She has better things to be doing. Better people to be seeing."

"Like your criminal friends?" he shrieked.

Jordan's eyes widened and she looked around. There were a few people out on the street as the daylight faded away, but most just hurried past, giving us uneasy glances.

"Absolutely. She's going to find a biker to fall in love with and forget all about your pathetic ass." Anger bubbled up inside of me. It was getting harder to ignore what he was saying.

Jordan tugged at my hand again. "We should go."

I started to turn, willing to walk away from this fight. That was until Trent uttered the next sentence.

"I'm going to wait until you're out one night…"

Glancing over my shoulder, I scowled at him.

"Then I'm going to let myself into your girlfriend's house. I'm going to fuck her so hard she won't even remember your name."

Turning, I ignored Jordan's request to stop. I moved back toward Trent, leaving Jordan a safe distance away. We were practically nose to nose by the time I stopped. "Who said she'd want a limp dick asshole like you anyway?" I growled.

"Who said I'd take no for an answer?" Triumph flashed in his eyes when he saw that remark had pushed me over the edge.

I wasn't sure why he was picking a fight with me, but that was all it took. My fist was breaking his nose before I was even aware that I was throwing the punch. I wasn't about to stop there, though.

Next thing I knew, we were down on the ground and I was whaling on him. Every once in a while, he'd throw a feeble punch of his own, or try to block my hits, but even though Trent had a big mouth, he didn't have the skill to back it up.

Despite his inability to throw a punch, he took them surprisingly well. I kept laying them on him and he just kept coming in for more. I'd been in dozens of scraps, hardly anyone could take this many hits. At least when they were sober. I had no clue what he was on, but it made him all the more dangerous.

There was yelling and grabbing hands, but none of it penetrated the fog of my fury. This scum of the Earth had just threatened to rape my old lady. He was going to die and I was going to enjoy sending him to hell.

Someone grabbed me around both arms, hauling me backward and off Trent. I lurched against their hold, trying to get back at him, but it was two men holding me back. Slowly reality began to intrude upon my fury. The red at the edge of my vision was clearing up.

A third man helped Trent to his feet. He bent over, spitting blood out onto the sidewalk. He was grinning like a fucking maniac.

My brows drew together. He shouldn't be standing upright, not after the beating he just took, yet here he was swaying, but standing. "What the fuck are you on?"

"Nothing," he spat, spraying blood. "Just implementing the next part of my plan." He backed away slowly, watching me. "You're going to regret this."

He was probably right. For all I knew he had someone filming this and he'd take it to the mayor to try to get the next steps for construction of the school shut down. Worst case scenario though, the guys could just take me off the crew. His 'plan' made no sense.

The men holding me back didn't let go until Trent had stumbled off down the block. They were muttering something about 'let him go', 'just drop it, dude', but I wasn't really paying attention to them. Once Trent was gone I wasn't going to waste any more time on him. I was already pissed that he'd egged me into a fight, but no one was going to threaten my old lady and get away with it free and clear.

I turned and my gut dropped down onto the sidewalk.

Jordan's face was pale and she was looking at me like I was the monster. She hadn't heard what Trent had said, she'd been too far away. It was better that way anyway. I didn't want her terrified to be home because that asshole had threatened her.

She swallowed hard as I walked up to her. She was fighting for control and I could see both fear and anger in her eyes.

"Sunshine-"

"Don't-" she barked the word out, looked around, then lowered her voice, "Don't call me that."

I sighed. "Look, he had that coming."

"You know how I feel about starting fights, Ricochet," she said, choking a little on the words.

"I'm sorry I scared you," I told her, reaching out to her. I had to bite back a curse when she stepped away from me.

"I can't. Don't touch me."

"You can't what, Baby?"

"I thought I could do this," she whispered.

Fear crept into my heart hearing her speak like that. "Give me a chance to explain, Jordan," I demanded.

She shook her head, her black hair shining under the streetlights that were just starting to come on. "I can't do this."

"Can't do-" My jaw dropped as she spun and hurried down the street. "Jordan!"

She didn't look backward, just kept going. As much as I wanted to chase after her, I knew that would just make things worse. I followed her and kept my distance, just watching over her, until a car pulled up and she got inside. It hadn't taken long for whoever she'd called to pick her up.

"That better be a fucking family member," I muttered, pissed off that she'd called someone else to come get her instead of letting me explain and going home with me.

I stepped into the shadows of a building as the car passed by, then kicked an empty bottle that was left on the street. It clattered across the sidewalk. "This is fucking horse shit!"

It didn't matter to her the reason that I'd just lost my temper and beat the shit out of Trent. I'd scared her. Reminded her of her shitty ex and now she was running away from me.

My fists balled up and I tipped my head back, heaving a sigh. I'd come so fucking far and for Trent to fuck this up for me… It was beyond pissing me off. I wanted to track him down and finish what I'd started. But that was what had scared Jordan off in the first place.

Breathing heavy, trying to rein in my rage, I pulled my phone out of my pocket and hit a number. The phone rang a few times before Smoke answered.

"Bro, how's it going?" he asked, laughter in his voice. The sounds of the bar filtered through the phone. He was back working there temporarily while we waited for everything with the school to be cleared up.

"I need your help."

"What happened?" He was all seriousness now, hearing the fury in my words.

I quickly explained what happened with Trent. "It was a fucking set up. I just have no clue what he wanted. But the things he threatened…" I swallowed down the emotions storming through me. "Could you go out to Jordan and Gwen's and watch over them?"

"Consider it done. I'll hang out until you get there, or have Hell replace me halfway through the night if you need to have a drink with the boys to calm down. Don't worry about a thing, Ricochet."

The line cut out as he hung up. He knew me too damn well. Booze always called my name after a fight. Not getting blind drunk. I just needed to take the edge off, rant to my brothers, and figure out how to unfuck this. I wanted to go straight to Jordan and fix it, but even if she would see me again tonight, I wasn't in any condition to talk with her. I needed to numb the anger churning in my gut.

Scraping a hand through my hair, I walked back to where my bike was parked. Why did relationships have to be so fucking difficult?

CHAPTER 28

Jordan

I watched out the window, trying to catch another glimpse of Ricochet. It didn't matter that I was angry with him, I still needed to see him. Shaking my head, I forced myself to look down at my lap. "Thanks for coming to get me, Dad."

The panic had mostly subsided while I'd waited on the street for my ride. My heart was already settling into a normal rhythm again. I'd almost gone back to speak with Ricochet. To clear everything up. In the end, I hadn't, because I was too confused about everything and unwilling to trust myself or him. I knew where this behavior led, and ignoring things would eventually hurt those I love.

"Anytime, Pumpkin," he replied. His calm brown eyes landed on me. He wanted to ask me what was wrong, but knew I needed a few minutes.

It wasn't hard to see that I'd overreacted, I already knew that, but seeing Ricochet lay Trent out and just start beating on him had terrified me. It was far more intense than anything Dan had ever done. It wasn't a drunken brawl. It was just plain frightening. I'd known better than to try to get in the middle of it and pull Ricochet off the other man. I didn't want to accidentally catch an elbow to the face. No thank you. So, I'd just stood back and waited. I hadn't even bothered to call out to my boyfriend to get him to stop. He wasn't going to.

It wasn't even that I cared about Trent. Honestly, if it wasn't for my hang ups about the men I date fighting, thanks to Dan, I probably would have been rooting for Ricochet to do more damage. Trent was a snake and he had been egging Ricochet on.

But from the first crack of fist into bone, I'd been ripped out of the moment and shoved back into that night. The sounds from the bar, the grunts of pain, and then Dad's face when he'd been lying in that hospital bed. The fear had overtaken me again and no matter what I did there was no convincing myself that it was different. How could I trust Ricochet to control his temper? It was obviously on a short leash if he let a few taunts get to him like that.

I wasn't even judging him. I really would have liked to hit Trent too for some of the stuff he was saying to my boyfriend, and about my friend. But I didn't. I'd controlled myself. It was more than just Trent. He could do this with anyone, lose his temper like that.

"Okay, Pumpkin," Dad said, breaking into my thoughts and bringing me back to reality.

Looking up, I realized that we were parked in his and Mom's driveway.

"What happened?"

"What do you mean?"

He gave me 'the look'. He wasn't buying my innocent act. The man knew me far too well.

I sighed and told him what had happened.

Dad pursed his lips as I fell silent, thinking through it all. "So what's the problem?"

Staring at him in shock, I asked, "What's…what's the problem?" I repeated, completely baffled.

Dad shrugged, shifting on the seat so he could see me better.

"Sounds like your young man stood up for you. And his sister. And himself. What's the problem?"

"Dad." I searched for the words. For how to explain to him why I was so scared. "First off, Ricochet isn't just a 'young man'. I mean, he's only twenty-eight, but he was a Navy Seal. He's strong. Knows how to fight."

"Okay?"

Huffing out an exasperated breath, I fought for the words. "He needs to be able to control himself."

"Did he kill the guy?" Dad's brow arched up and his lips twitched.

"Well…no. I mean some other men pulled him off him."

"But he knows this…Trent fellow?"

"Yeah," I said, hesitating. I wasn't sure where he was going with this.

"So, theoretically he could track him down anytime and pummel him to death?"

"I…guess." Folding my arms over my chest, I narrowed my eyes. "What are you getting at?"

"Look, Pumpkin. I'm not going to lie. I'm thrilled you found a man like him." He gave me an encouraging smile.

"You don't even know him."

"A veteran. Strong. Loyal. Protects his lady, which just so happens to be my daughter. Yeah. I'm fine with you dating him."

I shook my head, blinking in shock. "He's in a motorcycle club." My inside voice was berating me for telling him anything negative about Ricochet. But honestly, this was the one hang up I expected my parents to have about my new boyfriend. Better to just get it all out in the open now.

"I know."

Scowling at him, I muttered, "How?"

"You think I haven't looked into every man you've spent your time around?" He gave me a chastising look, as if I should have known better. "There really haven't been many…"

"After Dan, I just sort of-"

"Lost the ability to trust yourself." He sighed and wiped a hand over his mouth. "I haven't known how to talk to you about this. I should have left you home that night."

"Like I would have stayed while you went to bail my ex out of the newest trouble he'd gotten into." Mom and Dad had always made it clear that they hadn't approved of Dan once he started drinking and getting into trouble.

"True," he chuckled. "We raised you to know your own mind. That means stepping back and letting you make your own mistakes. Answer me truthfully. Do you really not see a difference between that night with Dan and what just happened with Ricochet?"

Shame coated my words as I whispered. "I do. But…how do I get over all of this?"

"All of what? It was one fight. Guys like that are going to live for fighting, Sweetheart. It's kind of who they are."

"What do you know about MCs?"

He laughed. "I was young once, you know."

I gave him a questioning look.

"I may have prospected for a club once." My jaw dropped, but he just kept going. "But, I met your mother and even though I liked to throw fists in my youth, I was starting to grow out of it. So, I walked away."

"You…never told us any of that."

"You, Noah, and Jenna are more like your mother. Thank God. There was no point in bringing any of it up."

"So you don't care if I date a biker?"

"I'm alright if you date *that* biker."

Staring at him suspiciously, I pressed. "Why though? I thought it was going to be a fight to get you to accept him. Noah already read me the riot act about being with him."

"I have my ways of finding things out, but the events from today just proved me right. He's a good man and he'll do whatever he has to in order to protect you and his family. That's what matters most. At least to your mother and me." He patted my shoulder.

"You don't care that he lost control and-"

"Jordan," he said, cutting me off. "I love you. You need to let what happened with Dan go. Taking a damn pool cue to the chest would have knocked anyone for a loop, but I wasn't in any real danger. Stop worrying about me, I'm not as fragile as you seem to think. And something else you need to realize is," he searched for his words before continuing, "yes, I like that he's willing to lose control and beat the shit out of a guy that was obviously harassing the two of you. It's your job to stay in control and to keep him on an even keel most of the time. During those few times when there's a threat? I want a man who's going to step in front of you and be willing to lay down his life for yours. For your future children. Call me selfish, but that's what I expect of any man who wants to marry you. He wasn't drunk, he wasn't looking for a fight. The fight found him and he took care of it."

"Dad," I said, a little choked up. "No one said anything about marriage."

He shook his head, a soft smile on his face. "You don't know much about men, Pumpkin. That's okay, you've still found a good one. Do me a favor?" When I raised my brows, he cupped my cheek. "Don't make him suffer for too long before you forgive him."

With that he got out of the car. Before he went inside, he poked his head back in. "Oh, and I don't know how much longer I can hold your mom back."

"Hold her back from what?" I asked, wary.

"She's dying to invite him over so she can grill him in person," he warned me. He winked, then went inside the house, leaving me to think about everything he'd said.

I sat in the dark car, wondering how my dad could see everything so clearly when my own feelings were so muddled. It hadn't taken me long to realize I'd made a mistake, but to see it from someone else's perspective, someone I trusted, made me feel a lot better.

Dad clearly didn't see an issue with what Ricochet did. That meant the problem was with me. How could I get past the fear of those I loved getting hurt every time some asshole picked a fight? How was I supposed to move forward with Ricochet, knowing that being a part of his club meant he'd be putting himself in danger more often than most men?

Somehow, I had to adjust my mindset. I just wasn't sure how to do that. I thought back to the fight tonight and realized that while I stood there watching, it was the past, not the present, that had terrified me. I wasn't at all scared that Ricochet was going to lose and that Trent was going to come after me. Maybe that was the place to start. With trusting Ricochet.

It'd been so long since I'd been in a relationship, I wasn't sure how to do it anymore. If he could forgive me for bolting tonight and the many screw ups I was sure I'd make in the future, maybe I could learn to accept him the way he was and get over this fear of mine.

Feeling a little better, I got out of the car and went inside to spend the evening with my family. I had to work tomorrow, and that was probably a good thing. Give both of us a chance to really cool off. Maybe afterward I could see if we could talk.

CHAPTER 29

Ricochet

I walked up to The Bunker and stared at the door for a few minutes before I turned and sat on a bench outside. I wasn't in the mood to go inside yet. For once, drinking myself stupid wasn't that appealing. "Good job, asshole. You did it again," I muttered to myself.

Now what?

There was no sense in chasing after her tonight. She was scared. Following her would only freak her out more. I'd just add this to the list of things I needed to unfuck. Apparently, Trent was on a mission to mess with me. I'd warn Lock and Rip in the morning, but I knew what they'd say. They'd tell me to stay away from him.

Normally, we'd roll a little fuck stick like Trent up and make him disappear for fucking with our business. But this asshole had a leg up on us. The last thing we needed was the mayor or the DA looking our way. And since he seemed to be connected to both, the best thing to do was stay away from him as much as possible. I didn't like this, being at his mercy. But I had others to think about. The women and children that had escaped the cult were depending on me not doing something stupid. As much as I hated to say it, I needed to be an adult.

I looked down at the ground, staring at the weeds pushing up through the gravel. For some reason their presence irritated me. An imperfection ruining everything.

Getting off the bench, I knelt down in the gravel, grasping the nearest weed by the roots and pulling. I ignored the voice telling me I had better things to do and focused instead on the weeds. Something about pulling them was easing the tension that was coiling up inside of me.

From down here I could see how out of control they had gotten. The entire perimeter and every area with gravel had the damn things coming up. I kept pulling and moving along. It was helping me keep my mind blank and my temper managed.

No one needed to tell me that I was the weeds. That was what some jack off therapist would tell me. Our aunt had made us see one when we'd come to live with her, after our parents had died. I'd come by my dislike of them naturally. The guy had been a jerk and had kept pushing when I wasn't ready to talk. Shaking my head, I focused back on the weeds.

I was the imperfect thing ruining other people's lives. My sister's. My club. The school that the women and children from the cult needed. Now Jordan was running from me. How could I blame her? The one thing she was afraid of was the one thing I did best. I wasn't sure I could quit fighting. It would mean that I had to stop protecting people. Let people like Trent make disgusting threats to the people I loved. I couldn't do that. She couldn't ask that of me. It was as much a part of me as my eye color. There was no changing it. But I didn't want to lose her either.

Snarling in frustration, I ripped at the encroaching vegetation. I might not be able to contain my temper, or alleviate my girlfriend's fear, but I could at least make the club look like it wasn't abandoned. It was the only thing I had control over and I was happy settling for any semblance of calm.

I kept moving along in a slow, but methodical manner, leaving not a single blade of grass untouched. The area behind me was immaculate. At some point during my fixation with weed pulling Toxic had decided to step outside.

His boots filled my vision as I squatted there. I didn't need to look up at his face to see the look on it. I knew him well enough to imagine what his expression looked like, something between confusion and disbelief. That tended to happen when you found one of your brothers manically pulling weeds in the middle of the night.

"Want a beer?" he asked.

Instead of answering, I hopped up onto a picnic table that was nearby. The realization of just how far I'd gone while weeding struck me. There was a trail of dead weeds all around the perimeter. I had nearly come full circle back to where I had started pulling them. Accepting the beer, I watched as he sat on the table next to me. I was sure some talk was coming. It was the last thing I was ready for right now, so I took a swig from the bottle, then started tearing at the label.

I could see from my peripheral vision that he was staring up at the stars. After a few minutes he finally spoke. "When you were in Afghanistan, what food did you crave the most?"

Taking another drink, I considered his question. Instead of answering, I asked, "What?" He always managed to throw me off kilter. And somehow the question gave my searching mind something to focus on. The unsteady, desperate desire to control everything around me started to fade away.

He stopped looking at the stars and stared at me. His expression was a mask of patience. "What food? Everyone has something they crave in Afghanistan, since your food options are limited to whatever the chow hall provides. What did you crave most?"

I blinked at him a few times, no idea what he was getting at, but an answer rolled out all on its own. "My sister's prime rib. She bakes it with this amazing spice and the edge crusts over." My mouth was suddenly watering at the thought. Where had that come from? The reminder further drove away the loss of control and the emotions it evoked.

Toxic smiled. "On my first deployment, I wanted…everything. Pizza from Georgino's, tacos from Guadalajara's, fresh baked donuts from that bakery by the university. I wanted every damn plate you could think of."

He looked at the beer bottle hanging from his hands and laughed before continuing. "When I got home I stayed with my dad for a few months while I was on leave, trying to figure out what to do next. I finally had the chance to eat everything I'd been craving. Thing is, I couldn't decide. I went from having no options on food, just what the chow hall was serving, to having everything available. I was so overwhelmed at the options that I was paralyzed."

I shifted on the wooden surface, stretching my legs out and looking over at him. "Seriously?" It was all I could mutter. All I could give at the moment, but it was something. Toxic didn't seem to mind.

"Oh yeah. I was so concerned that if I got pizza I was missing out on tacos, or that the donut might be stale. And of course, what to choose off the menu. So many fucking options. There was always this worry that I would choose wrong. I went to a grocery store instead, and when I saw all the items I was paralyzed again. I knew how to cook, it wasn't like I'd forgotten. But cooking food took even more decision making than going out to eat.

I'd spent the last year making decisions on combat missions, weapons loads, routes in and out of target areas, but here I was paralyzed by what to eat." He laughed again and took a long pull from the bottle.

I was floored. I looked at the dirt on my hands, behind me at the trail of weeds I'd uprooted. And it all made sense. *He* was making sense. I'd spent months finally learning how to live like a normal guy again, and all it had taken was one fight with my old lady to knock me back on my ass. That was just something I was going to have to live with because everything that had happened to me would live on inside of me for the remainder of my life. That didn't mean I had to let it paralyze me. I didn't have to give in and let it take control of me. "What did you finally eat?"

He smiled. "Beef jerky and granola bars."

"What?" I laughed with him. Something loosened inside of me at his admission. Something I'd never really stopped to consider before. These men understood me. They knew more about me and the things that I'd gone through than many could, because a lot of them had been through similar experiences. I'd never really given them the chance to help me before. It was a sobering realization, but one that made me feel that much more connected to my brothers.

"That's like…that's the only snack we had in abundance in Afghanistan," I said with another chuckle. People from all over the U.S. would send care packages to us, and they always had granola bars and jerky. They were snacks that wouldn't melt and never went bad. You would eat more of those on a deployment than a normal person would in a lifetime.

"I went back to what I knew. When I had too many options I just defaulted to what was familiar. I ate nothing but jerky and granola until my dad noticed. He didn't say anything, just took me out to pizza and ordered the meat lovers. It was what I always ordered as a kid. He knew just what I needed. It broke the spell. After tasting that greasy, cheese and meat covered delight I was able to function again."

I wiped my hands against my pants in a futile attempt to get the dirt off them. "I…uh, I guess weeding the parking lot at midnight isn't much better than eating jerky and granola."

"Everyone comes home and faces something that's supposed to be normal that turns out to be terrifying, so we all default to something we can control. Some of us find a productive outlet. Lockout remodeled the whole bar. Rip runs the damn thing now. Some of us…eat granola."

"Hmm," I grunted

"Thing is, you can't distract yourself forever. Eventually you run out of weeds. Then what? You can only control something that's irrelevant for so long until you realize it's irrelevant. It's a distraction that's keeping you from doing what you really need to. Sooner or later you have to integrate back into the real world."

I knew he was right. I wasn't fooling myself by weeding a parking lot by hand. I stood up and placed a hand on his shoulder. "Thanks Toxic."

"Good talk" He said, leaning back across that table and looking back up at the stars. "Now, go away."

Laughing, I walked toward the bar. I was only a few feet away when Hellfire opened the door.

"There you are. Figured you'd be stopping by. Smoke should be here anytime." He must have seen the worry on my face, because he was quick to reassure me. "Butcher offered to take over for him for the night. The girls will be perfectly safe while we get you blitzed."

"I don't think I need blitzed."

"Oh," he replied, with a grin on his face as he slapped a hand on my back, "you, my friend, definitely need to get blitzed. Then you can tell me the details about smashing in Trent's face. And what happened with Jordan."

There was empathy shining there in his eyes, though he knew better than to express it. This was the way we comforted each other. I glanced over toward the picnic table. Toxic raised his beer in a salute. I mimicked the gesture, then stepped inside.

The music was loud, the air was stale, and it was packed full of friends and family. Somehow Toxic had talked me down and now that I was settled, I knew Hell was right. I needed to let loose and have a good time with my brothers. For once I could drink with them and not have to get blackout drunk, not have to dull any pain.

I sat down at the bar and nodded in greeting at Kit. It took everything inside of me not to ask her if she'd heard from Jordan. Gwen had mentioned all the women, my sister included, now had a group chat where they texted each other constantly throughout the day. It pleased me to no end that both my old lady and my sister had found friends in these women, but it was also a bit terrifying. I didn't want to imagine the things they texted. With this crew, there were probably plenty of secrets being spilled about their old men.

Kit set another beer in front of me. "She's staying the night at her parents'."

My brows shot up. "Isn't that a breach of some kind of girl code?"

"Maybe, but I don't want you worrying about her all night." Kit put a hand on her hip. "I expect you to fix this, Ricochet. We're not willing to lose her because of whatever bone headed thing you did."

I laughed and shook my head. "I plan on it."

"Good." She gave my forearm a squeeze. It was her way of reassuring me. Then she was off, tending the bar, and barking at the patrons who were getting impatient.

Hush sat down on the other side of me. "Mind if I join this party?"

"Thought you went to bed, Old Man," Rip said, walking up. "Let's take this over to a table. Lock has one over there."

We all got up and moved. Hush glared at Riptide. "Fuck off. Just wait a few more months. When your pregnant old lady kicks you out of bed because you were snorin' and woke her up, I'll remember this."

We all hooted with laughter and tossed digs and taunts at Hush. Lock's eyes met mine and I gave him a nod of acknowledgment. He was going to need a full report of what had happened tonight. And I knew he would end up talking with me about Jordan too. If anyone knew how to give good advice it was him. And…apparently Toxic. Who knew?

I sat back in my chair, relaxed for the first time in hours. I hadn't realized how long I'd been out in that fucking parking lot. Kit kept the beers coming and though my thoughts didn't stray far from Jordan, I was back under the newly acquired control I'd found over the last few months. There would be time to fix this. My sunshine loved me as much as I did her. This wasn't going to break us apart. We'd figure out how to fix it.

CHAPTER 30

Jordan

I was driving home from work the next day and nerves danced in my belly. My plan was to go home and change, then meet Ricochet in town. I'd texted him that morning to see if we could talk.

He was in church right now, but once he was done we were going to get dinner and talk about what happened yesterday. I was so nervous to see him after I'd ditched him. I wasn't sure what I was going to tell him, I just knew I had to do something. After thinking about the situation all day, I realized Dad was right. Ricochet hadn't gone looking for that fight. He'd been about to leave with me when Trent started spewing more hateful things. I needed to apologize to him for reacting the way I had.

Frowning, I turned onto my road and saw the abandoned car that Gwen had noticed a few times. I slowed down, searching the area. No one was around it. I considered hiking down into a nearby wash to see if it really was kids messing around, but it was getting dark. The javelina loved to come out right at sundown and the last thing I wanted was to be caught down in the wash by the rat-pig looking creatures. They were extremely territorial and every Arizona native knew not to mess with them.

We had a family of them who'd lived near our house growing up. More than once Noah and I had been chased inside, screaming our heads off, by the animals. Mom wouldn't allow Dad to 'take care' of them, so eventually Dad had called The Wildlife Sanctuary to come relocate them.

Deciding to keep driving, I made my way home. As I pulled into my driveway, I glanced over at Gwen's house. In the dying light I could see her front door was wide open.

"That's weird." I left my purse in the car, slipping my phone into my back pocket and locking the car behind me as I made my way over to my friend's house.

I'd only made it a few steps inside when I heard a crashing sound in the kitchen followed by a sob. Running toward the sound, I skidded to a halt, my heart in my throat when I found Sean and Grace huddled up together in the dining room. My eyes widened, mouth opening in shock.

They were under the table, arms wrapped around each other, and Grace was crying silently. Sean had his arms over her like he was trying to hide her. Huge fat tears dripped down her face. I ran over and landed on my knees next to the table. "What's the matter?"

"He's here," Sean whispered, casting a fearful look at the door to the kitchen.

There was only one person it could be. I nodded. "Okay. Sean, listen to me." I pulled my phone out and handed it to him. It didn't have a password on the lock screen, so I knew he wouldn't have any issues using it. "Take your sister. Go hide upstairs in your closet," I whispered. "Call your Uncle Gage."

He nodded, swallowing hard as he clutched the phone to his chest. "Mom is-"

"I know, Sweetie. I'm going to help her, okay? But I need you to hide. Stay with your sister. And call your uncle."

"Okay."

I helped them out from under the table. As much as I wanted to hug them close, the sounds coming from the kitchen were unbearable to hear. I waited until they rushed up the stairs, looked around and cursed. There wasn't anything in here I could use as a weapon. I ran to the front hall and yanked open the closet door. Nothing.

Damn.

I weighed my options. I could take the time to run to my house and grab the shotgun my dad insisted I keep there, or I could charge into that kitchen empty handed. The scream made my mind up for me.

The door slammed open before I realized my feet had begun to move. Trent was standing over Gwen's prone body, about to kick her.

"You fucking asshole!" I bellowed as I launched myself at him.

He was off balance since his leg was cocked back and we both went tumbling into the oven. His head hit the glass door hard enough that the sound made bile rise in my throat.

I pulled myself up onto my knees, breathing hard from the adrenaline, and then scrambled over to Gwen. "Oh God," I whispered, my hand shaking as I touched her bruised and battered face.

Her eyes fluttered open. "The kids?" she croaked.

"They're okay. They're-" I yelped as I was yanked backward by the hair.

Trent had it wrapped up in his fist as he glared down at me, blood dripping down the side of his face. "You stupid bitch. I'm going to fucking kill you for that."

I squeaked in pain as he yanked my hair again to emphasize his words. The way his eyes were glinting with madness, I believed him. He had every intention of killing me to get to Gwen. I wasn't going to allow either thing to happen. The only one losing here tonight was going to be him.

My hand clenched into a fist, which I then used to punch him straight in the junk. Since I was kneeling and he was standing over me, it was the perfect shot. Satisfaction at the keening cry he released made me smile.

As soon as he let go of my hair to cup his balls, I was on my feet. My eyes were locked on the counter. His hand latched around my ankle right as I reached the knife block.

He pulled me back, making me lose my footing and my chin smacked the edge of the counter. He was saying something, but the sound was distorted as my ears rang from the blow.

My vision was swimming as I fought not to black out. I couldn't. He'd kill us. I wasn't sure what Trent's fucking problem was but his eyes were bloodshot and his pupils were so large they'd nearly taken over the section of color. He had to be high. That made him incredibly dangerous.

I scrambled backward on my hands and feet, the knife in my hand clanking against the tile. Watching him as he stalked toward me, I tried to still my frantic mind and make a plan. I was trying to lead him away from the corner that Gwen was lying in. She wasn't moving anymore. Fear clawed at my throat. For her. For myself. For the kids. If I failed them, Ricochet was going to lose his whole family. As if I needed one more thing to be scared of.

Shoving all the thoughts away, I decided to go on the offensive. Getting to my knees I slashed outward with the knife, catching his forearm and making him stumble back. He barely seemed to notice that I'd just cut him. I held the knife out, pointing towards him. "Don't come any closer," I warned him. Blood dripped from the blade to the floor, staining the air with a metallic copper smell.

He paused, eyeing the knife, then giving me a deranged smile. Like he wasn't scared of anything.

Meanwhile, the knife was shaking in front of me because I had everything to lose and I was terrified. No one was going to get to us in time. I was our last hope. Me. The girl who'd never even been in a fight before. Dad and Noah had taught me to throw a punch. To shoot a gun. To swing a bat. I had none of those right now. All I had was the third smallest knife in Gwen's butcher block. The blade was barely longer than my middle finger. It would have to do.

While Trent was debating on how to disarm me, I got to my feet. My heartbeat was pounding in my ears. My entire focus was on the man in front of me. At least, until he turned toward the door and disgust washed over his face.

"What do you think you're going to do with that? Huh?" he taunted.

I wasn't sure if I had a concussion, but his voice was a little distorted. The blow to the head was making it hard to hone in on everything all at once. I turned my head and gasped.

Sean was standing in the doorway that separated the dining room and the kitchen. And he was pointing a pistol at Trent.

"Get out of our house," Sean growled. The gun shook in his hand, belying his brave words. He was as terrified as I was.

The gun looked so big in his grasp. I knew it was Gwen's. We'd compared weapons the night my dad had brought over Trusty. Yes, I'd named my shotgun. I wasn't sure how he'd gotten it from the safe I knew she kept it in, but there wasn't time to worry about that now.

"Trent," I called out, trying to get the psychopath standing between us to focus on me. "You don't want to do this."

"Sure I do," he replied as though he'd just asked to take his son to a basketball game. He was answering me, but his eyes were fixed on Sean.

"He's your son, Trent. Don't do this. Don't make *him* do this." I risked a glance at Sean. His face was pale and his lower lip trembled. "Sean, go back upstairs." Anything to get him away from his father.

"You don't think I have one of those?" Trent asked, reaching behind him.

I saw the flash of metal at the small of his back and cursed. Lunging forward, I crashed into Trent a second time. All I could do was hope that Sean didn't accidentally shoot me in all the commotion. I couldn't let Trent get his hands on the gun he had hidden in the waistband of his jeans.

Trent wasn't as easy to take down this time, he outweighed me by forty pounds, at least. Still, I darted in low and took him down at the knees. He landed on top of me, making me grunt out a pained breath. He grabbed the wrist of my hand that held the knife, and squeezed until I thought he'd grind my bones into powder.

I cried out in pain, trying to bring my knee up to hit him anywhere I could. He was too heavy and too much of his body was lying across mine. He jerked the knife from my numb fingers and my eyes widened at the intent I read in his gaze. He brought the blade toward me and I did the only thing I could think of. I reached up and grasped his face in my hands. My thumbs dug into his eye sockets and the feeling of the soft tissue giving in to the pressure nearly made me gag.

His scream was loud and abrupt, but it did the trick. He dropped the knife and jerked away from me. Trent backed away, rubbing at his eyes, but then his lids opened and he glared at me.

Damn. I hadn't blinded him. I'd needed more force, but being pinned under him hadn't allowed for it. I scooted away just as he started toward me.

The noise made us all freeze. My ears rang as the gunshot sounded in the small space. I gasped and looked over at Sean. He'd pointed the gun up and toward the far wall of the kitchen when he'd squeezed the trigger. Then he lowered it and pointed it straight at Trent's chest. "I'll do it," he said, voice firm now.

I was terrified to move and startle him. He was only eight years old. He shouldn't have to live with the horror of killing his father, but I couldn't get to him. It became clear that someone was going to die tonight. I couldn't prevent that. Hopelessness settled in my chest. I didn't know what to do anymore.

CHAPTER 31

Ricochet

Thank fuck I'd already been on my way back to Gwen's place. Church had ended early and instead of waiting in town for Jordan, I'd decided to go to her.

I was only ten minutes away when Sean had called me on Jordan's phone. As soon as I'd heard his voice I knew something was wrong. Hearing him tell me that Trent was there and had hurt his mom and that Jordan was protecting her had made my blood freeze in my veins. After the threats that Trent had made yesterday, my imagination was set to run wild.

It was the longest drive of my life despite the fact that I was pushing my bike to its max speed. The fact that I didn't pass a cop was pure luck. As soon as I pulled up to the house, I dumped my bike, letting it fall to the side. There wasn't time to park it. All I could think about was my family.

The gunshot rang out through the night. My mind fought to pull me back into the past, when the sound of gunfire had altered my life so irreparably. I ran to the door, images of Afghanistan merging with what was in front of me. Gwen's house faded into an adobe hut. I shook it off as I ran. I had to stay in the here and now.

Shaking off the memories, I rushed into the house, weapon drawn. I always carried my pistol, but it was usually my last resort. The sound of a gun being fired had prompted me to draw my weapon without hesitation.

As I made my way into the dining room my heart was beating a mile a minute, but what I saw had fear clawing at my chest.

Jordan was sitting in the doorway to the kitchen, her face pale, blood dripping down her neck. My eyes searched her for more injuries, but it looked like the blood was coming from split skin on her jaw. Otherwise she looked okay. Her eyes landed on me and as much as I wanted to comfort her, I took in the rest of the situation.

Sean was on one side of the dining room table, a gun in his hand, while his father was on the other side, a few feet away from Jordan. Trent was completely focused on his son and was taunting him, the same way he'd been railing at me yesterday. I looked back to Sean and was hit with another barrage of the past. Jack taking up a position in front of me, a young boy holding a rifle. My past was replaying in the present, only this time it was through my family.

Gritting my teeth, I re-holstered my weapon. The only one with a gun right now, that I could see, was Sean. Jordan had a small knife in her hand, which she was holding out in front of her. Trent was unarmed, but clearly deranged.

As much as I wanted to kill Trent, I knew I couldn't. Lockout had outlined that one clearly today in church. His connection with the DA would land me in jail. Not that it mattered if he was threatening my family. But right here and right now, it was so much simpler and so much worse. If Sean killed his father it would ruin his life. Forget any other reason, I had to save Sean from a life of horror. Save him from my life. I hated the man who was standing there, who'd hurt my family, but the last thing I could do right now was kill him.

He didn't matter at the moment. Only Sean did. Only Jordan did.

Gwen and Grace. My family was what was important. Trent would be dealt with later.

"Sean."

His eyes flashed over to me and I saw the panic there, then he focused back on Trent. His jaw tensed. I knew the signs. I'd seen that look before. Right before Jack was killed. He was willing to pull the trigger. He was going to end Trent's life.

I couldn't allow that. "Give me the gun, Sean." Inching toward him, I took my eyes off Trent. The only one I could focus on now was Sean.

"He hurt Mom." His voice wavered, but his hand didn't. It was steady as he held the gun aloft. "He always hurts her. He's not going to stop." More images were flashing in and out now. One of them stayed. Lodged firmly in the present.

I could see Jack now. He was standing behind Sean. He was watching me with a desperate plea in his eyes. It was saying *save him*. I stepped forward in front of Sean, between him and his father.

"He'll pay for that. I promise you." I knelt down, my hand outstretched. "But not like this."

"He…he wanted to kill her. Kill me!" Tears dripped down his cheeks.

"I know. But you stopped him. You protected your mom, and Jordan, and now you need to give me the gun." I was within reach, but I didn't dare yank the weapon from his hands. Not with Jordan here. I didn't know where Gwen was, but if I had to guess, I'd say the kitchen because my sunshine was guarding the door fiercely with her little pig sticker. "Give me the gun. I'm here now, and I'm never leaving. He's never going to hurt you again. He'll never hurt anyone."

My tone was soft. This wasn't the time to bark at the poor kid. He'd been through enough. His life was already changed forever. But it didn't have to be ruined. I knew how he felt at that moment. Only I'd been a trained member of the military with a choice to make. "You're just a kid, Sean. This isn't for you to fix."

That got his attention. He looked over at me, taking his eyes off Trent. The gun lowered a few inches.

From my peripheral I saw motion. Trent had wizened up and was bolting out of the dining room, toward the front door. There was nowhere the rat could hide that I wouldn't find him. I let him leave.

Sean was focused on me now, his gun hanging limply from his hands, pointing toward the floor. When I flexed my fingers, he handed it over.

Sighing in relief, I stuffed it in the waistband of my jeans, then pulled him in for a hug. Jack was still there behind him, a smile on his face. Slowly he faded away, and a weight fell off of me. "Where's your sister?"

"Upstairs. Hiding."

"Go sit with Grace until the police get here," I told him. Before I let him go, I squeezed him tighter. "You were incredibly brave tonight. You did your family proud. Thank you for protecting them."

He gave me a small smile and that was when I knew he was going to be alright. I waited until I heard his shoes slapping on the wooden stairs before I turned.

"Jesus, Sunshine," I murmured, moving over to her.

She shook her head. "I'm okay, but Gwen. Oh God, Ricochet, Gwen." She backed up from my reach and scrambled into the kitchen on her hands and knees. She was in pain, if the way she was moving was any indication.

"What did he do to you?" I asked, following her. As soon as I saw my sister crumpled in the corner I swore. My knees hit the tile as I knelt by her side. I rolled her over, holding her in my arms. My heart froze as I watched her chest for movement. She took a breath and I let out a long breath of relief.

My hands skimmed over her lightly, looking for broken bones. Her face was a mess. I was betting she had a few broken ribs, but otherwise she seemed to be okay.

"Holy shit."

My head jerked to the side at the new voice, but I relaxed when I saw Smokehouse standing in the doorway.

"Get the fuck out of the way, Smoke," Lock barked, charging in through the door. His eyes flashed in fury when he saw the three of us lying there in Gwen's blood. "Is that fucker still in the house?"

"He ran as soon as Ricochet took the gun from Sean," Jordan told him.

I swiped a hand over my sister's hair, being as gentle as I could. "Rip. Could you come hold onto her?"

They were all here. I'd called Lock as soon as I'd hung up with Sean. Told them to call the cops and get here when they could. They'd beaten law enforcement. No shock there. It felt like hours had passed when, in reality, from the time I stepped through the door until now it had been just a few minutes.

Riptide sat down on Gwen's other side and rested her head in his lap. "I got her, Brother."

"Go search the house anyway," Lock ordered Hush, Butcher, and Toxic. "Find the kids. Don't…don't fucking scare them."

"I'll go with them," Hell offered. "They know me."

I gave my brothers a grateful look as I moved over to inspect Jordan. She had a nasty cut on her chin and her whole jaw was turning black and blue. "Did that fucker hit you?" It was clear he'd beaten on Gwen. I was just tallying up the injuries that he'd have to atone for.

"Grabbed my leg when I was going for the knife. I smacked my face on the counter," she told me with a wan smile.

Gently, I grabbed her face in both hands, tilting her head toward the light above. Her pupils weren't responding correctly. I was pretty sure she had a concussion.

"Priest. Go wait outside for the cops and the ambulances, and everyone put your fucking guns away. Last thing we need is a miscommunication with the police." Lockout told him. He squatted down next to me, putting a comforting hand on my shoulder. "Speaking of guns, are there any weapons I should take care of?"

"Trent's is over there," Jordan pointed to a corner. "It slid there when I tackled him."

"When you…tackled him." Lockout's lips twitched. "Thatta girl. We'll leave it there," he said. "It'll make it that much worse on him when the cops get here."

"Fuck the cops," I snarled, pissed off that this had happened. I'd had the guys watch over the houses last night, but I thought Trent's fixation landed solely with me. I hadn't really thought he'd go after my sister and his own damn kids.

Lockout's hand squeezed my shoulder hard. "No. Not fuck the cops," he said. He gave Jordan a considering look before he decided to speak in front of her. She was one of us now, and he made that determination in the moment. "You can't go after him."

"There's no fucking way I'm letting him get away with this."

"And he won't," Lockout said, "but *you* can't go after him. You'll kill him and after yesterday's brawl with him in the street, if anything happens to him you'll be the number one suspect. Think about it, Ricochet. Do you really want to spend the rest of your life behind bars?"

The look of fury was the only answer I needed before Lockout continued.

"You just stopped Sean from making the biggest mistake of his life. If you kill Trent, you go to jail. We won't be able to hide this one or protect you. Sean grows up not just with a scumbag father, he grows up without you. What do you think happens to him? What is his future after tonight without you there?"

That hit me like a knife to the gut. I knew he was right. Jack wouldn't see me through something like this just to blow it at the end. Gwen's injuries were bad, and Sean had a long road ahead to recover from this, but it was the end of the bad days. It was the beginning of a better life. I just needed not to fuck this last part up. I growled out a frustrated breath, but the anger from all of this was fading away. It'd never left me so quickly before. The red was trailing away like the glow of tail lights disappearing into the night. It left me clear headed, mostly. "Fine."

Lockout's brows shot up. "Good. We'll get these girls to the hospital, give the cops our statements, then figure out what to do about Trent."

Nodding, I shuffled around until my back was against the oven. It had a massive crack in the glass, making me wonder who had hit it. Pulling Jordan half onto my lap, I cradled her to me while her eyes fluttered closed. "Fine. But if those fucking ambulances take much longer, we're bringing them to the hospital ourselves."

Right about that time EMTs and cops flooded into the house. It wasn't easy for me to give my girl or my sister over to them, but I took that opportunity to scoop both Sean and Grace up into my arms. We watched as they loaded the women into the ambulance.

Lockout somehow got the cops to agree to interview us at the hospital, so I buckled the kids into Gwen's car. Hush got into the passenger seat next to me.

"Mind if I catch a ride?"

I shook my head and started the car. "Who's watching the club?"

"Dash, Bear, and George. They've got it under control," Hush replied. He gave me a long look. "You okay?"

Sucking in a deep, shuddering breath, I nodded. "Surprisingly, yeah." We sat in silence for a few moments before I looked in the rearview. Both kids were passed out in the back seat. "I almost lost them all, Hush." My voice cracked as I thought about what I'd nearly lost. "That would have been the final straw. I wouldn't have come back."

"But you didn't," he insisted, turning his head and staring straight at me. "They're here, alive, if not a little banged up. We'll get that fuckin' little prick and we'll make sure he never does this again."

"That's why I want to kill him. It's such a strong urge I'm fucking shaking from denying it." I held out one hand to show him. "I want to tear him apart."

"We all do. But if you do that, Ricochet, you'll lose your family anyway."

"I know that," I finally relented. "I knew it when Lockout told me. I know it now. I just don't fucking like it."

Hush chuckled. "You and me both, Kid."

We rode in silence for the rest of the trip to the hospital. All I wanted was to make sure my old lady and my sister were going to be okay. Then we'd deal with Trent. A plan began to form in my mind.

CHAPTER 32

Ricochet

My eyes were dry and scratchy the next morning when I woke up. I was sitting in a chair, hunched over Jordan's bed, holding her hand while I slept. Groaning, I stretched and the popping of my spine sent a wave of euphoria through me.

Jordan's eyes were closed as she rested, so I quietly made my way out into the hall. They'd kept her awake for most of the night as they kept an eye on her concussion, but around three in the morning, they'd finally let her get some sleep.

I'd bounced back and forth between her and Gwen's rooms. My brothers were spread out between each room, keeping an eye on things. Butcher was sitting on the floor, head back against the wall, mouth hanging open as he snored.

The nurses passing by kept eyeing all the men in the area and giggling. I had no idea how Lock had managed to convince the hospital staff not to kick them out after visiting hours were over, yet here they were. There was no way for me to describe the emotional storm building inside of me. These men meant everything in the world to me and knowing they were here by my side through all of this was a comfort I never thought I'd have.

I squeezed Lockout's shoulder as I went past. He and Hush were sitting in chairs on either side of Gwen's doorway. Two monsters standing watch, willing to kill anyone who came for her or her kids. Hush's arms were folded over his massive chest and his eyes were closed, but I knew he'd be at full alert if anything were to happen.

Looking up, I saw Smokehouse and Hellfire walking toward me holding cups of coffee. I took one gratefully.

"How's Jordan?" Hell asked.

"She's still sleeping. I want her to rest as long as she can. They said it was a pretty nasty concussion."

"The fact that she fought that asshole off even after sustainin' an injury like that is damn impressive," Hush rumbled, not bothering to open his eyes.

Pride for my old lady and her actions rushed through me. "Yeah. It is. She's fucking perfect."

The others chuckled, but no one disagreed with my statement.

"What's the plan?" Smoke asked, giving me a sly look before checking to see if Lock had seen. He still thought I was going to kill Trent.

As much as I wanted to, Lockout was right. I couldn't do that and risk being taken from my family. Not for my own sake, but I couldn't be the cause of more trauma for them. I needed to show Sean there was another way. "I actually have an idea," I said.

Lock's brows shot up. "Does it involve Trent breathing at the end?"

"Yes. Unfortunately," I added. "Though his breathing will come with some difficulty."

"Then I trust you to take care of it. Take as many brothers as you need."

"Smoke and Hell should do. I know most of the guys have their own old ladies to go home to, but-"

"We're staying here until you get back or they get released," Priest said as he walked up from behind us. "Then we'll be wherever they go from there."

"He's right," Lock replied. "We're not leaving them alone."

"Thank you." The relief was nearly overwhelming. "I'm going to call Jordan's parents, then we'll go deal with Trent." The last thing I wanted to do was speak to her parents for the first time and have to tell them that she was in the hospital, but it had to be done.

I went into Gwen's room and checked on my sister. Her face was a myriad of colorful bruises. "I'm so sorry I wasn't there for you."

"You were," she croaked, opening her eyes. "You saved Sean."

Brushing my hand over her hair, I shook my head. "I was almost too late."

"But you weren't. Your girl was there for us. She's an extension of you now," Gwen said with a small smile. There was pain in her eyes, but I was so grateful she was still here with me.

"I love you, Gwenny. I have something to take care of, but then I'll be back."

Worry flooded her gaze. "Gage, don't. Just let the cops handle it."

"Trent will be alive to go into custody, I promise."

She narrowed her eyes. "You didn't say he'd be unharmed."

"No, I didn't." Grinning at her, I leaned in and placed a gentle kiss on her forehead. I turned and found Sean watching me. We'd already talked a few times throughout the night. He was doing okay. As good as could be expected.

"Hi," he said as I came over and sat next to him. Grace was curled up in a recliner, asleep.

"Hey, Bud. Do you still have Jordan's cell?"

He shifted and dug in his pocket before handing the phone over. "I figured I'd watch over it for her."

"Thanks for that," I told him. "I'm going to call her family now that visiting hours are open again."

Walking back out into the hall, I opened her contacts and frowned. Did I press the number entitled Dad, or Mom? Making a decision, I called her father.

"Jordan? You're late for work. I've been trying to call you. Are you okay?" A man's worried voice peppered all that at me before I had a chance to speak.

"Hello, Sir. My name is Ricochet." There was a brief silence while he processed why his daughter's boyfriend might be calling him instead of her, so I continued. "I don't want to worry you; Jordan is mostly okay. There was a break in at my sister's house and Jordan fought off an attacker."

"Jesus. What do you mean by 'mostly okay', Son?"

"She has a pretty severe concussion and some bruising on her face, wrist, and legs," I told him. "Otherwise, she's okay."

He blew out a calming breath. "And Gwen and the kids? Are they okay, too?"

"It was Gwen's ex," I told him. "I wasn't home and he broke in and attacked my sister. She's pretty banged up, but they'll both be released today according to doctors. If it wasn't for Jordan-" I broke off and swallowed hard.

"Trent is a dead man," he growled into the phone.

I couldn't help the grin that formed on my lips. "I think you and I are going to get along just fine."

"The name's Leo. Which hospital are you at?"

I gave him the name and answered a few more questions. "It's highly likely that I won't be here when you arrive," I warned him.

"Good. Go take care of that piece of shit."

"I plan to."

Hanging up, I put the phone on Jordan's bedside table while I checked in on her. Her beautiful eyes opened. "You're leaving."

"Only for a little while," I told her, cupping her cheek gently.

"Trent?"

"That's why I have to go."

She frowned. "You stopped Sean from killing him."

"Don't worry, Sunshine. As much as I want to, I'm not killing him either. I have something much better in mind."

She nodded in understanding. "I'm worried the cops won't be able to hold him," she admitted. "That she will be in more danger."

Sighing, I leaned down and brushed my lips over hers. "I promise you, he's not slipping through the system. Not this time. His connections are going to work against him."

"I trust you, Ricochet. I'm so sorry that I-"

"Don't," I told her, silencing her apology. "We can talk about it later. When you're feeling better. But just so you know, there's nothing to apologize for. I owe you the apology."

Her expression softened. "We'll talk later."

"I called your parents. They should be here soon to sit with you."

"Oh," her eyes widened, "they must be so worried."

"I explained everything to your dad. Until they get here, Riptide, Butcher, and Toxic will be sitting with you. Feel free to ignore them and sleep," I told her as they came into the room.

"Just no snoring," Butcher told her with a grin.

I kissed her again and left her in the capable hands of my brothers. It wasn't easy, but we needed to catch up with Trent before he skipped town or was able to shore up some kind of alibi.

"Do you know where he is?" Smoke asked, as he and Hell fell into step beside me.

Everyone moved out of our way, giving us uneasy looks as we walked toward the elevator. "Best place to start is his apartment. Gwen told me the address."

"What's the plan once we get there?" Hell asked.

"We could add a few more bruises to his face. Though, between you and Jordan, I bet he's looking pretty worse for wear. But I know you told Lock you weren't going to kill him," Smoke said under his breath as we got down to the main floor of the hospital. The last thing we needed was people over hearing us talking about killing someone. As it was, it'd taken hours last night before the cops had been satisfied and left.

"We'll see what happens once we find him," I replied. "I need the two of you to be the level headed ones today."

"Shit," Smoke spit out.

"Maybe you should have brought Rip and Hush," Hell said with a laugh. "We're not really known for our patience."

I gave him a long look until he admitted, "Okay, fine. The two of you aren't known for your patience. I'm a fucking saint."

"Saint my ass," Smoke said with a snort. "But you do have better control of your temper."

Relaying the plan to them while I started up Gwen's car, I shrugged. "Figure it's worth a shot."

"It's a damn good plan," Hell replied. "Let's go catch us a dirtbag."

CHAPTER 33

Ricochet

My foot slammed against the door, ripping the deadbolt and lock apart, sending the door crashing open into Trent's apartment. I stepped in casually, as if shattering a door was a normal way to enter a building. "Oh Trent, come out and play!" I said in a sing-song voice. Smokehouse snickered from behind me.

Trent had been sitting on his couch. He shot up as I strolled in, Smokehouse and Hellfire at my back. "What the fuck do you think you're doing?!" he yelled.

I stopped a few feet past the entrance and surveyed him. He was standing there in his underwear, disgusting tighty-whities. I glanced down at the coffee table in front of him. There were lines of coke laid out, a mess now since he had hit the table when he jumped up. He was holding a card in his hand and had power under a reddened nose. Literally, caught him in the act.

"What in the fuck are you even supposed to be? Besides a useless piece of shit?" I stared condescendingly at the man who'd attacked my family last night. This was the man that had caused so much trauma, nearly killed my sister, and almost forced his own son to kill him. And this was all he was? A strung out cokehead. I shook my head, disgusted with him.

"Get the fuck out of my house. You just don't fucking learn do you, Gage? Get out or you'll be identical to your twin sister, I'll make sure of it." He was pointing at me as if to threaten, but his hand was starting to shake.

I narrowed my eyes on him and silently counted to ten in my head, calming the rage and ensuring that I stuck with the plan. When I reached ten I spoke. "You know, Trent, a few days ago I would have killed you for talking shit. Still tempted to, if I'm being honest." I started to walk toward him. He backed away, stumbling over the mess on the floor.

"I'm serious, don't fuck with me right now."

"I'm serious, too," I snapped at him. "So serious I brought my friends to make sure I didn't give in to temptation and wring your scrawny, pathetic neck." I pointed my thumb over my shoulder. "Thing is, I made a promise to the people I care about. Do you have those Trent? People you care about? People who you love so much that you *won't* kill a piece of human garbage, because doing so would send you to jail, breaking their hearts? I do, Trent. I have people that I love, the same people that *you* should have loved. I won't ruin their lives any further by ending up in jail. I'm not going to jail over you, Trent. You, however, are."

Trent wiped his nose and sniffed hard, amping himself up. "Fuck that. I work for the DA. I fix his problems. He wouldn't dare arrest me, I know too much."

"Wanna bet?" I asked, a smile tugging at my lips.

Trent was done arguing, he charged at me. I stuck my left arm out, catching his shoulder while simultaneously bringing my right arm up and over in a vertical haymaker. I caught the side of his face with my fist, sending him slamming to the ground with a satisfying crunch of bone. I looked at him, limp on the floor. "Come on Trent, I said I wasn't going to kill you, I didn't say I wouldn't fuck you up. Get up. Do better, you coked up loser."

Trent shoved off the ground and lunged again, wrapping his arms around my waist. I grabbed his head with both hands and drove my knee into his face. Another crunch. He must have a broken nose and jaw by now. This felt good. He might not be feeling the pain now, thanks to the drugs, but when he sobered up, it would be painful. That's what I wanted, to give him a small taste of what Gwen and Jordan were feeling.

This time he didn't get up. Smoke was already wiping off any surfaces that I went near. We knew better than to get our prints all over the place. Nodding, I said. "Alright. Since he's down and out, let's go to the next phase of the plan."

We tied his hands and feet together, gagged him and shoved him into the trunk of Gwen's car. I shut the door behind us, leaving it unlocked. Why would I make it harder for the cops when they eventually got here?

***

The ride to the DA's office only took a few minutes. It was located downtown, which made the next part harder. We had to roll Trent into a tarp to make sure that no one saw us going in with him. Explaining why I was carrying an almost naked, beaten half to death coke head was not something I needed right now.

Getting into the building was easier than I thought it would be. Smokehouse just looked at the secretary at the door and said, "We're here to see DA Fremont, we're his painters," and kept walking right past her. The secretary's eyes bugged out of her head when she saw three large, tattooed, men walking past her desk. I wasn't sure she even heard Smoke's excuse.

"Uh…um…do you have an appoint- Hey! You can't go in there!" By the time she got around the desk we were shutting ourselves inside the DA's office.

He didn't even blink when he saw us. "I'm going to have to call you back," he said into the phone before setting the handset back into the cradle on the desk in front of him. "Gentlemen." His blue eyes were shrewd, cool. Nothing shook this man.

I dropped Trent on the ground, letting him unroll from the tarp. He groaned when he hit the ground, but was still unconscious. Smoke rolled the tarp back up to take with us when we left.

Walking over, I plopped down in the chair across from Fremont. "Name's Gage Barrett." Recognition flashed in his eyes. "I see you've heard of me." I leaned forward, my elbows on my knees as my gaze bore into his. "Well, we have a problem."

"What kind of problem?" He stared down at his assistant as though that didn't necessarily constitute an issue for him.

"Trent Baker." I pointed to him.

Fremont spared another unamused glance, then looked back at me "What about him?"

"He's going to be arrested soon. Arrested for possession of cocaine. Arrested for domestic violence. For nearly beating his ex-wife to death," I said, eyes locked onto him.

"Wanna bet?" he replied, unblinkingly.

I sat back and stretched my arm over the chair. "You see, somehow I knew you'd say that. Didn't I say that would be his response, guys?"

Smokehouse and Hellfire acknowledged at the same time. "Sure did."

"I know Trent is some kind of lackey for you. Maybe he's a fixer, or he obtains or plants evidence as needed. I really don't care about the details. I don't care about your political ambitions or what dirty deeds you have going on. What I care about is my family. My sister, her kids, my future wife.

Trent tried to kill them. I'm giving you the opportunity to make it right. And you can further elevate your career in the process."

His eyebrow raised at this. "I'm listening."

"You're another of the generic 'tough on crime' DAs. You're going to lean into that, hard. When you discover that your own assistant was using and distributing coke, that he was a woman abuser, that he nearly killed his ex-wife, well, you *had* to act.

You won't tolerate that from anyone, especially not in your own back yard." Here I leaned forward again. "That's why when he came crawling into your office, demanding help and threatening you, you personally oversaw his arrest." We both looked at Trent, neither one of us impressed with what we saw. I continued, "And why you'll also head up the prosecution. Conflict of interest be damned, you'll personally see justice served. You'll ensure the maximum sentence. And finally, you'll ensure that he ends up in the General Population of the prison, where they treat women beaters with extra love."

I smiled at the thought of Trent being beaten every day in prison before adding, "Because the alternative would be a disaster. A DA trying to cover for his own staff. Who was caught with enough cocaine to kill a herd of elephants. A staff member who beat his ex-wife so badly she nearly died? The media would crucify you. I can guarantee that."

Fremont looked at Trent and sighed, then turned to me. "You leave me with a bit of a problem. Trent was a very useful assistant. And he knows…things I don't want known."

Was a useful assistant. I thought. *You've already given up on him.* "Sounds like putting him in Gen Pop works for both of us then." Neither of us would say it out loud, but Trent's odds of survival in Gen Pop were about zero. And that's without the DA bribing someone in the prison to make sure of it. The problem was just about resolved.

"True enough," Fremont said. "This still leaves me needing to replace a…formerly reliable asset. I'll not forget the burden you placed on me."

"I would expect nothing less." With that, I stood up and walked between Smokehouse and Hellfire, who fell in line behind me. We walked out without saying another word until we were back at Gwen's car.

"You think it worked?" Hellfire asked.

"Oh yeah, Trent's done for." I said. A malicious smile crossed my face. If I couldn't kill him personally, this was the next best thing.

"What about that last part, what did he mean by 'won't forget'," Smoke asked.

"It means that the drama isn't over. Lockout expected as much, Fremont confirmed it. But that's tomorrow's problem. We have better things to do until then.

CHAPTER 34

Jordan

My head ached fiercely, but I kept it to myself. My family was sitting around my bedside talking with Butcher and Toxic, and I didn't want it to stop.

Laughing made my head throb, but I was now convinced you couldn't do anything else with these two around. The rest of the guys were moving in between Gwen's and my rooms. Having them there made me feel so much better, but I wasn't going to relax until Ricochet got back. My insides were twisted up with nerves over what might happen when they confronted Trent.

"How you feeling, Pumpkin?" Dad asked.

Glancing over, I realized he'd been watching me while I'd watched everyone else. "I'm okay," I told him with a weak smile.

"You're hurting."

"A bit," I admitted. I knew it wasn't nearly as bad as poor Gwen, so I didn't want to complain.

"We're so proud of you," Mom interjected, her eyes filling with tears. "You saved them."

I let out a small laugh. "I only distracted him, if I'm being honest. Ricochet and these guys showing up is what scared him off."

"Well, we're so glad you and Gwen and the kids are all okay. And we're grateful to all of you for watching over them," Dad said, turning his eyes to Butcher and Toxic.

"It's what we do for family," Butcher said with a shrug.

"Family..." Mom replied, looking over at me with a hopeful smile.

"Yeah, once Jordan became Ricochet's old lady-" he paused when he caught my expression, then glanced at my mother.

Her hands were clasped together and she was tearing up again. "Oh, when do we get to meet him? It's been too long since you've had a boyfriend. I was getting worried that you'd end up alone out in that big house."

Toxic bit the insides of his lips, giving me an apologetic look as he tried to smother his laughter.

"I'm twenty-five, Mom," I told her with a laugh. "Hardly a dried up old spinster."

"Yeah," Mallory said, "besides I'm twenty-five and still ringless. Just because you have a guy doesn't mean anything." She gave Noah a look of mock disdain.

We all laughed at that, especially because my family knew Noah had something special planned for Mallory coming up soon. My brother grimaced, his eyes pleading with us not to spill the beans.

"True," Mom said, sounding a bit strangled because it ruined her perfectly good speech to have to admit such a thing.

"Don't worry, Mom," I said, patting her hand. "At least you have Haze as a grandchild."

She scowled at me. "Don't even joke," she muttered.

"Haze?" Toxic asked.

Grabbing my phone, I pulled up a picture and showed him.

"That's a fucking bird," he said with a laugh. "What the hell are you doing with a hawk?"

That started a conversation that both me and the rest of my family could talk on for hours. The other guys joined us, listening in about how we hunt with our hawks.

Word must have spread because Kit, Seek, Sloane, Jenny, and the other old ladies showed up. They were taking turns holding Grace and snuggling her close, while Sean talked with Riptide about something to do with technology.

The air in the room was relaxed as my family and Ricochet's all sat speaking together.

"Who's throwing a party?"

We all looked up as Smokehouse and Hellfire came into the room. I searched behind them, looking for Ricochet, wondering where he was.

"He's checking in on Gwen for a moment," Hell told me, as he came over and sat down near me and Jenna.

Jenna's eyes widened as she took in the huge man with all his tattoos, beard, and leather cut. Her eyes darted over to me and I had to bite back a laugh because I knew my fourteen-year-old sister was already half in love. At least she hadn't picked Smokehouse.

"Hi," Jenna said, fluttering her lashes dramatically.

Hell didn't notice a thing. "Hey, Kid."

Cocking my head, I watched as his gaze tracked the room, landing on Kit. Jenna was chatting with him and he was holding up his end of the conversation, but his eyes always ended up back on my friend. One side of my mouth kicked up into a smile.

Suddenly people started making excuses about leaving my room and once the crowd parted, I saw why. Ricochet was making his way inside.

"Is it taken care of?" Lockout asked him. At Ricochet's nod, Lockout slapped him between the shoulder blades and left, taking his bikers with him.

It happened so quickly my head swam, or maybe that was the concussion, but soon it was just my family in here with my boyfriend. I glanced over at my mom and sighed. I could already hear her making to-do lists for the wedding. There were practically hearts in her eyes. It wasn't just me. She'd been harping at Noah to lock down his girl for years now. She just wanted more sons and daughters through marriage and she was practically dying to get her hands on some grandbabies.

Not that any of us were ready for that step. Remembering what Ricochet had said about kids made my cheeks heat, and I tried to shove that memory out of my mind. This wasn't the time to be thinking about it. "Everyone, this is Ricochet. He's my…boyfriend."

The quick discussion we'd had before he'd left my hospital room gave me hope that the fight we'd gotten in hadn't ruined the relationship. I sure hoped it hadn't. With everything that had happened over the last few days, I now realized that Ricochet wasn't Dan. He wasn't going to ever make the kind of mistakes that Dan had.

"Why don't we give these two a chance to talk?" Dad suggested, and I gave him a grateful look as he steered my mother out of the room.

She was still talking to Ricochet. "You'll come over for dinner," she declared.

Ricochet laughed. "I'd love to, Mrs.-"

"Call me Carol," she insisted. "Or better yet, Mom."

I groaned in embarrassment, but deep down I loved how accepting she and my dad were. *They're going to love him as much as I do.*

That thought made me freeze as he walked over. When had that happened? Oh yeah, probably when he was saving my life. But in all reality, I'd been falling for him longer than that. The man had ruthlessly pursued me. It was hard not to give in when he made me his sole focus like that.

He sat next to me and grabbed my hand. "How are you feeling, Sunshine?"

"I'm okay. How's Gwen?"

"Awake and trying to eat some of the hospital food," he said with a grin.

Wincing, I motioned to where the plate of food was sitting down on the ground, untouched. "Not even Butcher or Toxic wanted to eat it."

"I'll get you something delicious on the way home," he promised.

"What happened with Trent?" I really wanted to know, but I was also nervous to talk about the elephant in the room.

Ricochet walked me through his talk with the DA. "There's no way he's going to be able to slip out of any kind of punishment. The DA is overseeing the arrest personally."

"Strung out on coke, that explains the erratic behavior." I shook my head. "He was acting bat shit crazy. Crazier every time."

Ricochet chuckled. "That's the truth."

Sighing, I pulled on my big girl panties, metaphorically of course, and met his gaze. "I'm so sorry for how I acted the other night. It wasn't fair to leave you standing there like that."

"I get it, Sunshine. You were scared. You have every right to be. I'm known for my temper and not controlling it very well."

"You did, though," I insisted. "I don't know very many people who would have lasted as long without getting pissed at Trent. He deserved the beating you gave him."

"What happened, with you I mean. Why did you run off?"

"It was sort of like I was right back in that bar with Dan taunting those guys and then Dad getting hurt. I know it sounds stupid, but I was terrified that you were going to get injured and then I just sort of freaked out." I gave him a wan smile. "It was stupid."

"No," he said, shaking his head. "I actually understand exactly what you mean. That happens to me a lot thanks to my PTSD."

"Really?"

Irritation swept over his features. "Yeah, I swear I've relived that night in Afghanistan more times than I can count. Though it's happening a little less frequently now." He squeezed my hand. "I'll try to be better about controlling my temper, but I'm never going to let some asshole threaten you, or speak badly to you without there being some kind of consequence."

"I think I can learn to live with that. Who knows maybe I'll end up some bad biker bitch and will beat up some woman for trying to take you from me." Giving him a wide grin, I laughed at that idea. It was ridiculous.

"My money would be on you, Sunshine," he said, lifting his hand to brush his thumb over the bruise on my jaw. He was careful not to touch the split in the skin, or hurt me in any way. "You just proved you know how to handle yourself."

Scoffing at that idea, I shook my head. "If I never have to be in a fight again, I'll be happy. That was crazy. I was honestly just trying to survive."

"And you did. And you saved my sister and my nephew and niece. I'll never be able to repay you for that." He lowered his forehead to mine. "I'll never be able to thank you enough for what you do for me each day."

"What I do for you?" I asked in confusion.

"You make this life worth living," he confessed.

The breath caught in my throat as he lifted his head and searched my gaze. "I love you, Ricochet." My eyes widened as I realized that those words had just popped, unbidden, out of my mouth.

He was just watching me, possessiveness and heat creeping into his eyes. "Can't take it back now," he teased, his voice rough. "I love you too, Sunshine."

His mouth slanted over mine and I sank into the kiss. This was where I belonged, with him. He made me so happy and looking back on it, I'd only been existing for the last few years. Maybe I'd just been waiting for him. Either way, we were together now and I wasn't going to let my stupid hang ups ruin what we had. That didn't mean I wouldn't mess up again. I probably would. He definitely would, but we'd work through it together.

I sighed in contentment as he crawled onto the bed next to me and held me until I fell asleep.

CHAPTER 35

Ricochet

"We're having a barbeque today. Bring your old lady down," Lockout told me.

Sidestepping his jab, I frowned. "Why am I just hearing about the barbeque now?"

It'd been a few days since the attack and Trent's subsequent arrest. Everything was settling down and going back to normal. Still, we'd set up a rotation at the girls' homes. When I wasn't there, one of my brothers was. I wasn't going to be able to relax fully for a while. It didn't matter that Trent had been transferred to the state penitentiary in Florence. An hour's drive away wasn't nearly enough for my peace of mind. We wouldn't need to keep the guard up much longer. Trent was being housed in Gen Pop, just as I had advised the DA to do. He wouldn't be around for much longer.

I threw a jab, testing Lock's reflexes and focus as we circled each other inside the boxing ring. He'd put this thing in a few years ago and it was by far the best investment the club has ever made. All of us used it on a regular basis.

"It was sort of last minute. Listen, some Army friends of mine are swinging through town. I convinced them to stay for a day, catch up. Turns out Hush and Toxic know them, too, so we decided to make one big party of it. You should be here. It will be good for you. Trust me."

Since this whole thing started Lockout had been good about giving me space. He hadn't pushed me at all. This was the first time he was really trying to get me to do anything, and I couldn't help but feel the pull from him. It was an easy way to show my support, especially after all the help all of my brothers had given me. "Okay. We'll be there."

Things with Jordan were slowly getting back to normal. We'd talked a few more times about expectations around emergency situations. She knew now that if I felt there was any kind of threat to her safety, I would handle it in the way I deemed best. She agreed to that and also laid down her own rules. Mostly, that she was going to try to get me to shake things off and not fight as much as possible. She wouldn't be successful every time, but knowing how much she disliked it, I was willing to do my best for her. Unless necessary, I planned to keep the fighting to the inside of this boxing ring. That is, unless we were out on missions.

"Good, looking forward to it. They should be here around six."

"Perfect," I muttered, barely missing a haymaker. His glove swung past my face so hard the wind ruffled my hair.

"You're not paying attention," he said with a grin.

Laughing, I went in low and landed a solid strike on his side, then blocked his return hit to the side of my head before moving back. "Can't have the old man beating me." I grunted as his hit landed this time.

"Fuck," he muttered, glowering at me. "Just because I'm turning forty this year doesn't make me old, asshole."

"True. That's still Hush's title."

"Shut the fuck up!" Hush called from the sidelines where the others were watching.

Lockout and I both laughed as the buzzer went off, ending our session. I had to admit it was nice to be wanted back in the club. Not that my brothers had ever given me cause to think I was unwelcome. That was something I did to myself.

Tapping my gloves on Lock's, I left the ring. Every brother who was standing around watching or waiting for their turn said goodbye to me and for once, I acknowledged them all. Gone were the days where I just slunk through life like a kicked dog.

Sure, the nightmares still woke me at night. That would likely always be a thing, but having my life back in my waking hours was worth any price. The flashbacks were more manageable, and for once I was looking forward to the future instead of immersed in the past. Butcher had been right. I was living for today and the future now. Jordan had given me that.

The drive back to my sister's place didn't take long. Once she was healed up and the kids were in the right headspace, I'd likely be moving back into the clubhouse. It was going to be quite a bit different than living next door to my old lady, but I was hoping I could charm her into moving in with me eventually. It meant I'd have to get a bigger space at the club, but Lock had plenty of apartments. The dorm style rooms had always just worked for me in the past and I'd had no need for more space. Now I did.

I walked over to Jordan's house. Better to do this in person. I knocked on the door and waited.

She opened the door and leaned against the frame, giving me a seductive look. "Hey," she said.

"Hey." I reached forward and brushed my thumb over the bruise on her jaw. It was lightening up, but was still very noticeable. It was a badge of courage and a reminder to me of what I could have lost. "There's a barbeque at the club tonight, just club members and a few special guests. Some of the guys' Army buddies are coming through town so Lockout is throwing a party. Just the guys and their old ladies. I'd like you to come with."

"That sounds like fun," she hesitated, her eyes darting over to Gwen's house, "but what about your sister?"

"Don't worry about her. I have another friend who's going to be looking after her and the kids tonight." Gwen was healing up too, but it was still painful for her to move around thanks to some broken ribs. I'd been helping out as much as I could with everything, and when I couldn't, Jordan was there. The sound of an engine roaring filled the air and I grinned. "There he is now."

"Well, that's something I didn't expect to see." Jordan crossed her arms over her chest and grinned.

Looking over my shoulder, I saw Static, still in his suit, getting off his bike. "Yeah. He's fucking fancy."

"He's handsome." My glare made her laugh. "For an older man. Don't worry, I already have my old man." She pushed off the doorframe and wrapped one arm around me. The other tugged on my neck, silently asking me to bend enough to kiss her.

Everything about her was intoxicating. Her scent, her taste, the way her body wrapped around mine. I wanted to bring her into the house and show her exactly what she meant to me. I groaned against her mouth. "We're going to be late. Go get dressed." I forced myself to let her go. When she turned, I slapped her ass, chuckling at her squeal of indignation.

Leaving her to dress, I walked over and shook hands with Static. We didn't know each other well, but he knew Lock and Rip and he'd helped the club out a few times. According to what I'd heard, if he had accepted back when Lock took over the club, Static would have been our VP. I was glad things had played out the way they had. Riptide was the perfect VP for us. He was laid back, but he got shit done. When Lockout was working with all cylinders firing and burning the candle at both ends, which he did far too often, Rip was there to take some of the burden from him. Lockout was the classic overachiever and Riptide was the surfer guy who just barely made it on time anywhere. Somehow they evened each other out and made each other better.

Add in Hush and Priest and the rest and we had the perfect set of officers for our club. It ran like a well-oiled machine thanks to them. That didn't mean that Static wouldn't ever have a place. I was pretty sure Lock was trying to talk him into joining. It would mean prospecting, though, and I wasn't sure the lawyer's ego could handle that.

"Thanks for doing this, Static."

"No problem. I'm happy to help. I was sorry to hear what happened to your sister. How's she doing?" His intense blue eyes were on mine. Everything about him radiated intensity. I understood living in that state of mind. It was only recently that I'd been able to take a step back and breathe.

"Better, though she still needs help with things. Come on, let's go introduce you to her and the kids."

He followed me into the house and we found Gwen and her kids wrapped up in a blanket on the couch, eating popcorn and watching a kids' movie.

"Gwen, this is Static. Static, my sister, and her son, Sean. And this little angel," I said, while catching Grace up in my arms as she rushed up, "is Grace."

"Nice to meet you," Static told her.

Grace gave him a shy smile. "Nice to meet you," she parroted.

"Static is going to be hanging out with you guys tonight, okay?" Glancing over at Sean, I arched a brow. He'd been nervous about having a man around he didn't know. He'd grown accustomed to my brothers, though, and I knew he'd do fine with Static. Sean gave a nod of agreement.

"That's a pretty suit," Grace told him.

"Thank you." Static looked amused, but his eyes kept drifting over toward Gwen.

I wasn't sure if it was because of all the bruises and cuts, or something else. I sure as fuck hoped he was just pissed about the state she was in. I wasn't sure I was ready for my sister to be in a relationship. Hell, she probably wasn't ready.

"Hi," she said, tone quiet, but the smile she gave him was friendly as Static sat down in the recliner.

I settled on the couch with Grace, and by the time I left, the anxiety and unease had fled the room. Grace helped with that. She was open and cheerful. It was a permanent state for her.

Twenty minutes later we were on my bike and heading over to the club. I grabbed Jordan's hand and held it in mine as I drove. Everything that had gone down had just shown both of us how much we loved each other, and how one stupid fight wasn't worth losing the good thing we were building. I was grateful for that, though I wished none of them had to go through the shit show that Trent brought to our door.

We walked through the door of the club and the first thing I noticed was how bright it was in there. Had it always been like this? The permanent shadows that seemed to overtake my life had slithered off into nothingness somewhere along the line.

Toxic was hanging out near the entrance. He walked over and bumped our knuckles together. "Glad you made it, Brother. Good to see you, too," he said, turning to Jordan. He gave her a sly grin. Jordan blushed, then narrowed her eyes at him. She wasn't about to talk about seeing him naked, which I was grateful for. It had been bad enough that it'd happened, I didn't need the reminder that my old lady had seen some of my brothers bare assed.

"Everyone's in the bar." Toxic led us to the bar where everyone was gathered. "Hey Shep, look who I found."

Sitting at a table, surrounded by everyone, were the last two people I had expected to see in here. My jaw dropped and I stood there in stunned silence for a few heartbeats before shaking off my immobility. "Chief Sheppard? Captain Walker?" The words fell out of my mouth before I knew I was saying them. Sheppard stood up from the bar and walked around, shaking my hand before pulling me into a bro hug.

"Don't be so formal. I'm retired now. It's just Mark and Jen." His smile was infectious, I was grinning, in fact my smile was so large it was hurting my damn face. "We want you to meet someone."

Jen was standing slowly. Wrapped in her arms was a happy, giggling baby. "Ricochet, meet Tyler. Tyler Gage Sheppard," Jen said with a smile.

My mouth opened and closed several times but nothing was coming out. Jordan nudged me in the ribs, snapping me back to reality. I left Mark standing near Jordan and approached Jen and Tyler. "Could I..."

"Of course!" She plopped Tyler in my arms so fast, it startled both me and the baby.

He studied me with inquisitive blue eyes before he gave me a drool soaked smile. I bounced him and looked back at Jen. "I can't believe you guys are here."

"Don't you look fucking natural holding that kid," Smokehouse said with a laugh as he and some of the others walked up. "Ready to have some of your own?"

"Damn right I am," I told him, my gaze sliding over to Jordan. Her cheeks were pink and she was staring wide eyed at me, as though she couldn't believe I was saying this in front of the others.

"Better you than me, Bro," Smoke said, leaning in to tickle Tyler under the chin. "I'm staying far away from the likes of you," he cooed.

"Can't believe you don't already have twenty the way you whore around," Hush said with a laugh.

Smoke joined right in. He loved the ladies and they were infatuated with him. "You know how it is."

Looking over as Lockout walked up, I shook my head in amazement. "What are the odds that you all know each other?"

"Deployment is a small place," Lock said, handing Jordan a beer. "You know that."

"True. Also, Mark, Jen, this is Jordan. Jordan, Mark and Jen were in Afghanistan at the same time I was. They helped me out when I was in a spot of trouble."

Mark grasped my shoulder and squeezed as I handed Tyler back to Jen. "He's got it backward. He saved my ass when *I* got into a spot of trouble."

We all sat at the nearby tables while Mark went through the story. He and Jen were both pilots. He flew Apache attack helicopters and she flew Black Hawks, for MEDEVAC and search and rescue. Up until today I had no idea that they were in a relationship.

His helicopter had some malfunction that had caused him to crash land in hostile territory. I was with Jen in the chow hall when she got the news. I didn't have time to call back to my command, I just followed her out of the chow hall and into her helicopter. Together, with her team, we went out into the desert and found Mark and his copilot.

"So Jen flies in right above us, Artie and I grab onto the hoist cable and up we go, Jen flying out of there like a bat out of hell. Imagine my surprise when we get into the bird and we see this guy behind a machine gun."

"Well, I owed you." I told him. Shep smiled and gave a subtle nod. He could see the appreciation in my eyes. Shaking off the downer mood, I pointed to little Tyler. "So what's the rest of the story?"

Jen answered. "When the deployment was over Mark put in his retirement papers, then we got married and well…" She held up Tyler as evidence. "Really Ricochet, I don't know that I can ever thank you enough for that day." Her eyes were so bright and full of love, I knew she meant it. And I was thankful I'd been there to help.

Without Shep, I might not have been. Then who knew what would have happened to him and Jen during that incident. She and I had fended off insurgents together on the ground while we searched for Mark and his co-pilot. It all came around full circle and I just chalked it up to the fact that we were meant to have met each other.

Maybe Jack had sent Shep to me. Who knew? I didn't really believe in all that occult and ghost shit, but after seeing Jack that night with Sean, I wasn't ruling anything out. I'd talked to Hush about it later, since he'd mentioned once before that he'd sworn he'd seen his late wife. I tried to play it off, but Hush had just shrugged and said something along the lines of, "Fuck if I know what's really out there. Far be it for me to turn away help." Then he'd gone back to drinking his beer.

I decided then and there to take a page out of his book. Likely, it was just my memories clashing with reality, like they often did, but this time had seemed different. I wanted to believe it was. That Jack was helping me out, yet again. A band of emotion squeezed around my heart. The things I owed to that man were immeasurable. It was time to do what I should have done long ago. But first, I was going to spend a fun night with my brothers, their old ladies, and the woman I loved.

Toxic and Hush stole Mark and Jen away to tell more war stories, apparently Hush had saved Mark once as well. Deployment created an unbreakable bond for those of us lucky enough to have met each other a half a world away.

Jordan and I sat back as the convo moved across the room. She grabbed my hand, getting my attention. "You told Mark that you owed him, what did you mean?"

There was no holding back now, not if I wanted to keep her. "I met Mark after the darkest night of my life. It was right after my best friend and teammate Jack had been killed.

"Between Jack being killed because of me, and having killed a kid, I was spiraling bad. I was ready to shoot myself. Literally. I couldn't face my team, couldn't face Jack's family, I felt I had let them down and didn't deserve their help. I didn't dare ask for any. I hid myself from my team to stop them from trying. And even though I'd talked to Gwen, I was still struggling. I'd made her a promise, but I wasn't sure I could keep it. I was in the chow hall, sort of a last meal, but really a last ditch effort before I…gave in. I saw Mark at a table with his crew and well, there was something there in his eyes. It was a look I recognized."

Emotion flashed over Jordan's face and her eyes filled with tears, but she didn't stop me, so I continued, "Crazy thing is, he recognized it in mine, too. He invited me over to their table, so I went. And little by little, I talked about what had happened. I'm not really the type to lay my troubles on the table, but he was just… He knew. He knew somehow that I was hanging on by a thread. He stayed there with me until well after the chow hall had closed. But by the end of it, I was stable. I was still wracked with guilt, but he'd talked me off the ledge. I think he would have sat there with me all night if I'd needed it. Without him, I wouldn't be here today." There were many sitting around these tables who'd done the same in the months and years afterward, but he'd started it all.

"Looks like I owe him a debt of gratitude, too," Jordan said. Her voice was thick with tears. "Look at those people in there, Ricochet. Look at the lives they're leading, that baby. It's because of you. That guilt you were carrying; you don't deserve it. You've been hanging onto it so tightly that you don't realize all the good you've done; the lives you've *saved*. You're a good man, you deserve your own happiness."

I pulled her into my lap and kissed her, fucking grateful for her, and for all the people surrounding me. Somehow, I had every single person who I owed my life to in one room. It was a cleansing for a darkened soul and I'd never felt so light.

CHAPTER 36

Jordan

I woke as Ricochet picked me up off the couch. My bleary eyes opened and I saw the other men picking up their old ladies as well. The party had gone on into the early morning hours and Seek, Kit, Jenny, Sloane, and I had all fallen asleep on the uncomfortable sectional of couches and chairs the guys had in the rec area.

Rubbing my eyes, I smiled as I saw Hush holding Seek close as they went upstairs. The smile turned wicked as I saw Smokehouse toss his sister over his shoulder and head out toward the parking lot, with Hellfire in tow. "What's the deal there?"

Ricochet looked down at me, then over his shoulder. When his eyes met mine again we were grinning at each other. "You see that, too?"

"How could I not?" Hellfire hadn't been more than a few steps away from Kit all night.

He chuckled. "You're observant, Sunshine. Most haven't picked up on that yet."

"I won't say anything," I replied, stifling a yawn with my hand.

"Stay with me tonight," he whispered into my ear.

His husky growl sent shivers racing down my spine. I wrapped my arms around his neck. "I'm not going anywhere."

"Good."

"What about Gwen and the kids?" I asked as he ascended the staircase with me in his muscular arms. My inner girl swooned at the fact that he was so easily carrying me from place to place.

"I called Static. He's staying overnight."

There was a tightness in his tone that worried me. I searched his face. "What's wrong?"

"Nothing. Just not sure I cared for the way he was looking at Gwen."

A slow smile formed on my lips. "He's not part of the MC, right?"

"Not yet."

"And how was he…looking at her?"

He gave me a playful scowl. "No matchmaking. I think we all need a break for a little while."

"Gwen's been on a break for years," I reminded him. "Trent doesn't count."

He grunted, then shut us up inside his room. "Can we please stop talking about my sister, so I can do this…"

His lips trailed over my neck, making goosebumps rise on my skin. "You don't need to ask me twice," I told him, tipping my head to the side to give him more access.

"No?"

I hummed out an answer as my eyes drifted shut. We were on his bed and I was wrapped up in his muscular arms. There was nowhere safer for me and it allowed me to drop my guard fully. This man loved me and wanted to marry me. I would do anything for him. And tonight, I wanted to make him feel as good as he did me.

Squirming out of his grip, I straddled his hips, looking down into his smiling face as he laid back on the bed. His arms were pillowing his head, causing the biceps to bunch and look massive. My guy was seriously ripped and I wasn't complaining.

"What're you doing, Sunshine?" he asked. His eyes were a direct contrast to the rest of him. His body was relaxed, mellow, but his gaze was predatory as he watched me.

I didn't bother to ask him to move so I could pull his clothes off, I just shoved his cut open and yanked his shirt up to his chest while I kissed every inch of skin I bared. Alternating between quick pecks and licking his skin, I realized I was enjoying myself. His body was something I would never get enough of. My hands skated over muscles, all hard planes as they roamed over his abs.

"You're killing me here, Jordan," he rasped.

Looking up, I saw the muscle in his jaw bunching as he clenched his teeth. I bit back my grin. There was just something about reducing a man this hot down to a melted pile of need that turned me on, apparently. This was a new revelation for me, but one I was fully committed to exploring.

I unbuckled his belt, watching him as I flicked open the button on his jeans and tugged the zipper down. His breathing had changed and he was taking these deep chugs of air that had his whole chest rising and falling heavily as he watched me. I was forced to swallow just to get some moisture back in my mouth. Why was that so sexy?

"Give me a second," he muttered and started to sit up.

Seeing all his hard packed muscle flex as he did a sit up made me want to continue rubbing my lips and tongue all over him. Only I had another destination in mind, so I put a hand on his chest and shoved him back down.

Surprise flooded his face, but he laid back again. He even lifted his hips as I tugged at his clothes and left his jeans and boxers down at his calves. He'd wanted to take his boots off, but I wasn't about to wait that long.

Shimmying my way down his body, I laid on the mattress to the side of his legs. My hand wrapped around his dick and I grinned when he hissed out a curse word. I wasn't very practiced in what I was about to do to him, but he made me want to try. I wanted to please him.

"Suck it." My eyes flashed up to his. "Go on." His voice was a deep growl and I could see how tense he was now, waiting for me to start. "I can't wait to feel your lips around me."

Dipping my head, I swiped my tongue over the tip. A bead of pre-cum transferred from the slit to my tongue and I hummed again at his taste. His deep groan sounded tortured, so I quickly encased the tip inside my mouth.

The sounds he was making were incredible. I hadn't realized men made so much noise in bed. The husky groaning and heavy breathing was turning me on to the point where I wasn't sure I'd be able to wait long enough to make sure he enjoyed this enough. I wanted to straddle him and ride him until we were both sweaty and satisfied.

Instead, I tucked my lips over my teeth and settled into my task with an earnest appreciation for the specimen below me. As my mouth skimmed up and down his length, I'd let my tongue lick the underside of his shaft.

"Fuck, Baby. That's it, take me deeper." His arms were behind his head again, holding it up so he could watch what I was doing to him. His pretty blue eyes were heavy lidded with desire and a thrill raced through me.

I had him in the palm of my hand, at least for the moment. Speaking of… I squeezed my hand around the base of his dick and my brows rose as he gave a hoarse shout of pleasure.

"Fuck. What a good girl. Do that again. Stroke it."

There was no way for me to smile, not with his cock shuttling in and out of my mouth, but if I could, I would. Even in this, he took the control I'd enjoyed and put it back in his hands. I didn't mind so much. It was arousing to hear him demand things from me.

I gasped as he grabbed a fistful of my hair, then wrapped his other hand around my throat. My eyes widened as they met his.

"I want to feel it when I go in here." He squeezed my throat gently.

Oh God. I'd never done that before. I started to shake my head, but he hushed me.

"Just for a minute. We'll eventually work up to that." His eyes glittered and I swear he looked feral. I nodded, mouth still too full to speak. He wasn't a small man, I was worried about him shoving his length all the way back, but I knew he'd look after me. "Good. Relax. Let me do the work."

Trying to obey, I let my muscles loosen. My hands were on his hip and the bed, steadying myself as he flexed his hips upward. He hit the spot where I'd been stopping.

"Take a breath."

As soon as I did, he slid further. Deeper than I'd thought possible. The urge to gag nearly overwhelmed me.

"You can do it. Just relax your throat." His hand was still there, but now he was stroking my skin.

I swallowed down the uncomfortableness and he slipped a little deeper. There was no breathing while he was lodged so far back, but I knew he'd let me take in air in a moment.

He held perfectly still, wasn't trying to thrust, and for that I was grateful. I'd have choked for sure if he had.

"You look so damn hot," he groaned. Then he was pulling out. Saliva hung from my lips as his cock popped out of my mouth, but he didn't seem to care. He yanked me up until our mouths met with a crash.

The kiss was deep and sensual and knowing I'd pleased him had me glowing with pride. I was back to straddling him and couldn't help but grind against him.

He set me aside and this time I didn't stop him when he sat up to remove his boots and the rest of his clothing. He stripped me much slower than he had himself. He peppered my skin with kisses and nips and had my nerves buzzing.

A squeal left my throat unbidden when he suddenly flipped me over. Before I could ask him what he was doing, his hands were jerking my hips up until I was on my knees, chest down on the bed. "Ricochet!" I couldn't reprimand him for the abruptness of the move, however, because my eyes were too busy rolling into the back of my head. This man was kneeling behind me, eating my pussy. I couldn't even think about what the view must look like, clearly he wasn't complaining, because rolling waves of pleasure were breaking over me. How was it possible for that to feel so good?

It was like he knew exactly where to lick, where to suck, to give me the most satisfaction, and before I knew it I was grinding my pussy back against his face. The sounds of him eating me out would have embarrassed me if my system wasn't in complete meltdown. His tongue dipped inside of me, then swiped up—or maybe down—and flicked over my clit, and that was it. Lift off. My orgasm hit me so hard my knees started to slide over the comforter. I couldn't hold my own body up anymore.

Ricochet sat up, grabbed my hips, hitched me back into position, and slammed inside of me so hard I swear it made a second aftershock of ecstasy ripple through me. I let out a scream of pure bliss and rocked back into his thrusts as he fucked me.

It was fast, rough, and so fucking delicious I never wanted it to stop. The sounds echoing through the room were so dirty and yet I reveled in them. The wet sound of his flesh hitting mine told me that my pussy was sopping. The comforter was bunched up in my fists and my feet were wrapped around his legs as I held on. It was all I could do because the slide of his cock inside, at this angle, was hitting every pleasure spot inside of me. I was going to come again and it was going to be brutal.

"Please," I whined, not sure exactly what I was asking for. I didn't want him to stop, but this was overwhelming. A tear formed and tracked down my cheeks as I gasped and moaned.

"Does my dirty little girl need some help coming?" he crooned in my ear as he covered my back with his chest. His hips were still surging forward into me as he asked.

I shook my head, unable to speak. I was trying not to come, afraid of breaking apart completely and never being put together again. That was what he did to me.

"You're going to come. You're going to come hard on my dick like my good little girl, aren't you?"

I gasped in a breath, but when he reached around and started rubbing my clit in circles I knew I'd lost. Whether I was ready or not, he was bending my body to his will. And it was divine. I knew in that moment it was safe to let go.

"That's it, Sunshine. Come all over me."

He'd never let me stay in pieces. I was his, just like he was mine. He'd already completed me, like a puzzle that had been missing a piece. He tethered me here, to him.

Closing my eyes, I let go and the orgasm hit me so hard, I couldn't even make a sound. It was all blinding lights and bliss soaked sensations. I was vaguely aware of him slamming inside of me and groaning, but I was too busy enjoying the aftermath.

His forehead dropped down onto my back as we both caught our breath. Too soon, he was pulling away from me, but I smiled as he flopped over onto his back and dragged me halfway over his body as if he wanted to wear me like a blanket.

We were lying there, wrapped up in each other afterward. My heart rate was just starting to come down, when he brushed a kiss on the top of my head.

"Would you come with me somewhere tomorrow?"

"Of course." It was my day off. "Where?" Tears filled my eyes when he told me his plan. "I'll go with you anywhere, Ricochet, but I'd be honored to go with you tomorrow especially."

CHAPTER 37

Ricochet

Pretty much from the time I'd met Jordan, she'd started chasing the numbness away. It was gone now. The pain and grief wasn't, but the soul searing agony of losing Jack and what I'd had to do in order to protect myself and others was fading. There would always be a missing piece of my heart. It belonged with my best friend. The man who'd saved my life. But I could finally move on and actually live my life.

Holding out my hand, I helped Jordan off my bike. It was early, but I knew the people we'd come to see would be awake. I stood outside the house. It was situated inside a community of other homes. All the stucco buildings looked like each other, rows upon rows of houses, and yet I knew this one like the back of my hand.

Jordan's fingers linked with mine as she grabbed my hand and held it. She didn't say anything, just waited for me to be ready. That was what she did for me. A steady ray of light in my otherwise bleak world, urging me to live instead of shutting myself away.

I'd tried this once before, after I'd come home from the deployment where I'd lost my friend. I'd never made it up to the front door. The door had remained closed and I'd just stood outside, staring at the outside of the home. Not today.

It opened and I saw the woman who'd once been a constant in my life in between deployments. Swallowing hard, I watched as she stepped out of her home.

"Took you long enough, Gage." Her voice was exactly as I remembered it. Her smile was warm, tinged with humor.

The last time we'd seen each other had been Jack's funeral. I'd wanted to beg for her forgiveness, but that day hadn't been about me. It'd been about laying my friend to rest and helping his widow and children get through the hardest moment of their lives. I'd remained a stoic, quiet rock for them to lean on as they'd cried.

"You look good, Mary." I squeezed Jordan's hand and as one unit we moved up the path until I was standing in front of her. Jordan let go of my hand and waited while I wrapped Jack's widow up in a hug. "Sorry I stayed away for so long," I told her.

She held me tight and when she pulled back, I saw the tears in her eyes. "Come inside. The kids will be so excited to see you."

"Are you sure that's a good idea?" I asked, voice rough. I'd told her everything. She'd insisted, after the funeral, on hearing everything that had happened.

"Gage Barrett. My husband was a hero. He saved your life. My kids know that and they know that his death wasn't in vain. None of us blame you for it." Her eyes softened. "You did enough of that, there was no need for us to pile on."

"He isn't here...because of me." I shoved my hands into my jean pockets, unsure of what to do with them.

"He made the call. Don't take away what he did by blaming yourself, Gage." She hugged me again. "He wouldn't want you to be blaming yourself like this. We don't begrudge the fact that you lived and he didn't."

"You're a good woman, Mary," I told her.

"Speaking of, are you going to introduce me to your lady?"

Smiling, I turned and pulled Jordan closer, "This is Jordan. Sunshine, this is Jack's wife, Mary."

The women shook hands and we followed her inside. "Steve! Jeremy!" she called out.

Two scrawny pre-teens came barrelling out from the back of the house. They skidded to a halt, eyes comically wide when they saw us. "Uncle Gage!"

Even though it'd been years and they'd grown like weeds, it was like no time had passed. They looked so much like Jack it was heart wrenching. The eleven and twelve year olds crowded around me, peppering me with questions about where I'd been.

Looking up at their mom with an apology in my eyes, I told them, "Sorry it's been so long. I'll be coming around more often now."

All of us sat down at the dining room table and I asked the boys what they'd been up to. Somehow, being here, in Jack's home again, wasn't as hard as I'd always imagined. It was comforting to see his wife and sons doing well after so much time had passed.

The last bit of weight lifted off my shoulders. Somewhere deep inside it was as though the last bit of despair was freed. I didn't have to hold it inside anymore. Breathing a sigh of relief, I smiled over at Jordan. The love shining there was all I needed to see to know that everything was going to be okay.

We stayed and talked for a few hours. I told the boys stories about their dad, helping to keep his memory alive for them. I'd keep my promise. This wouldn't be the last time I visited them. I should have never waited so long in the first place, but I hadn't been able to dig myself out of the hole of misery I'd been living in. Until I had, I couldn't help them. Now, they'd never want for anything. I'd make sure of it.

It was noon by the time we left the house. I drove us toward my next planned activity for the day. This one, Jordan had no idea about. I grinned beneath my helmet.

We were cutting it close by the time I parked in The Wildlife Sanctuary's lot. It was mostly deserted though it was almost one p.m. on a

Tuesday afternoon. There were a handful of cars and a bunch of motorcycles parked near the entrance.

"What's going on?" Jordan asked. She scanned the parking lot with a frown. "It's never this slow, even on a weekday." Her beautiful eyes met mine. "Why are we here?"

"Come on." I grabbed her hand, linking our fingers and all but dragged her to the designated spot. I then sat her down on a singular chair in a gazebo, which was mostly only a roof with four poles to hold it up. Her father had picked the place since he knew the Sanctuary so well. I left her there while I went into the back where usually only the employees were allowed.

"There you are," her dad said, motioning me over. "You're all set." He handed me a glove, then opened one of the cages where the birds were set.

The male hawk and I eyed each other for a brief moment before Scuff jumped onto my fist. "You sure this is going to work?" I asked him.

Leo chuckled and slapped my back between the shoulder blades, causing both Scuff and I to jostle. The bird shot the older man a look of disdain, as if he didn't appreciate the abrupt movement. I laughed. "I never knew they had so much personality."

"Oh yeah. It's amazing. Trust me. Scuff is a super friendly bird and he works with Jordan almost every day. The plan will work." He studied me. "You ready?"

"Never been more ready for anything," I told him. There was no backing down for me. There was no other path for me.

Leo nodded, a pleased smile on his face. "Good luck." He attached a microphone onto my cut with a clip, then left.

I walked back out to where I'd left Jordan. As soon as I came out of the back, Scuff took flight. He looped through the air, giving my family and hers, all of whom were standing nearby behind a railing, a show. They ooohhh'd and awwww'd as he flew.

"Usually you guys would have a gorgeous woman telling you all about hawks while you watched Scuff fly," I told them, the mic projecting my voice.

"You've never seen my show," Jordan said with a suspicious smile.

I glanced out at the crowd and saw Leo take his wife into his arms. It was more to hold her back before she could leap over the railing and ruin Jordan's surprise than anything else. Noah gave me a thumbs up, his arms around his own fiancée, and Jenna held her hands clasped together at her chest.

Gwen mouthed 'I love you' as she watched, while I set about proposing to her best friend. All my brothers were standing around, grinning. Their old ladies were wiping tears from their eyes while their kids ran around playing. I knew they were all damn glad to see me back with the living, back with them. Everyone here—at least my family—knew it was because of the woman in front of me.

I ignored Jordan's comment and kept going. "But you're going to have to just put up with me."

Butcher and Toxic let out loud boo's. I chuckled. Moving forward, I knelt between Jordan's knees. The shocked look on her face made me smile. I knew the minute she saw our families here she'd have an idea about what I was up to, but Gwen and the old ladies had assured me that she'd still be surprised and very happy.

"You brought me back from the dead." Tears filled her eyes. "I was barely hanging on. Drifting through each day, constantly shrouded in darkness. Then I saw you." I shook my head in disbelief. "I know it sounds corny as hell, but seriously, you brought light to my life, Jordan. I never want to live without you." My body jerked as Scuff landed on my shoulder. There'd been no cue that I could tell; I cut a look over at Leo, but he was just grinning.

He'd said that once I got close to Jordan, Scuff would end up coming around to investigate. The bird loved her. He'd told me more than once she'd petitioned The Sanctuary to let her keep him permanently. He was confident that one of these days they'd give in and agree.

The bird's talons tightened around my shoulder, as though to remind me that I had something to finish. My leather cut kept his lethal talons from cutting into my flesh. Thankfully, he was a small bird, so he wouldn't have done too much damage even without the leather.

"Will you marry me, Sunshine?" I reached over and untied the ring from Scuff's leg. Leo had secured it tightly in the leather ties, so it took a minute to untangle it. Better than it falling while Scuff flew around.

By the time I looked up again, there were tears flowing down Jordan's face. Uncertainty crept in, but I held out the ring, waiting on her answer.

"Of course I will," she cried, flinging her arms around my neck and catapulting her body forward out of the chair. Scuff took off, not wanting any part of what was about to happen next.

Not expecting the sudden movement, I tried to catch my balance, but she took us down in a tangle of limbs. I couldn't help but laugh while she peppered my face with kisses. Chasing her lips, I caught them in a soul-searing kiss.

The crowd erupted with cheers and she was breathless by the time I came up for air. I found the appropriate finger and placed my ring there. My claim. I'd told her once that she belonged to me and she'd scoffed in my face. Now she really did, for the rest of our lives. I had every intention of building and living a long life with her.

Hands dragged us apart and up onto our feet. Jordan was passed around by my brothers, their wives, and my sister while her family pressed close so they could welcome me. Even though it was just the beginning for us, it felt like the perfect ending. Somehow, I'd found the one person made for me and I'd be damned if I'd let her go.

Jordan would wear the title of wife and old lady simultaneously and one day we'd add mother to that list. I couldn't fucking wait.

CHAPTER 38

Ricochet

Two days later, we all piled into the meeting room inside the clubhouse. It was only seven a.m., so a few of my brothers looked pretty rough from a night of celebrating, but they were here. I pulled Jordan down onto my lap. There were enough chairs for everyone, but I liked having her close.

"Don't you dare," Seek told Hush, slapping his hands away as he tried to do the same. "I'm as big as a house and I'm going to end up squishing you."

"Shut up, Woman," he grumbled and pulled her down onto his lap.

"When the hell is your wedding going to happen?" Riptide asked. "You're running out of time if you want to have it before the baby gets here."

"Nope, screw that," Seek said, shaking her head. "It's waiting. I pushed it back. I'm not walking down the aisle as big as a whale. Besides, then I get a super adorable flower girl."

She waited a beat, her eyes wide with excitement. She was looking around at all of us. Everyone was present, but Lock hadn't started church yet.

Jordan gasped. "It's a girl?" she squealed.

I grinned, and so did the other men as the women jumped up to congratulate her. There would be multiple rounds of beers to be had in order to congratulate Hush, but that would have to wait.

Lockout smiled at Seek. "We're so happy for you both." He waited a few more minutes while the girls all hugged, then took their seats again.

Lock had even asked Kit and Gwen to be here today, plus Static. We'd start the meeting with the news that Static had for us, then send everyone out to finish celebrating Seek's news while we finished up church.

"Go ahead, Static," Lock told the man.

He cleared his throat. "As you know the DA was pressing charges against Trent-"

"Was," Gwen interrupted, her eyes wide and fearful. "Is he getting out?"

"No," Static told her, his eyes softening. Even his gruff, formal way of talking eased into something more gentle for her. "Gwen, Trent is dead."

Her mouth worked a few times as she processed that information, but didn't say anything else.

"What happened?" I asked.

"Shanked. In his cell. They found him this morning," Static replied.

We all looked around at each other. Riptide frowned. "That's a bit…"

"Convenient," Hush finished for him.

"So this guy is connected somehow with the DA and the mayor," Toxic said, "gets arrested, tossed in prison, and dies less than a week later?"

"It's not that surprising, given what he did to Gwen. I may have insisted that he be placed in General Population," I admitted.

"He wasn't there when it happened," Static said. "They'd brought him back to the county jail, while he awaited a preliminary trial. They found him when they came to bring him into the courtroom."

"Sounds like shady shit to me," Butcher clarified in case any of us weren't picking up on the vibe.

"I'm fucking glad he's dead," Smoke interjected.

"Agreed," Hell said, wrapping his burly arm around Gwen's shoulder to give her comfort. "He deserved to die. Since we couldn't do it ourselves, I'm glad someone took care of it."

"Word probably got out about what he did," Smoke shrugged.

"Maybe," Lock said, but his expression was worried. "Something tells me it's more than that. It's too much of a coincidence. Someone wanted him shut up. For good."

"Fremont did tell me he wouldn't forget about this. We expected as much, but he moves quickly," I said.

"Fuck me," Priest muttered. "Shit was just starting to calm down from the whole cult incident." He rubbed a hand over his chin. Jenny patted his chest.

"I could ask some of the guys I know at the station," Seek offered. "See if they heard anything about it. They don't have any say about what happens over at county lockup, but they might have heard some rumors."

"That'd be great," Lock told her with a smile. "Just make sure you do it in a way that doesn't arouse suspicion. If this was an inside job, I don't want you becoming a target. We suspected that Trent was some sort of fixer. If Fremont had him killed this quickly, then he's definitely up to something bad, and in a big way."

A dull red crept over Hush's face at the thought of someone coming for his pregnant old lady. "I'll fuckin' kill them all if they try." His promise was a low growl.

"We don't know anything yet," Lock told him. "Calm down. Rip, could you and Dash look into it?"

"Definitely. We haven't found the link yet, but something tells me we're getting closer," Rip told him.

"Do you think it had something to do with Ethan?" Sloane asked hesitantly. She was still incredibly quiet around everyone, but each day she came more and more out of her shell.

"No," Rip told her. "There's no way that Ethan would have worked with anyone, let alone a politician. He's dead. The cult is gone," he reassured her. "I couldn't even find traces of bribes going to the DA. Some county inspectors, of course, but no link between him and Fremont. This is something else entirely, unfortunately."

"We're telling you all this," Lock said, looking around at the women, "so that you all know to be on watch. Trent was a real piece of shit and what he did was awful," Lock's eyes fell on Gwen, "but if the DA wanted to silence him, there's no telling who he'll go after if they think we know his secrets. The best thing for the women and kids is to lie low while we try to figure this out. Agreed?"

Everyone nodded their heads. "Keep a watchful eye whenever we're not home with you," Hush added. "Those of you livin' at the clubhouse have extra protection since we always have members patrollin' our place."

"If it comes down to it, we could always have the rest of you come live on property until we get this sorted out," Lock added.

"There's plenty of room," Priest said. "I could make sure the extra apartments get cleaned out. That way they're prepped in case anyone needs them. Would only take a few days."

"Good idea, do it," Lock told him.

"If any of you want to come stay prior to trouble finding us," Rip offered, "you can. Like they said. There's plenty of space." His eyes fell on Gwen.

"If that's on the table, I want Gwen and the kids here," I said. "And, of course, Jordan will stay with me."

"Hey, wait," she said, turning in my arms. "I can't just abandon my house-" The look I gave her made her swallow her arguments. "I guess I could have Mom and Dad take Haze for a while," she amended.

Gwen was scowling at me, but I knew I'd be able to talk her into it as well. It was the safest course of action and after they'd already been attacked, I wasn't going to accept anything less than them living here.

"Besides," I said while eyeing Gwen, "Priest's girls have taken a liking to Sean."

Priest growled at me, but Jenny smiled. It was going to be so much fun to torture him since his second oldest, Taylor, was already giving my nephew love struck looks.

"Kit, you, too," Smoke told his sister, getting back to the subject at hand.

She looked around at the others, brows furrowed, but then sighed. "It'll be fun," she relented.

The other women seemed to get on board easily after that. It was going to be a lot of people in one area, but at some point down the road we all wanted our families living together on this property anyway; it was just a jump start to that.

"Any ideas on what you think is going on with Trent's death? I mean, specifics beyond Fremont 'cleaning house'?" Lock asked Static.

The older man shook his head, his light brown hair falling onto his forehead. He was in jeans and a t-shirt today instead of his usual suit. Minus the lack of a cut, he looked more like a biker today than a lawyer. "I haven't heard anything, but I'll keep my ear to the ground."

"Thanks," Lock said. "Alright. Static, ladies, if you could give us the room. Feel free to enjoy the bar outside. We'll discuss moving arrangements after church."

"It's not even eight in the morning," Jenny said with a laugh.

"Sounds like the perfect time for mimosas," Kit declared.

My eyes were glued to Jordan's ass as she left the room. It was hard to pay attention to the rest of the meeting. It was mostly finalizing plans for everyone to move in and more ideas on how to figure out what Trent was into.

"Alright. That's enough for today," Lock said. "We'll find out what's going on soon enough. Someone will end up slipping up and we'll be there to see it. Get the fuck out of here."

I went out into the rec and bar area, looking for my sunshine. Frowning when I didn't find her, I pulled Seek to the side. "Hey, have you seen Jordan?"

"Oh, yeah, she stepped outside real quick." Her dark brows rose.

"Some girl came through here as we were coming out of church and Jordan and Gwen knew her."

I blinked at that. "Did they say who she was?"

"Nope," Seek said with a shrug. "They just asked if we could watch the kids while they went to speak with her."

"Thanks, Seek." I turned and pushed the door open. It didn't take long to find my girl. She and my sister were standing near the gate, watching a car drive off.

I made my way across the property. "Who was that?"

They turned, giving each other secretive looks. "A friend we know."

"What was she doing here?" I asked.

"I think she spent the night with one of the guys," Jordan said. "She wouldn't say which one, though."

"She was in a real hurry to get out of here," Gwen added.

"How do you know her?" I asked, eyeing the tail lights that were disappearing down the road suspiciously. With everything that had happened I wasn't feeling very generous and everything was on my radar.

Gwen sighed. "She's one of Sean's teachers."

My head jerked back in surprise. "What the hell? Teachers aren't usually the type we attract."

"No?" Jordan asked in a sugary sweet voice. "What kind do you typically attract, Ricochet?"

That was a trap if I ever heard one. I grabbed her and leaned her back into a dip. "Gorgeous, courageous, wonderful women," I replied.

"Good answer," she laughed, then moaned as I kissed her.

"That's my cue to leave," Gwen said, giving my shoulder a pat. "I'll be inside when you're done."

I couldn't respond because I was all wrapped up in my sunshine. With her in my arms, I had no worries. We'd figure out the situation with Trent and resolve it. The school was back on track and my family was happy and safe.

I planned to find out later who the teacher had stayed the night with, but first I planned to drag my old lady off somewhere secluded so we could have some alone time. If I took her back inside the others would distract us before we could get up into our room. I'd have to ignore Lockout's directive of no sex on the property.

Lifting Jordan up onto my shoulder, I strode away from the clubhouse. Her laughter cut through the morning air. If I heard that every day until my last, I'd be a happy man.

* * *

Thanks for reading!

Keep flipping to find a sneak peek for book four of The Vikings MC: Tucson Chapter, Ricochet. It's available for pre-order now!

Sign up for my newsletter to receive an updates on new releases and much more! https://www.cathleencolenovels.com/bonuses.

Join The Book Bunker-A Cathleen Cole Reader Group https://www.facebook.com/groups/thebookbunkercathleencole

SNEAK PEEK

DANICA

I sat up on the bed and covered my face with my hands as the realization of what I'd done overwhelmed me. Last night had seemed like a fantasy come true, but now, in the light of day, I saw it for the mistake it was. All I'd been thinking about was letting loose a little. Maybe getting a tiny bit of revenge on my cheating husband. But that was supposed to have stopped at maybe some light flirting, or kissing. It had turned into going home with a biker.

I was the quintessential good girl. I'd been married for years, since I turned nineteen, and straying had never crossed my mind. The same couldn't be said for my husband. *Ex-Husband.*

Glancing up, I looked around for the man who'd introduced himself as Smokehouse last night, but he was nowhere to be found. I was both relieved and slightly worried.

I sighed, wondering what I'd been thinking. Sure, Smokehouse was handsome, well, gorgeous. Muscles for days, and charming...my God, I'd never been spoken to like he had. But I wasn't the kind to tangle with pick up artists like him. I wasn't the type to ever get hit on either. He'd charmed me, though. And I'd been upset and a little buzzed. I wasn't drunk, or in any way not under full control. I knew exactly

SNEAK PEEK

what I was doing when I agreed to go home with him. This mistake was one I would have to embrace.

Blankets were pooled at my waist and I was naked from the top up. I was willing to bet it wasn't much different beneath the sheets. There were enough memories of last night that I knew I'd slept with him. I also knew I'd enjoyed it. A lot. I was still numb and tingly in a way I didn't know was possible.

He hadn't left me hanging high and dry. In fact, if I remembered correctly he'd given me the best night of sex I'd ever had. He'd delivered on the subconscious need I'd had to find someone who treated me like I was beautiful and cherished, if only for a few hours.

I got up and dressed. Shame was edging in and I needed to get out of here before he got back. I remembered he'd brought me back to what he'd called his clubhouse. It was clear other people lived here, though we hadn't run into any last night. It was imperative I also escaped without being seen. The walk of shame I was about to do was bad enough without an audience.

Pulling out my phone, I called my sister.

"Do you know what time it is?" she grumbled when she answered.

"Early. Sorry. Hey, Carly…"

"What's wrong?"

The shift in her tone went from sleepy to sharp. I didn't need to see her to know she was sitting up in bed and worry was marring her face.

"Can you come pick me up?"

"I'm putting pants on and will be right there. Text me the address." She didn't bother to ask questions. It didn't matter that I was supposed to have stayed over at my friend's house. I was in need and she'd be there.

"Thanks, Sis." At twenty-eight, she was older than me by three years and she'd always looked out for me. It was a point of pride for her. Most of the time, she didn't need to bother. I'd always been the brainy kid while she was the sports star. School had been easy and I'd graduated early. Then I'd worked hard to get my teaching degree and ended up with the premium position for me. It was outside of the city in the small town of Picture Rocks.

I was back living with my sister in the city though, since I'd caught Eli cheating on me. It would only take her about ten minutes to get here. That didn't give me much time to sneak off the property.

Making sure I had all my things, I prepared to leave Smokehouse's room. *You never even got a real name from him.* I stuck my head out into the hall, my heart racing as I scanned the hallway. Clear. They were probably all asleep. For all I knew, Smokehouse did this every time he brought home a woman. Snuck off somewhere until the girl got the hint and skedaddled so he could go back to bed.

His light brown hair, green eyes, and charming smile were enough to knock the socks off most women. I wasn't anything special, so I'd been shocked when he hit on me. The man was drop dead gorgeous with all his muscles and tattoos. He had abs you could wash clothes on, which I'd discovered later. It had been flattering to have him pay attention to me.

I'd also been irritated that my so-called friend had already ditched me to go make out with some guy in the corner. Trina had promised to stick by me and she'd dropped me after the second drink and the first guy who'd hit on her.

I was about to leave when Smokehouse had shown up. He was funny, and had been sweet, and I'd let him win me over. If I was being honest, I didn't try too hard to resist. But that had been last night, two drinks in. In the light of day, I knew this hadn't been my best decision.

Tiptoeing down the hall, I made my way down the stairs. A small gasp forced its way between my lips, causing heads to turn my way. There were a bunch of women and a man standing in the living area of the building. My eyes widened when I recognized the mother of one of my students.

"Oh...oh, no," I whispered to myself. There was nothing left for me to do. I bolted past them and out the door. My cheeks were on fire as I ran across the gravel parking lot. This was the worst case scenario.

I'd met Gwen this year when her son Sean had started at my

SNEAK PEEK

school. We'd had multiple meetings about the best way to make the quiet eight-year-old feel at home in a new school.

"Mrs. Carmine!"

Groaning, I slowed my pace, but my breaths were still coming hard and fast. It was hard to say whether embarrassment or horror were winning out in this game of emotional rugby happening inside of me. I turned and pasted a bright smile on my face that I knew didn't reach my eyes.

"Gwen, hi. Please, you can call me Dani."

"Okay. Dani, you remember Jordan?" The two women smiled at me. There was no trace of a smirk or judgment on their expressions. We all knew there was only one reason I was sneaking out of here this early in the morning, but they weren't mentioning it. At least, not yet.

"You've picked Sean up a few times. I remember."

"Good to see you." Jordan shifted from foot to foot. "Is…everything okay?"

"Of course." If my face got any hotter my eyebrows would catch fire.

"Good," Gwen sighed. "You just took off so fast, we were worried…"

"I…wasn't expecting to see so many people." I gave them a weak smile. My feet were itching to get moving again, to carry me away from the excruciating awkwardness.

"My brother belongs to this club…" Gwen told me.

"And I'm engaged to him," Jordan said with a laugh.

"Oh… That's nice." It was evident they wanted me to elaborate on why I was here. I wasn't about to tell them that I'd had a one night stand with an unbelievably sexy biker last night, though. No reason to admit it out loud. To anyone. Ever.

"Well, it was great seeing you two again," I said, inching backward. "But my ride is here, so…" I left them standing there, looking between the empty road and myself.

I refused to run again, not with them watching, but my legs carried me swiftly down the road. It didn't take long before Carly's car

SNEAK PEEK

appeared and we met in the middle. I got inside and slumped down in my seat.

"Uh oh. What happened?" Her eyes flashed with concern

"I had a one-night stand," I admitted. "And I just ran into a student's mom while doing the walk of shame." I covered my burning face with my hands.

Carly was quiet enough that I peeked at her through my fingers. "Well damn. Good for you," she finally said. "I mean, sorry you're upset, but good for you." She scowled at the road as she made a U-turn. "Eli never deserved you. Your marriage is over, even if not officially with the courts. No reason not to hop back on the horse, or biker in your case."

I sighed. "It's not like me."

"No. You sort of skipped over the wild years. But there's no time like the present," she said with a smile. She was trying to make me feel better. It was working.

"I think that's the only night of 'wild' I'm planning on having."

"That's it?" She frowned. "Was it at least worth it?"

I thought back to the mind numbing orgasms he'd given me. "Oh yeah."

"Well that's something." She reached over and stroked a hand over my hair, something she'd been doing to comfort me since we were kids.

Closing my eyes, I tried to put it all out of my mind on the drive home. I'd had my fun. Now it was over. Life would return to normal.

* * *

One month later

"Oh. My. God," I whispered in horror. My hand shook as I stared down at the object I held. The plus sign on the pregnancy test mocked me as my vision wavered. This couldn't be happening.

ACKNOWLEDGMENTS

A huge thank you to my partner in crime and Co-Author, Frank Jensen. I couldn't do this without you.

To my amazing beta reader Heather Ashley, thank you so much for all of your time and effort you spent helping me make these books the best they can be!

Also a heartfelt thank you to my editor, Ce-Ce Cox of Outside-Eyes Editing and Proofreading! Thank you for catching everything I always seem to miss, especially those pesky commas.

Thank you to the awesome Kari March of Kari March Designs for giving me gorgeous covers each and every time.

To my wonderful and perfect fans! Thank you all for giving an unknown author a shot and for reading my books! I hope you love them and I can't show my gratitude for you enough.

Lastly, to my family, you're the best. Thank you for the love and support.

ABOUT THE AUTHOR

Cathleen and Frank live in SE Oregon where they have a family farm. They split their days between working with their animals and writing. Both left a law enforcement background to pursue their passions and for Cathleen that meant picking back up a long-forgotten hobby with writing. They strive to bring readers steamy, action-packed stories that provide hours of entertainment.

Sign up for our Newsletter to receive free extra chapters, as well as sales and updates.

Join our Facebook Reader's Group to interact with us.

And check out our Website to order signed paperbacks!